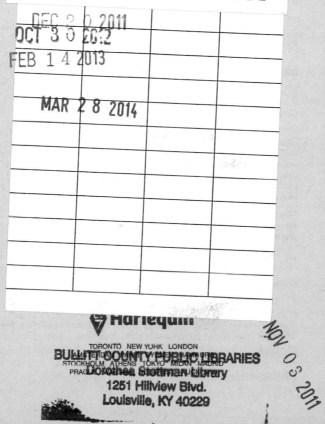

♥ Harlequin

TORONTO NEW YORK LONDON
AMSTERDAM PARIS SYDNEY HAMBURG
STOCKHOLM ATHENS TOKYO MILAN MADRID
PRAGUE WARSAW BUDAPEST AUCKLAND

Recycling programs
for this product may
not exist in your area.

ISBN-13: 978-0-373-61870-5

LORD OF THE WOLFYN

Dear Reader,

Blood drinkers, werewolves and warlocks. Oh, my! Welcome to the Royal House of Shadows.... Do you dare enter this dark, dangerous and sexy world?

I loved, loved, loved writing the story of a secretive magical prince and a redheaded cop with a penchant for archery and no luck with men. When sorcery plucks them from their rightful homes and prophecy throws them together, mayhem, adventure and a hot, sexy romance ensues...and asks the age-old question: Who's afraid of the Big Bad Wolf?

*Lord of the Wolfyn* follows Gena Showalter's *Lord of the Vampires* and Jill Monroe's *Lord of Rage,* and next month comes Nalini Singh's *Lord of the Abyss.* It was an absolute blast working with these talented ladies and imagining how these royal siblings would avenge their parents and save their kingdom.

Happy reading,

Jessica Andersen

*To lone wolves and life mates.*

# Prologue

Once upon a time in a magical land, a dark sorcerer—the Blood Sorcerer—coveted the only power denied him: the right to rule. So he led his army in a vicious attack on the Royal Castle of Elden, vowing to wipe out the royal family and take the throne. But he hadn't counted on the king and queen's love for their children, particularly the rebellious, headstrong Prince Dayn....

Branches stung Dayn's face and lashed at the bloodred chestnut stallion he rode, but neither of them flinched. They were trained for this, had been born for it: Dayn was the king's second son, Hart a royal war-horse descended from generations of beast-chasers. Together, they guarded Castle Island and the villages surrounding Blood Lake and kept the foul monsters of sorcery trapped in the Dead Forest.

It was a noble role, a dangerous calling...and an incredible rush. At least, it usually was. Tonight, though, he rode in anger with his reins white-knuckled in one hand and his loaded crossbow in the other, his mind not on protecting his castle or the country folk, but on the kill itself.

Full of his master's mood, Hart snorted, grabbed the bit in his teeth and leaped a thorny tangle they normally would have dodged around. Dayn shouted and grabbed the sturdy beast-chaser's flowing mane, and the two landed together and pounded away, now with a clear view of the monster they pursued.

The bristling, pony-size gray creature could have been one of the giant wolves that hunted the high country beyond Elden, save for the saddle of reddish fur at its heavy nape and the golden stripe that ran along its spine. Those things marked it as something else entirely: a wolfyn.

The older hunters told of the wolfyn taking human form and seducing the most beautiful women they could find...and then killing and eating them. Those were just stories, though. And the legendary shape-shifting was a way to explain why, back when they first set out to exterminate the creatures, the ravenous beasts would retaliate by attacking at a village's weakest point and go straight for the strongest warriors and then their beautiful wives, as if they were at war, not hunting.

Those days were gone now, the wolfyn nearly wiped

from the kingdoms. The few that remained, though, were deadly and had to be killed for the safety of all.

At the moment, though, all Dayn cared about was riding hard enough to leave everything else behind— his father's anger, his mother's disappointment…and the look on Twilla's face when he'd broken it off with her after hinting at marriage.

His father's words echoed in his mind. *You must wed a proper princess. You are the protector of the royal forest and your brother's right hand.* And the gods knew that dark, seductive Nicolai wasn't settling down anytime soon, so the king and queen—and their advisers—had pinned their hopes for profitable alliances on Dayn and his sister, Breena. The very thought of it—and the argument he'd had just now with his parents—had Dayn riding hard away from the castle and its politics. He was twenty and six, and his kind lived for hundreds, sometimes thousands, of years. Yet his parents wanted to sell his life to whichever royal house bid highest. Gods and the Abyss, he wished he had been common-born.

But he hadn't been, so he kicked on until the wind stung his face and the ground blurred beneath Hart's hooves.

His man-at-arms, Malachai, who was riding well behind them on his sturdy gray gelding, whipped around the thorny brake Dayn and Hart had just sailed over, bellowing, "Damn it, wait!"

Dayn's former-tutor-turned-companion said something more, but it was lost beneath Hart's loud snort as the trees thinned and they caught another glimpse of the wolfyn. The stallion accelerated after the beast, which looked back at them with too-intelligent amber eyes, and Dayn gripped with his knees and raised his crossbow as the gap narrowed. The trees opened up around him, but he focused on the reddish saddle mark, which outlined the target for a kill shot.

The wolfyn gathered itself for a last burst of speed, and—

Mindspeak screamed suddenly in Dayn's skull, filling him with pounding emotions that weren't his own: *rage, defiance, fear, betrayal.* Before he could do more than jerk with surprise, wind whipped up around him, squeezing him in a giant's fist of spell-power, and then yanking him clear out of the saddle and up into a rapidly forming whirlwind that suddenly spun overhead.

"Ambush!" Malachai shouted, his voice wind-distorted and quickly growing faint as the tornado sucked Dayn inward and air screamed past him.

He fought the magic that held him, but it was too powerful, too all-encompassing, a physical force that roared and keened, and then flattened, reverberating in his soul as he reached the calm at the center of the whirlwind. There, he hung suspended—seeing nothing but the moving wall of gray-brown surrounding him, feeling nothing but the magic. His pulse hammered and his muscles screamed for him to fight or run. But there was nothing to fight, nowhere to escape. Gods. What was happening? Mindspeaking was usually nothing more than shared thoughts between blood-drinking kinsmen. He and his father shared the bond most strongly, though he also had it with Nicolai. But this was something different entirely. "Hello?" he shouted. "Father? Are you doing this?" Maybe his sire sought to punish him for refusing to—

The chaos of battle sounds suddenly rang clear in his head: terrible screams, bloodcurdling roars he couldn't place, the clash of steel on steel, bow-twangs and bellowed battle commands. And his blood ran cold at the realization that this was no punishment. It was a warning.

"Alvina!" he heard his father shout to his mother, "Go back, damn it!" Then there was a wrenching jolt of magic and Dayn was suddenly *inside* his father's head, seeing what he was seeing, feeling what he was feeling.

*Horror and grim determination thudded in Aelfric's veins as he slashed at the creature confronting him on the narrow open staircase. He didn't know how the Blood Sorcerer had gotten his army onto the island undetected, but the castle was overrun.*

*Monstrous scorpion creatures filled the great hall below the curving staircase, knocking aside elite guard-soldiers with their poison-tipped tails, then slicing through their armor with razor-sharp claws. As blood splashed and men screamed and died, the king slammed a bolt of magic down the stairs, driving back the ettins that were trying to win their way up the steps to the upper level. The huge three-headed ogres stumbled back, dazed, but not for long.*

*Aelfric spun to charge up the stairs and found himself on his wife's heels. Which didn't surprise him, because his lovely Alvina was a fighter, fierce and powerful in both love and war. What surprised him was the panicked ache he felt at the sight of her rushing up the stone steps ahead of him, the inner whisper of,* Please, gods, no. I'm not ready for this.

*Worse, he saw the same emotions reflected in her eyes when she ducked into an alcove just short of their chambers and turned to him, holding out her hands for his. "We must act quickly," she whispered as the stones trembled beneath their feet with the force of the battle. "We can still save the children."*

*He wanted to argue, but knew in his heart that it would only waste time.*

*Folding his hands around hers, he moved in close and laid his cheek on her brow. "Ah, my queen. My love. I am sorry." Sorry that he had waited too long to go after the Blood Sorcerer. Sorry that he had no hope to offer. Sorry that they had so quickly gone from talking about little Micah's fifth birthday to this.*

*Her next breath was a sob, but she said only, "We must hurry."*

*He eased away, keeping hold of her hands, which trembled in his. "Tell me what to do."*

"No!" Dayn shouted, pain searing through his chest as the vision dissolved. "Gods, no!" More, as the mindspeak faded he heard the distinctive buzz that said it was a memory, that what he saw had already happened. He struggled against the invisible force that held him at the center of the whirlwind, lashing at it, cursing it. "Malachai!" he shouted. "To the castle!" But there was no response, and the forest suddenly seemed very far away.

*Dayn.* The word was spoken inside his head, in a familiar low, rumbling voice.

"Father?" Hope burst through him. "Thank the gods. Get me out of here. I can gather the villagers and—"

*It is too late. The castle has fallen, and us with it.*

"Don't say that." His voice went ragged, his breathing choppy. "Hang on. Just hang on. I'll get Nicolai. If we work together—"

*The spell is cast, our lifeblood gone. I don't even know how much longer I'll be able to reach you, so you must listen.*

*"No!"* Dayn shook his head wildly, denying both the statement and the whisper of echoes that said his father had passed on to the psychic space between dead and alive. "Father...Mother...gods..." He felt no shame in the sobs that tore from his throat, jumbling his words with terrible, awful guilt. "I shouldn't have lost my temper, shouldn't have ridden out. If I had been there—"

*Cease!* Aelfric snapped, much as he did to his men in battle.

Dayn came to attention, but his voice shook when he said, "I await your orders." He had said the words many times before, though most often lately with resentment. Now it took on a new, sharper meaning, because he didn't know what to do next. Find Nicolai?

Muster an army? A magical attack? A retreat? Never in his wildest dreams had he imagined the castle taken, his parents gone. But he couldn't waste whatever time his father had left in the in-between, so he whispered, "Speak, Father. I will do whatever you tell me."

*Good, then listen well. Because of our wounds and the sorcerer's power, the spell turned warped as your mother and I cast it. The magic has sent you and your brothers and sister far away, as we intended, but it has also tied the four of you to the castle and begun a count-down. When this count enters its final four nights— and not before then—you must all return to the island, retake the castle and kill the Blood Sorcerer. If you do not, you will die and Elden will be lost. But you must wait until the time is right.*

Dayn's breath rasped in his lungs; his mind spun. "How will I know?" Gods, was this really happening?

*A woman will come to guide you home. The count-down begins when she arrives and ends on the fourth night. You must let her guide you, but remember: stay true to yourself and know your priorities. Promise me that.*

A sob backed up in his throat. "I promise. Gods, Father—" He was cut off as the tornado suddenly accelerated with a roar. Seconds later, he was flying away from the calm center and back out toward the whipping wall of air. "No!" he howled as the wind grabbed him, latched on and flung him forward into the spin. In an instant he was moving, tumbling over and over, leaving him to shout into the roaring wind, "I'm sorry I wasn't there to help fight!"

Thunder cracked and energy detonated inside him, searing his flesh and driving the breath from his lungs. Pain consumed him, convulsed him, as his body suddenly sought to tear itself apart from the inside out. Flesh and muscle ripped; sinews snapped from one place to another and his bones *bent*. There was a sharp jolt, and agony javelined through him, so terrible that he screamed and his senses went dim for a few seconds.

Then, between one second and the next, the howling stopped and the tornado disappeared, blinking out of existence as if it had never been. He hung for a second facedown in midair, eight or ten feet above a grassy clearing surrounded by strange stone pillars. Then his weight returned and he fell.

"Son of a—" He hit hard, with a rushing *boom* of impact that made his eyes blur, his ears ring and his brain spin. Surely that explained why, as he struggled to his hands and knees, the world around him seemed too bright, the sky too pale, the trees too tall. But no head injury could explain the cold that cut through his tunic or the way he could see his breath on the air. Or why the sky was a strange color and the ringed stones and tall, thin trees didn't look like anything he'd ever seen before.

Where was he? Had the spell sent him to the High Reaches? Even farther? Gods, what if he was all the way out by the Barrens? It would take him months to get home. His father had said he needed to wait for a woman guide and a four-night countdown that started when she arrived, but impatience stirred at the thought. What if he didn't wait? What if he returned on his own? He was a hunter, a Forestal. If anyone could make it safely through the kingdoms alone, it was him. What if—

He jolted when movement blurred in his peripheral vision, and his pulse thudded thickly in his ears as he turned, hoping to see his guide.

Instead, men emerged from the trees. One was a gangly youth in his late teens, while the other appeared to be in his third or fourth decade. They shared long-nosed, forbidding features that suggested they were related, and they wore brightly colored clothing that wasn't made of any hide or textile Dayn had ever seen before. The strange fabric crinkled like parchment when they moved, coming toward him.

Dayn dragged himself to his feet, belatedly realizing that the magic had stripped him of everything but his clothing, leaving him unarmed and wearing only the common laborer's homespun he favored. But if he was in hostile territory, that was probably for the best. He needed to lay low and keep his true identity hidden until he knew whether it was safe for him to reveal himself as a prince of Elden.

"Ho, there," the older man called. "Don't be afraid. We're here to help you." Aside to the younger man, he said, "Okay, pop quiz. What do you make of him?"

Dayn frowned. He understood the man's hard-edged, almost guttural accent, but what was a "pop quiz?"

"Well, the outfit says he's from the kingdom realm." The teen's teeth flashed. "Or maybe a human renaissance faire. But I'm going with the kingdoms. Homespun, nothing fancy, no weapons? Probably just a regular guy who stumbled into a vortex with zero clue what just happened. I say we drug him and send him home, no harm, no foul."

"I'm not sure about that. There's something in his eyes."

"You know how most of them are when they come through. Hell, half of them are so whacked from the trip that they don't need the drugs. I bet that's his deal. I mean the kingdomites don't believe in science, never mind the realms or realm travel, so it's not like he's got any point of reference to start from."

"Maybe." The older man paused at the edge of the stone ring. "You, there. What is your name, and who is your king?"

"King—" Dayn broke off as his throat closed on the knowledge that the answer wasn't "Aelfric" anymore. His older brother was the rightful king now. *Gods, Nicolai. Where are you? What has happened to us all?*

"See?" the youth said. "He doesn't remember jack shit."

"Language, youngling," the older one chided. "You've been spending too much time with the human guests again."

"Better to borrow from the humans than the kingdoms. They're backward, their magic is unpredictable and half of them are led by those foul bloodsucking parasites." The teen made a gesture near his heart, as if warding off evil.

Dayn was suddenly very glad that he'd been unable to name his king. Where was he that blood drinkers were reviled so?

Before he could figure out how to ask the question, a blur flew out of the woods and came toward the men: a gangling, puppyish creature with gray-buff fur. It wasn't until it skidded to a halt, furiously wagging its tail in greeting, that Dayn saw the pale reddish saddle and the hint of a golden stripe. He couldn't hide his flinch at that, or his gasp when the young wolfyn reared up on hind legs that became suddenly fluid as its outline stretched straight and tall and its fur shimmered all over…and then became strange, shiny blue fabric, glossy black boots and gloves and the pale oval of a boy's face.

Dayn stared, stunned. Dear gods, it was true. The wolfyn *were* shape-shifters. Did that mean that the other stories were true, too? Was this their homeland?

The child's eyes were alight with curiosity, his features a younger version of the others'. "Aw, I missed a vortex? Bummer. Where did he come from? Is he staying?"

The teen tousled the youngster's reddish-buff hair. "We're working on it. Though I'd say from his reaction just now, we can safely say he's from the kingdoms."

The older man's eyes narrowed. "Question is whether or not he's one of those murderous bloodsucking bastards or not." He and the others moved forward, stepping into the circle drawn out by the standing stones.

Dayn's heart thudded but he held his ground and willed his secondary canines deep into hiding, so not even their small bumps could be felt if the men checked his gums. Because if they figured out who and what he truly was, he wouldn't live long enough to return home.

*Chapter 1*

*Twenty years later*
*Human realm*

Reda Weston stalled on the sidewalk outside the Cat Black Curiosity Shop with her hand on the latch and her stomach in knots.

The wide-eyed reflection that stared back from the tinted window wasn't anyone she recognized. Yes, the stranger had a wavy red-shot ponytail the same as hers, and she was wearing the ratty jeans and beat-up leather jacket Reda had pulled out of her closet that morning because there was no reason for her to dress like a cop these days. And yeah, those were her deep blue eyes at the back of the dark hollows that had taken up permanent residence. But if that was her, what the hell was she doing?

Normally, she wouldn't go anywhere near the kitschy magic, witchcraft and whatnot shops that lined the Salem waterfront unless someone called 9-1-1…but then again, normal circumstances had hit the bricks six weeks earlier. And she *had* asked MacEvoy, the owner of Cat Black, to find the book for her.

"It's here," his phone message had said. "And if you liked the picture you bought, you're going to *love* the rest of it."

Like it? Heck, she'd spent the past four days staring at the framed woodcutting of a dark, eerie forest of gnarled and twisted trees, with just a hint of eyes in the shadows. More, she had dreamed about the image… and others like it.

A clatter startled her and she flinched for the weapon she wasn't carrying, then winced when she saw that the noise had come from the shaking of her hand on the door latch. Worse, she didn't know how long she had been standing there.

"Don't be surprised if you have sleep disturbances, panic attacks, behavioral changes, even compulsions," the department shrink had told her. And yeah, she'd had all of the above…except for the last one. This was her first full-blown compulsion. Or rather, the strange urge that practically dragged her into the creepy-ass store earlier in the week had been the first. This was her second. And it was much stronger.

*It's not the same book,* she told herself. *It's just*

*another copy.* Except that her maman had said it was one of a kind. *You're just transferring, trying to solve something that's solvable because you know the real stuff isn't.* That was the practical part of her talking, her father's daughter. And suddenly she saw the major in the shape of the blue eyes that stared back at her, and in the ramrod posture that made her look taller than her true five-six. Inwardly, though, her mother's voice whispered, *At least take a look. What have you got to lose?*

"My sanity," she muttered under her breath, ignoring the ache that fisted beneath her heart. She hesitated another moment, then shook her head and pushed through the door, causing a distant bell to ring in the back of the cluttered shop.

As before, the place smelled disconcertingly like foot powder—gritty talc with a cloying perfumed undertone that made her think of funerals. Display racks near the door held the usual suspects: artsy postcards, books on the witch trials, copies of *The House of the Seven Gables* and such. But the racks themselves were made of wood rather than the usual cheesy wire, and the sides were carved with strange, sinuous curves and the hint of scales and teeth. The walls were painted black, with greenish white accents she bet glowed in the dark when MacEvoy turned off the lights. It would make the perfect backdrop for him to pull out the three-foot-high grim reaper statue that was locked in a glass case behind the register at the back of the store, and which she'd bet a hundred bucks converted, Transformer-like, into a giant bong.

Yeah. This was so not her scene. She should just leave.

"Miss Weston!" MacEvoy came through an employees-only door with his hands outstretched and his red-rimmed eyes holding an expression of pleasure that might or might not be faked.

A middle-size, middle-age grasshopper of a man, he was all arms and angles inside a faded black suit that made him look like a Victorian mortician and, she suspected, had come from the clearance rack at Cosby's Costumes a few doors down.

*Don't be bitchy,* she told herself as she shook his hand and returned his greeting. *It's not like he came looking for you.* And it wasn't his fault she felt totally out of place. The problem wasn't with the location, or with him.

"Right this way." He headed to the register area, where a wood-and-glass case held a collection of impressively ugly silver-and-moonstone jewelry, along with a sterling frog whose garnet eyes seemed to follow Reda when she moved. But that was just her imagination.

Right?

Holding back a shiver, she reminded herself that she didn't believe in magic, that this was all just a put-on for the tourists. If the atmosphere was working on her, it meant that MacEvoy was better at his shtick than she would've thought.

Disappearing behind the case, he rummaged around for a moment, then made a satisfied noise. When he straightened, he was holding a black, metal-edged cardboard clamshell box that was marked Acid-Free Archival Storage on the spine.

Reda's mental cash register went *cha-ching* and she wondered whether she should do a "thanks but I've changed my mind," and have another session with the shrink instead. *Certainly be cheaper.* Or she could go home and fill out the paperwork on her desk—applications to the forensic-science programs at Colby and New Haven. That wasn't the same as saying she was wimping out. It was just exploring options.

But those practical thoughts exited stage left the second MacEvoy set the box on the counter and flipped it open…and a skim of heat washed through her, followed by a prickle of gooseflesh that made her feel suddenly awake, though she hadn't been aware of being sleepy.

The shopkeeper grinned. "You like it?"

"Oh, yes," she breathed. "Yes, I do." Because it wasn't just any book. It was *the* book. It had to be.

The cover was intricately carved with another forest scene, this one with an achingly lovely girl front and center, running along a narrow path. She was wearing a long, flowing cloak over a peasant dress, and was looking back over her shoulder with an expression of mingled terror and excitement. There were no authors' names, just a title that stood up a little taller than the rest of the carving. *Rutakoppchen.*

"Red Riding Hood," she whispered, hearing the words in her mother's voice. *Not just one of a kind,* her maman had said on that long-ago birthday, *but yours alone. It was sent to me, darling, to give to you when the time is right.*

MacEvoy looked surprised. "You speak the language? The paperwork says it's some obscure Western European dialect, and doesn't make any promises on the translation."

"I don't need a translation." She already knew the story by heart. Pulse thrumming, she reached for the book.

The shopkeeper hooked the box with a spindly finger and tugged it back an inch. "You going to buy it?"

Her plastic was on the counter before she was even aware of having made the decision. More, she didn't yank it back when MacEvoy two-fingered it, even though her smarter self was inwardly screeching that they hadn't talked price.

She didn't care. She had to have it, regardless of whether it was really the same one or not, really one of a kind. Not because of the strange, fragmentary dreams she'd been having every night since she brought home the print—*a circle of stones like Stonehenge only not, a sense of pounding urgency, a flash of green eyes that brought heat and left her to wake up alone and aching*—but because it was a missing part of her past. And if that was transference, she didn't give a crap right now.

As he swiped her card, she brushed her fingertips

across the carved wood, and got a jolt of strange excitement. Nerves jangled and her smarter self asked what the hell was going on here, why was she acting like this?

"Is it true that the wolf doesn't just eat Red in this version?" MacEvoy asked as he waited for the slip to print. He glanced over at her, getting a gleam in his red-rimmed eyes. "The paperwork said that he seduces her first, enslaves her, plays with her until he gets bored… and *then* he eats her."

"Something like that," she said. She was dying to page through, but didn't want to do it in front of him, though she didn't know why, just as she couldn't explain the sudden pounding of her heart and faint clamminess of her hands, or the liquid churn low in her belly. All she knew for sure was that her hands were shaking as she scrawled on the slip, and then flipped the clamshell shut and tucked it under her arm. "Thanks. See you around." *Or not.*

"Wait," he said as she headed for the exit. "I wanted to ask you… Aren't you that cop? The one—"

She put her head down, clutched the box and beelined it out of the shop.

The short walk to her apartment on the outskirts of the "cool" district where the old houses were still getting restored seemed to take forever, especially when two of her neighbors pretended they didn't see her. Guilt stung, but Reda told herself—as the shrink had told her—that they weren't acting that way because they thought she was to blame for her partner's death in a liquor-store robbery gone bad. Like most of her friends and family, they just didn't know what to say anymore given that Benz had been dead for months now, and she was still ghosting around looking as if her best friend had died.

Except that he had. And it was her fault. Not because she'd done anything wrong, but because she hadn't done *anything*. She had frozen. Just stood there while a strung-out meth head looking at his third strike opened fire.

The news reports had said she was lucky to get away. The other cops hadn't said anything, really. Just like her neighbors didn't now as she hurried past them. But for a change the uneven thudding of her heart didn't have anything to do with the sidelong looks and whispers, or the knowledge that her father and brothers had been right when they said she wasn't the save-the-world type. Instead, it was the heavy weight of the box she held clutched to her chest, gripping it so tightly her fingers had gone numb.

She was breathing so fast she was practically light-headed by the time she let herself into her small, homey apartment. Not even pausing to shuck out of her leather jacket, she dumped her purse near the door and crossed to the narrow galley kitchen. The hollow sound the box made on the butcher-block counter reminded her that she hadn't looked at the credit-card slip, didn't know how much she had dropped on the thing. Didn't care.

"So open it," she told herself, the words sounding far too loud on air that had gone still around her, like the world was holding its breath. Or maybe—probably—that was just her. She was turning this into a way bigger deal than it needed to be.

Still, her fingers trembled as she flipped open the box, then reached in and touched the wooden cover. She told herself the faint tingle was her imagination, just as the hot dreams she'd been having the past few nights had been nothing more than memories of her girlish rescue fantasies with the temperature turned up by her adult experiences.

She traced the raised lettering. *Rutakoppchen.* A version of Red Riding Hood with the wolf as both sinner and seducer, the woodsman as the hero who saves the girl and takes her away from her old life to a new, better one. Seeing the book, touching it, made her mother feel closer than she had in years. Even if it turned out to be just a copy, it was worth whatever she had paid.

But she had to know, so she opened it. The cover creaked like an unoiled door, her throat became suddenly parched and tight…and then her eyes filled at the sight of a blank page with two lines of elegant script right in the center, done in blue ink that had faded over the past two decades.

To my sweet Alfreda on her eighth birthday, with the rest of the story to come when you turn sixteen.
    —Your maman

Reda's heart *thudda-thudded* in her chest as she

brushed her fingers across the last word. *Maman.* Her older brothers had teased her about putting on airs, calling her "princess" and poking at her because there was nothing remotely royal about any of them. They were army brats and proud of it.

*You'll never get anywhere by looking backward.* The major's voice suddenly came so clear he might have been standing right behind her. Which he wasn't; he was overseas. It was just that the words were such a familiar refrain: *eyes up and ahead; one foot in front of the other; look ahead, not back.* Words to live by.

"You're right," she said softly. "I know you're right." She should put the book back in its box and set it aside, maybe even lock it in the fireproof safe where she kept her unused passport. She should take comfort in knowing she had a cherished memory back, and then focus on more important things—like filling out those applications.

But she turned the page, anyway, unable not to glance at a picture of the young, innocent girl with her hamper. Then one of a huge wolf—her maman had called it a wolfyn—stalking her along the pathway and watching with too-human eyes as she entered her grandmother's cabin, only to find it empty. The next few pages showed the wolfyn and girl together, the story relying on the text more than pictures. But then the huge beast morphed to a shaggy-haired man with hot, feral eyes, and the girl looked up at him, face bright and excited, like she was looking at a handsome prince, not a leering wolfyn. But now Reda saw something she hadn't before: the girl looked disconnected, and she was almost smiling past the wolfyn, not at him.

Reda's stomach dipped. She had seen that look on the faces of roofie victims.

She skimmed the next few panels, realizing that her maman must have skipped some pages. Or had she seen the pictures as a child and not really realized what they meant? Because now, looking at them with an adult's perspective—and that of a cop who had worked rape cases, though mercifully far fewer than would be the norm in a larger, grittier city—the girl's vacant, glassy expression and rag-doll compliance to the wolfyn's G-rated yet highly suggestive demands smacked of drugs or brainwashing. Or both.

She hadn't been seduced. She had been compelled.

Reda shuddered. "That's not really the way I remembered this part." But then again, most fairy tales had started out dark and bloody, rarely reaching mainstream puppies-and-kittens territory until Disney got hold of them.

Something buzzed in the back of her brain, like a trapped bumblebee of a thought that wouldn't land long enough for her to catch its meaning.

"Poor girl," she murmured, touching an image of the young woman lying heavy-lidded near the hearth of the cottage, where a fire burned low. The wolfyn was halfway between his two forms, looking out a window with the fur at his nape erect as if searching the shadows for danger. It was hard to tell if he was protecting her or holding her captive. Probably both, depending on who you asked.

Reda found herself getting far too caught up in feeling sick for a two-dimensional character who had suddenly become a stand-in for too many of the victims she had worked with. She was so wrapped up in that theme, in fact, that when she turned the next page and saw the woodsman looking up at her from the page, she simply stared for a few heartbeats.

Then she whispered, "There you are." Which was ridiculous because, just like the girl, the woodsman wasn't anything more than a picture in a storybook.

Only he was more than that. He was the hero.

Standing in the cabin doorway with a long-handled ax held across his body, he should have looked like a lumberjack stereotype. Instead, he looked strangely out of place, as if a knight errant had been dropped into this story from another. His forearms, bared by rolled-up sleeves, were corded with a tension that carried from his taut-knuckled grip on the ax handle throughout the rest of his big, rangy body and up to his face, which was etched with disgust and determination as he took in the scene within the cabin.

Reda's perceptions tunneled down to the tousle of dark hair atop his noble brow and wide cheekbones, his narrow-bridged, aristocratic nose, full lips and square jaw, and his eyes...dear God, his eyes. They stared out of the page and cut right into her, seeming alive even though it was just an illustration, and a black-and-white one at that.

She knew those eyes, though. "Green," she whispered, suddenly yearning in a way that made no sense, for a man who didn't really exist. "His eyes are green."

*Help him.* The thought came in a voice that sounded like her own breathing turned into words that weren't hers.

A shudder coursed through her body.

"Great, now you're imagining things while you're wide awake," she said aloud, trying to use the words to chase away the sudden crackle that laced the air.

It didn't work. The air stayed heavy and thunder rumbled, hollowing the space beneath her diaphragm and stealing her breath.

This time it was the whistle of the rising wind outside that said, *Help him. Save him.*

Her heart stuttered when she looked out her apartment window and saw that the sky was as clear and bright as it had been when she left MacEvoy's shop. Yet thunder rumbled again, vibrating through the soles of her boots and up through her body, making her feel suddenly empty and alone.

*He is alone, too. Help him.* It was the sound of wind, yet the neighborhood trees weren't moving and the light, fluffy clouds hung motionless in the sky.

A whimper lodged itself in her throat, the weak noise unuttered, but the panic that spawned it remained, bringing a memory so deeply buried that she didn't remember even having it until it was right there, fullblown in her mind.

*"So what do you think—is she nuts?"* her father

*asked the doctor. She could see them both from the waiting room through the partly open office door, could hear them clearly, though their voices were hushed.*

*"We don't use labels like that," the stern-faced doctor said, but that made her father nod as if he'd gotten the answer he expected. The doctor sighed. "Look. The mind has a sort of framework it uses to deal with trauma and loss, a way of rationalizing how it happened, why and what it means. In this case, Reda's mind has chosen an atypical framework, one where she believes that her mother is not dead, but rather trapped in a land of magic beyond our own. Things like this can happen following the loss of a parent, especially in children her age. Usually it goes away on its own."*

*"How long?"*

*"Months, sometimes longer. In the meantime, it's basically harmless."*

*"You call sleepwalking out the back door and into the woods 'harmless'? What if she got lost? Or, worse, got found by the wrong sort of person?" The major's voice gained volume at the end, but then he glanced out at her and lowered his voice once more to say, "Help me out here, Doc. I need this to stop. The boys need it to stop. We all need to move on."*

*The doctor didn't say anything, and Reda's heart went* bumpity-bump *at the thought that he was going to tell the major that she was right, the kingdoms really did exist, and that sometimes visitors accidentally fell through the gates connecting the realms. Suddenly excited, she leaned forward in her chair.*

*"There are a few things we could try,"* the doctor said finally. *"The first thing I would recommend is getting rid of the book."*

The memory wavered and disintegrated, but the heartache remained, along with Reda's dull surprise at remembering how it had happened. Not because the major had tried to pretend otherwise, but because the months of therapy that followed had trained her not to think about the book, magic or monsters.

Or, really, even her mother.

The police shrink had wanted to talk about her mother's death, of course, but Reda had just shrugged and said, "It was a long time ago." And it would have stayed that way...if she hadn't found the book. Or rather, if it hadn't found her.

Thunder rumbled, closer now, though the sun still shone. Unbidden, her eyes went to the picture of the woodsman standing in the doorway, staring up out of the page at her and making her yearn. "Repressed memories," she said softly. "That's what this is all about, isn't it?"

Benz's death had put a crack in the dam, and the strange, cosmic coincidence of her seeing the woodcutting in MacEvoy's shop had washed out its base of support, meaning that now the entire construct was poised to come crashing down on her. Oddly, considering how much she used to pride herself on control and self-discipline, she didn't really mind. Since the shooting she had felt like she was running in place, or maybe hunkered down inside herself, waiting for something. And this was it.

Or was it? What if this was all just happening in her head? What then?

The rational, logical part of her said to call the shrink and have herself checked in somewhere. Instead, reaching out with a hand that suddenly didn't shake at all, she touched the page, resting her fingers on the woodcutter's chest.

It didn't take any effort now to remember the magic words her maman had taught her. The two of them used to sit on a mossy bank down by the duck pond, cross-legged, knees touching. "Concentrate," her maman would say, over and over again, though somehow it never seemed like a lecture, never like work. "Close your eyes, visualize the doorway and say the spell, and when you open your eyes again you'll find yourself where you were meant to be."

The words weren't magic, of course, wouldn't conjure some strange passageway to a magical realm. But they were exactly what her mind needed in order to wash away the dam once and for all.

So she thought, *What the hell?* And she said the words.

*Crack!* Lightning split the air around her and incredibly, impossibly, wind whipped past her, around her, though she was standing inside her apartment. Panic lashed through her and she froze, paralyzed by the fear. Her heart hammered in her ears, but that inner pulsation was the only movement she could manage.

She tried to call for help but couldn't, tried to tear her eyes from the book but couldn't do that, either. She was snapping, losing it. She screamed but made no sound, fought but didn't move. The woodcutter's eyes grew larger and larger in her vision, until she saw nothing but the inky black, heard nothing but the wind, and felt…

Nothing.

*Kingdom realm*

Moragh snapped out of her trance as the divination was interrupted by magic of another kind—a blood-linked power the likes of which she hadn't sensed in many years.

*"The prince!"* she hissed, excitement firing in her veins as she recognized the signal's source. Finally— *finally*—after all this time she could feel the spell that had snatched her prey from her. More, she could follow it. Even after the first flare of power leveled off, the connection remained inside her, throbbing like a heartbeat. One that said, *This way. I can lead you to him.*

The spell had reactivated. Thank the dark lords.

Her lips curved in a smile that the ornate, gilt-edged divination mirror showed as feral, with a hint of fang gleaming from behind the lips of a coolly gorgeous brunette in her forties. She had survived the Blood Sorcerer's wrath over her failure to kill Prince Dayn the first time, and had eventually won her way back into his graces. But she hadn't ever escaped the failure. And now… "Redemption," she said, the word echoing off the cool stone walls of the castle's upper reaches.

Over near the hearth, her servant, Nasri, looked up from his mopping. The old, crooked-fingered gnome—who now had only seven of those crooked fingers, having recently been caught filching a meat pie he'd had plenty of coin to buy—was cleaning last night's bloodstains up off the stonework. The water in his bucket was dark, the gray mop gory. "Mistress?"

"Send word to the bestiary. I want the largest two ettins ready to hunt in an hour." The three-headed giants were pure rage wrapped up with hunger, killing machines that need only be pointed toward their target. "And have the beast master reinforce their collars and control spells. I'll be handling them myself, with you along to help tend them."

He cringed and whined low in his throat. "Wouldn't you rather—"

"Go," she snapped with enough force to have him squealing and bolting out the door. When he was gone, she smiled again into the warped mirror. "By my life and blood, I'll get him this time."

She had missed before. She wouldn't miss again.

# Chapter 2

*Wolfyn realm*

As the blood moon edged over the dark tree line, a perfect blue-white circle visible through the windowed wall of the big bedroom, Dayn did up the last button of his plaid shirt and shrugged into his fleece-lined bomber jacket.

"You could stay, you know. Be here when I get back."

He glanced over. A cut-glass lamp shone from the bedside table—a Tiffany knockoff that had been imported from the human realm and converted to run off the quasi-magical energy that powered the wolfyn's gadgets. The pale glow lit the room's earthy brown walls and finely carved furniture, both of which were subtly worked with the Scratch-Eye pack's sigil: four parallel bloodred slashes crossing an amber wolf's eye. The bed was piled with luxurious crimson-dyed furs, but the room's true centerpiece was Keely. The pack's alpha bitch lay stretched, sinuous and satisfied, her scent musky with arousal and the magic of the blood moon. Graced with the toned body of a huntress and the ruddy hair of a bitch in her prime, she was unmated and independent, just like him.

Except that she was nothing like him. Not really.

They met and mated this one night each year, when sex sparked the strongest of changes and the wolfyn stayed largely in wolf form for the next three days, running together, renewing their magic and making or breaking new alliances. She didn't dare mate with a male of her kind during the blood moon lest he claim the Right of Challenge for the pack leadership, which had gone to her brother, Kenar, rather than down through her as was traditional. So, as the Scratch-Eye pack's "guest"—that was the name given to the few accidental realm travelers who by some quirk of the vortex magic couldn't return home through the standing stones—Dayn had become Keely's choice. She had laid it out with the blunt practicality of a wolfyn: sex once a year, nothing more or less. Which worked just fine for him for a number of reasons.

Their relationship might have begun as a transaction, but over time it had mellowed to friendship. Or what did the humans call it? Friends with benefits. But, friends or not, he didn't tell her that he was almost certain this had been the last time. He didn't dare. Instead, he said,

"Thanks but no thanks on the staying over. And you wouldn't have asked if you didn't know that would be my answer."

"You understand me too well. So…same time next year?"

"Of course," he said, and then added, as he always did, "unless you're mated by then."

Her eyes flashed. "Kenar is a good alpha."

That was debatable, but Dayn wasn't going to get Keely or any of the other pack members to admit that their alpha was more interested in himself than the pack or its traditions. Or that it had been wrong for him to twist those traditions around in order to run off the male Keely's father had brought in from an outside pack to be her mate and his successor. Granted, the male—Roloff—shouldn't have left. But that didn't make Kenar right.

Since there was no point in picking the fight, though—"been there, done that" was a particularly apt human saying in this case—he blew her a kiss. "Until next year, then." Which was a lie, but a necessary one. In the entire wolfyn realm, only the pack's wisewolfyn, Candida, knew who and what he truly was, and that it was almost time for him to go home.

"Of course," Keely agreed. "That is, unless *you* find a mate between now and then."

He had his hand on the door, but looked back, surprised. "Me? No. Not in the cards."

"The Stone-Turn pack's new guest is pretty."

"I'm not interested in taking a mate." Besides, the

newcomer wasn't the woman he was waiting for, the one he'd been dreaming of more clearly every night over the past week, waking each morning with the image of a heart-shaped face, dimpled chin and go-to-hell attitude topped with curly, red-streaked hair. *Hurry,* he wanted to tell her. *Please, hurry.*

Keely looked at him quizzically. "If that's not it, then what's bothering you?" To the wolfyn, problems always boiled down to politics or family. Since he wasn't involved in pack politics, that left family—or, in his case, his lack of one.

"I'm fine. I promise." Sketching a half salute in her direction, he said softly, "Have a good run." Already, he could see the amber fire at the back of her eyes. And, as he let himself out of her place, he could feel the hum of change magic on the air. It crinkled along his skin, stirring the restlessness that had been riding him harder and harder as the days passed and there was no sign of his guide. Frustration gnawed at him, making him feel itchy, twitchy. He wanted to race through the darkness, pick a fight, howl at the moon....

Instead, he headed for the small log cabin he'd built near the standing stones, zipping his jacket and shoving his hands in his pockets as he hiked along the two-mile path. The blood moon lit the night with the eerie blue-white light that was almost as bright as day, though monochromatic. By the time his cabin came into view, the air already carried a chorus of excited yips and deeper, spine-shivering howls.

His cabin, little more than a single long room with

a central chimney and big hearth, was laughably rustic as far as the pack members were concerned. He had used human-style insulated windows, though, and had a wolfyn-tech generator for power. He had left the lights off tonight, though, and the moonlight that bathed the cabin lit it blue-white, making it seem like it was...

*Oh, shit. Glowing.* Dayn's pulse kicked, because he knew from past experience that it wasn't the cabin doing the glowing. There was a vortex forming in the standing stones!

He took off at a run. As he came around the corner, thunder rumbled, vibrating up through the soles of his boots even though the sky was clear. He nearly cheered at the sight of blue-white lightning sparking among the standing stones. The electricity lit the air, charging the ozone and making his hair bristle as if he, too, were going through the change.

Magic surrounded him as he charged up the hill, suffusing him and running foxfire glows along his skin when he came to a halt just outside the circle. Electricity arced from one stone to the next and the next, lighting the entire circle with blue-white power. Then, suddenly, the grass and empty air within the circle grew blurry and started to move, making a slow inward spiral at first, but then spinning faster and faster, tightening within seconds to a gray tornado of everything and nothing.

Magic tugged at him, beckoning. *Come,* the vortex seemed to be saying. *Say the words and come.*

Dayn hesitated, though. The vortices had never

worked for him before, even with the spell that should return him home to Elden. But what if it was finally time? Maybe his guide wasn't supposed to come to him, but rather the reverse. *Please, gods.*

Thunder boomed and magic churned as he pictured the forest he had been snatched from and said the spell. Then, braced for anything, he stepped into the stone circle.

The wind surrounded him instantly, grabbing him up and tumbling him head over ass in a whirling maelstrom of power. Excitement seared through him. It was working! Thunder roared and lightning arced and snapped, and the universe seemed to hold its breath for an instant. In that moment, he glimpsed a modern, human-style kitchen and jolted with dismay. *No, not the human realm. Take me to Elden!*

Even as he thought that, pain flared behind his eyes, lashing through his skull…and everything winked out.

For a second, there was only darkness. Stillness. Silence. He couldn't even hear his own heartbeat.

Then everything jolted back into existence around him, and there was blue-white light in his eyes and the springy press of grass-covered earth beneath him. He blinked into the light, gut fisting on disappointment as things came into focus and he recognized the full moon pouring down on the familiar ring of standing stones.

"Son of a bitch." He hadn't gone anywhere, after all. He was still in the wolfyn realm. "Son of a sucking—"

A soft moan cut him off. A soft, very feminine moan. His heart started to *thud* in his chest as he turned toward the sound, telling himself not to hope, but hoping nonetheless.

And there she was. After all this time, there she was.

She lay curled on the grass with her cheek pillowed on her hands, but he recognized the oval of her face, the stubborn dent in her chin and the strong yet subtly curved lines of her body. More, he knew without seeing it in the light of day that her wavy hair was red-shot, her eyes a clear blue, like the deepest part of the Elden sky after a rainstorm. Not that it mattered whether or not she was beautiful—she was his guide, and he had his priorities well in mind.

Her clothes said she was human, which surprised him. Of the three known realms, the human realm was the most technologically advanced and used the least magic, which put them the farthest away from the pure magic of the kingdoms. Given that, how was she supposed to guide him?

*Have faith,* he told himself. His father had promised a guide, and here she was.

Which also meant that the four-night countdown had begun, and they needed to get moving. But there was a problem with that: she was out cold, and the Scratch-Eye pack was gathering for their run, which would include an hour-long serenade at the stones. Although the wolfyn were largely civilized on a day-to-day basis—in their home realm, at least—the blood moon unleashed the other aspects of their personalities. And while Keely probably wouldn't have a problem seeing him with another woman during the blood moon, others wouldn't be so forgiving.

Making a snap decision, though he would have rather stayed and called a new vortex right away, Dayn gathered the woman in his arms. She was lighter boned and smaller than Keely, and seemed to fit naturally against him as he carried her from the circle, with her head tucked against his neck and her curly hair brushing his cheek.

Inside his cabin, he put her gently on the couch near the hearth, where the remains of the fire were still warm. Then he shucked out of his too-hot jacket and knelt beside her, part of him still unable to believe that he had dreamed of her, and here she was. His eyes lingered on the fullness of her lips, and the faint blush of color on her cheeks. He reached for her, intending to try again to wake her, but instead he found himself easing a few fallen strands of her hair away from where they had caught on her eyelashes. Her skin was soft and warm, and although he told himself he shouldn't be touching her, not like this, he couldn't make himself pull away.

She stirred beneath his touch, and let out a soft sigh. He caught his breath, then held it as her eyes opened and locked on his. The entire universe telescoped down to those blue, blue eyes and her look of shock…and then recognition.

The woodsman smiled down at her. "Thank the gods you're finally here."

Reda stared mutely up at him as her head spun and the world tilted a few degrees away from normal.

It was the same dream she'd been having all week, where she would wake in a log cabin to find this man crouched over her while a fire *hiss-popped* nearby. He looked like she had dreamed him: rumpled dark hair fell forward over his brow and curled below his ears, accenting his sharply defined features and emerald-green eyes. He had a rawboned yet powerful body, wide-shouldered and long-limbed, with lean, loose muscles that folded economically where he knelt beside her. His skin was smooth and bronze, with a light dusting of masculine hair visible where the top two buttons of his shirt were undone. And, as in her dreams, the air smelled of wood, smoke and cinnamon. Fluid warmth coursed through her body, concentrating at the point where his fingers rested softly on her cheek.

But as the spins settled, nerves took their place... because the overall picture was right, but the details were wrong.

The cabin was made of rough-hewn logs, yes, but she was lying on a plush sofa rather than a cot, and on a nearby end table, a mosaic lamp gave off muted amber light. And the man was wearing clothes straight out of the Bean catalog rather than homespun. More, even the details of the details were off. The couch she was lying on had the soft nap of velvet, but the fabric moved oddly, as did the stuffing beneath. And the lamp didn't have a cord.

*What the hell?*

"I'm going to kill MacEvoy." The idiot must've

juiced the shop's incense burner with something really funky and hallucinogenic.

Like, say, acid.

"Who is MacEvoy?" The woodsman's voice was a smooth baritone with a raspy undertone that seemed to stroke her skin. But the question put another dose of nerves into the mix, as did the look in his eyes as he rocked back on his heels and stared down at her with a wary, confused air.

He'd never spoken before, never looked baffled before.

They were way off the script, and she didn't like it.

"He's… It doesn't matter." She pushed herself upright on the couch, waving him off when he made a move to help. "I'm good. I'm fine." Only she wasn't fine. This was all wrong, because whatever the hell was going on, the dream—hallucination?—seemed way too real.

"Fine enough to get moving?"

"Moving?"

He nodded. "We have four nights counting tonight, so we should get started as soon as possible."

Reda breathed deeply and told herself not to panic. There was some logical explanation for this. There had to be. "I'm not having sex with you." And oh, holy crap, she didn't know why that had been the first thing out of her mouth. Or, rather, she did: it was because of the dreams.

His eyebrows rose. "Of course not. You're my guide."

She flushed, but pushed on. "Seriously. I don't have

a clue what you're talking about." And she also didn't know why she was arguing with a figment of her over-stressed mind.

"Don't even joke about that."

"Who's joking?" She wasn't kidding around; she was confused as all hell. "Wait. Am I being punked?" Who would bother?

Expression suddenly clearing, he said, "Damnation. Vortex sickness."

"Vor-what?"

He rose and started to pace. "Sometimes when travelers come through the vortices from one realm to another, they become confused or even forget pieces of their past."

A low burn fisted beneath her heart. "I'm not crazy."

"I didn't say you were," he said, which she guessed was true as far as it went. But then he continued, "Memory loss and insanity aren't the same thing. I believe you call it 'apples and limes,' yes?"

"Oranges. Apples and oranges." His speech pattern was an odd mix of formality and slang, which just added to the weirdness. "Who *are* you?"

He stopped pacing and looked slightly shamefaced. "Sorry. I'm Dayn. Well, Prince Dayn, Forestal of Elden. But if anyone here knew that, they'd rip me to shreds." He said it so matter-of-factly that it took a moment to register. As her jaw dropped, he held out a hand. "So let's just go with 'Dayn,' okay?"

"I'm Reda." Head spinning, she took his hand on autopilot, registering the warm strength of his wide palm and long, elegant fingers. But instead of shaking, he lifted her hand to his lips and brushed a kiss over her knuckles. It was an unselfconscious move, as if he'd done it a thousand times before and it meant nothing more than a fist bump on the T platform or a cuff on the arm between buddies at Downtown Pizza. But her gasp brought his eyes to hers and made it far more than casual, as did the sizzle that tightened her skin and reminded her that this was a dream. More, it was her fantasy. *He* was her fantasy, had been since she was a little girl and dreamed of someone coming to her rescue.

He dropped her hand and took a big step back. "I'm sorry. I shouldn't have done that."

*Why not? It's my fantasy.* But he wasn't playing his part. He should have been whispering sweetly to her, kissing her, stroking—

The cabin door blew open with a bang, making her jolt as a cold gust of wind puffed ashes into the hearth and swirled smoke into the air. But that wasn't what had opened the door. Because as Dayn spun toward the commotion, a huge figure darkened the doorway. Reda shot to her feet. Then she froze and a three-headed giant stepped through.

So tall that it had to duck through the door, the monstrous creature had the body of a man, huge and muscular, but its skin was cement-gray and its broad shoulders supported three ogre-faced heads with protruding lower jaws, curved upthrusting teeth and fierce black eyes framing moist, snubbed noses. The thing was dressed in a leathery loincloth, boots the size of mailboxes and studded wristbands and neck collars, and it carried a huge, blunt-headed club that was ringed with spikes and banded with iron. When it caught sight of her and Dayn, all three faces grinned horribly.

Dayn lunged for a rack of weapons her mind had initially dismissed as decor, grabbed a crossbow and yelled, "Run!"

The middle head locked on him while the other two stayed leering at her. Which made it tough to figure out who was the target as the creature bellowed a roar, drew back and swung its enormous club of death.

"Down!" Dayn plowed into her. They slammed against the back of the sofa, which overbalanced and fell, taking them with it.

The club screamed over their heads and crashed into the chimney above the hearth, sending chunks of brick spattering around the room. Nearly flattened beneath Dayn—he might be rangy, but he was *solid*—Reda struggled to breathe through the white-hot grip of panic. *This isn't happening, can't be happening. It's just a dream, not real, none of this is real.*

Heavy footsteps thudded as the creature came toward them, growling low in its three-way throat.

*Not real. A dream. I'm waking up now. On the count of three, I'm going to open my eyes and everything will be back to normal.*

"Stay down," Dayn whispered in her ear, shifting as the monster stumped nearer, shoving furniture and knocking things crashing to the floor.

*One.*

Three heads came into view, six eyes locked on and the creature roared, reared back and swung. Dayn shouted something, lunged to his feet and fired his crossbow from the hip. The bolt buried itself at the top of the giant's middle throat.

Shaking, Reda flattened herself. She couldn't breathe, couldn't think, couldn't do anything but count.

*Two.*

The monster screeched, tossed the club, grabbed for its blood-spurting throat and reeled back. The club smashed into a window and hung up on the frame as Dayn fired a second bolt into the same head, turning the creature's roar into a high-pitched mewl that grated on her soul.

*Please, God. Three.*

# *Chapter 3*

Reda didn't wake up.

Instead, she watched in frozen horror as the three-headed giant staggered and went to its knees, and Dayn methodically fired bolts into the other two heads. As if that had finally hit the kill switch, the creature plummeted to the cabin floor, where it lay for a moment, twitching in its death throes, and then finally going still.

The sudden silence rang in her ears as she stared at the monstrous corpse, which smelled like chicken breasts gone very bad.

She yanked her eyes to Dayn, who stood looking down at the creature with an expression of pity, but also excitement, as if the attack had been partly a good thing.

Who was he? What in God's name was going on? She wanted to ask him but couldn't get out the words. She was locked in place. Frozen. Once and always a coward under fire. Was this, then, what her subconscious wanted her to see?

Maybe. But she'd seen it and the dream wasn't ending.

"You can get up now." He said it without looking at her, but she thought she saw the twitch of a smile. "There's a bag in the pantry. How about you load up some provisions while I take care of the other stuff?"

As he turned away, she slowly levered herself to her feet, suddenly wishing that a herd of pink elephants would walk past the broken window, so she could point at them and say, *Ha, I told you so. It's a dream.* Hallucination. Whatever. What mattered was that this wasn't really happening. It was all in her mind.

Except there weren't any pink elephants. Which left her with a stinky dead giant with two too many heads, and a really hot guy who thought they were going somewhere.

*MacEvoy, when I get through with you, you'd wish you just mailed me the damn book for free,* she thought. And then, because she couldn't think of a good reason not to, she went to pack some food.

The bag proved to be a single-strap rucksack, and the provisions at hand were heavy on the hard rolls, dried protein—she didn't ask, didn't want to know— and trail mix. She loaded up whatever she sort of recognized, trying to focus on the similarities rather than cataloging the differences. Her brain, though, kept a running tally that twisted the knots in her stomach increasingly tight.

And all the while, she was entirely aware of Dayn as he pulled on a sweater followed by his heavy leather coat, loaded a rucksack with his crossbow and bolts and strapped on a narrow leather belt that held an unusually short sword on one side, pouches on the other. As she finished up her packing, he slung a sloshing crescent-shaped leather pouch over his shoulder, glanced over at her and nodded.

He didn't seem to expect a reply, though, because his attention moved on to the overturned couch and smashed end table, the broken window and the scattered other things that defined a life: a journal bound in what looked like nylon but wasn't, a bunch of interesting rocks in a jar, a huge antler with a picture of a beautiful stallion carved into it, only half-finished. And while he looked at the room, she was looking at him. Decked out in a strange mix of modern clothing and archaic equipment, he should have looked as if he was late for Halloween. Instead, he appeared utterly comfortable in his own skin and—as evidenced by the giant's corpse—deadly capable. She couldn't take her eyes off him.

He turned abruptly toward the door. "Let's go."

She held her ground. "Go where?" They were the first two words she had managed to utter since the attack. Her mind might be racing but her body was still mostly vapor locked. That was the way it worked when she went into curl-up-and-die mode.

He tipped his head toward the dead creature. "That was an ettin, which isn't native to this realm. It had to have come from the kingdoms, which means the vortex has probably opened back up. And that means we need to go. Now."

Vortex? Realms? How could he stand there wearing a crossbow and sword and talk about things that belonged in science fiction? It didn't make any sense.

*Of course not,* her rational self said. *It's a dream, or a hallucination or something. But since counting to three didn't work, maybe this vortex will.*

So she nodded and followed him out of the cabin, her boots crunching on broken glass and then echoing on the short steps leading down.

"This way," he said, urging her along a wide path. His breath fogged the air. "If we can get back through the stones— Shit." His face fell. "It's not glowing."

"Which means?"

"The vortex is already gone." He glanced at her. "You know how to call one, right?"

"I…" She thought of the whirling wind in her kitchen, the spell her mother taught her. "Yeah."

"Then let's go. If we hurry we can be gone before the pack gets there." But he hadn't gone more than a few paces before a wolf's high, eerie howl rose into the clear night air, coming from very nearby. First one, then another and another joined in, swelling the note to a harmony, then to a chorus, as if they were intentionally singing together.

The hair on the back of her neck shivered at the sound, which was wild, feral and hauntingly beautiful. But at the same time, nerves twined through her, turning her skin to gooseflesh.

Dayn stopped in the middle of the pathway. "Damn it, we're already too late to get ahead of them, and we *really* don't want to interrupt the blood-moon ritual." He paused, considering. "Given that I don't want to cross paths with them tonight, especially not with you, we're going to need to hole up somewhere out of sight." He glanced back at the cabin.

"Not there," she said quickly.

He nodded, then pointed off to one side, where the trees ran up a steep, rocky hill. "There's a cave I use sometimes. We'll be okay there for an hour or two."

"A cave," she repeated, apparently only able to string together two words at a time, preferably one syllable each. Suddenly very aware of the cold that bit through her shirt and lightweight leather, she hugged herself tightly. This couldn't be happening; it was all too unreal. Yet, strangely, Dayn seemed more real to her than anyone had in a very long time. He was bright and vivid; he drew her eyes and made her want to stare, made her want to touch. She'd felt inner sparklers when he kissed her hand. What would happen if he kissed her lips? What if he did more?

*Focus. Stop transferring. You need to get out of here, not fantasize.*

"Here." He dug into his rucksack and pulled out a second sweater. "Figured you'd want another layer, unless your coat is one of those fancy jobs with the really thin insulation."

"It's not." She slipped out of her leather and took the sweater from him. It was dark in color, thick and lightweight, almost airy, and the material had a faint rasp that suggested some dream-version of wool. Needing to say something that involved more than two syllables and might defuse the strangeness of wearing his clothes, she said, "Okay, so you carry a sword but you know about Thinsulate. What's the deal here?"

He hesitated, then said, "There's some travel between your realm and this one, so a certain amount of your technology has leaked over and been adapted to work here. I'm from the kingdom realm, which is pure magic. Thus, the sword."

"Is there the same sort of sharing between your realm and this one?" She was stalling, asking about things she didn't begin to believe in because she had been having sex dreams about him while he'd apparently been waiting for her to show up and lead him somewhere. And she didn't want to wear his sweater. Except she did, because it was freezing out, and the sweater smelled like him—a mix of pine, moss and mint.

*I really am losing my mind, aren't I?* The thought brought a jab of new fear.

He glanced in the direction of the howls. "Things are far more complicated between my realm and this one.

And we should get moving before a pack scout catches sight of us."

"Sorry." Holding her breath, she pulled on his sweater and smoothed it down her body, where it clung unexpectedly to her rather blatant curves. But she didn't care about that because she was already warmer, on the way to growing toasty. Letting out a soft sigh, she said, "Ahh, yes. That's good." Not letting herself snuggle or even take a deep breath, she nodded. "Okay. Lead on."

He made a quiet noise at the back of his throat, adjusted his burdens and headed across the track and into the moon-dappled forest. There must have been some sort of path; she couldn't see any markings, but he led her up the steep, rocky slope with a neat economy of effort, his near-silent footsteps making her feel loud and awkward in comparison. After ten, maybe fifteen minutes, he motioned for her to join him on a wide, flat ledge near a triangular cave mouth.

"Wait here. I've got some lights and other supplies inside." He slipped into the darkness. Moments later a muted glow sprang to life and he called. "Come on in."

She ducked to follow him in, found him crouched at roughly the midpoint of a low tunnel that was formed where two huge slabs of smooth, porous stone leaned against each other. In his palm he held a small rectangular unit that emitted blue-white light and a low background hum.

"The wolfyn won't come up here," he said. "After they're done with the ritual, they'll run the lowlands for the rest of the night. Moon time, you know."

She only heard part of it, though, because the moment he said "wolfyn," her stomach hollowed out and she flashed back to the woodcutting and the sly, evil creature that had seduced innocent Red. She sank down opposite him, and then leaned against the wall when her head spun. "Those were *wolfyn* back there?"

He nodded. "You'd call them werewolves. They're shape-shifters. Human. Wolf. Back again." He paused, fiddling with the little light. "I don't know what the legends are like where you come from, but you don't need to be afraid of them here. They treat guests well in their own realm. It's part of the tradition they live by."

Her heart was beating so hard her chest hurt, and her legs and arms tingled with an oncoming panic attack. A big one. *Breathe,* she told herself. *You can deal with this.* The wolfyn were just part of the hallucination. They couldn't hurt her, couldn't roofie her into sexual submission and then eat her when their other needs were satisfied. So far, all they were was just noise on the horizon. Besides, her mother's stories about them taking young girls had been allegories about not giving it up too early or to the wrong guy.

Right?

*Breathe. Don't lose it.* He wasn't her fantasy prince and she wasn't really in another realm. She wasn't even really wearing his sweater, even though she was far warmer now, both because of the extra layer and the intimacy of the little cave, which forced them to bump knees and kept her system on a low rev of awareness.

Her racing mind was scared, confused and frustrated, but her body was entirely aware of his.

When he shifted back, so he was leaning on the opposite wall, his movements were controlled; after he settled in, he went very still, almost looking as though he wasn't even breathing. He moved like a martial artist, she thought...or a predator. A hunter. The realization stirred her blood far more than it should, and she caught herself collecting small details, like how his aristocratic nose had a faint ridge where it had been broken and just slightly offset, and the way his hands were long-fingered and elegant, yet tough and callused with hard labor.

Benz had used to tease her that she would need genetic engineering to create her perfect guy, because she wanted the whole package: brains, compassion, honor and romance in a laborer's strong, muscular body. And he wasn't far off, because that would have been a real-life approximation of her woodcutter hero... Like the one sitting opposite her now, staring out into the night.

*Except that he's not really here, is he?* said her logical, rational self. And the heat buzzing through her body racheted down because it was right. Her brain was tricking her, just like it had when she was a little girl and thought she heard her maman's voice whispering to her, sending her into the woods looking for answers. She didn't need the department shrink to tell her that.

*You have to get to the vortex,* logic reminded her. *He said that was the way home.* And if her mind had bought in so deeply to the illusion, then the rules of the illusion should work. Maybe. Hopefully.

But the place where the vortex formed was crawling with wolfyn, and…wait. "If the wolfyn are harmless, why are we hiding up here?"

He looked back at her for a moment, seeming to be measuring her mental state. Or maybe deciding how much to tell her. "There's some personal stuff between me and the pack leader. Tempers can run high this time of year, so I think it's better if he and I stay out of each other's way."

"And?" she prompted when her cop's instincts told her there was more.

He shifted, stretching his legs out beside hers, almost but not quite touching. The alignment of her battered jeans against his turned the differences in fabric and stitching from subtle to a shout as he said, "You know how I said things were complicated between my realm and the wolfyn? Well, there was a war. I don't even know what really started it—nobody here seems to, and it was a long time ago. But it was ruthless and bloody, and didn't end until a group of kingdom magic-users, the Ilth, got together and changed the nature of the vortices so that when wolfyn come through to the kingdoms they wind up stuck in the wolf form, unable to change back or cast the spell to return home. Eventually, they even lose their human thoughts, becoming purely feral." He paused. "The wolfyn came up with a counterspell, but by that time they had discovered the human realm and become fascinated with your science.

For the past few generations—and my people have very long generations—contact has been limited to the few wolfyn who get sucked up into the vortices without the counterspell, and the occasional guest who shows up here, like me. In fact, the people of the kingdoms don't even believe in realm travel anymore—it's faded to legend status, just like the wolfyns' abilities to shape-shift and enthrall beautiful women."

A shiver crawled up Reda's spine as the hallucination suddenly gained an uncomfortable amount of detail that dovetailed with the stories she knew. "Can they do that? Enthrall women, I mean."

He shook his head. "They wouldn't do that to a guest, not even during the moon time. The traditions are very clear on when and how enthrallment can be used."

Which wasn't a "no." Feeling the cold more than she had been moments before, she tucked her hands under her arms beneath her jacket, warming them in a sweater that was uncomfortably peltlike all of a sudden.

He continued, "So while the wolfyn are generally tolerant, they prefer humans over kingdomites, and there are certain bloodlines from the kingdom that remain kill-on-sight."

"Which is why you don't want them to know that you're a prince," she said, remembering his earlier comment. Then, without warning, a bubble of half-hysterical laughter rose up inside her, sticking in her throat and threatening to turn into a sob. "You're a prince," she repeated. "Of course you are." She used to dream of charming princes, ethereal princesses and magical adventures, so maybe it was no wonder her mind had gone back there now, turning her fantasy man into not only the woodcutter, but also a handsome prince. She buried her face in her hands. "You're not real. *None* of this is real. Go away and let me wake up in my real bed in the middle of my real life." She felt a tug of wistfulness at the thought of leaving the dream behind, and that couldn't be good.

"It's just vortex sickness," he said soothingly. "Don't worry. Just relax—it'll all come back to you soon."

She lifted her head to glare at him. "I haven't forgotten anything, damn it. My name is Reda Weston, my father is Major Michael Weston and my mother's name was Freddy. See? No gaps. No blank spots. And this isn't real."

"By the gods and the Abyss, this *is* real." A hint of temper licked at the back of his eyes, which had gone very green in the pale illumination. His voice gained an edge. "And it's going to stay real whether you believe in it or not, so how about you chuck the 'science is God' human attitude and consider that maybe this *is* happening, and that you're here for a reason? Because unless you help me out here, people are going to die."

"I..." She stared at him, throat drying to dust. "What?"

"People. Will. Die," he said, spacing the words through gritted teeth. "I need to get my ass back to Castle Island within the next seventy-two hours, and you're supposed to be helping me."

Her throat closed, but she forced out, "I've never

heard of Castle Island." Then, seeing it in his eyes, she held up a hand. "And if you say 'vortex sickness' one more time, I'm going to scream."

His expression eased. "Okay. At least you're listening."

"I'm…" She shook her head. "I don't know what I am, besides scared and confused. What's going on here? What's on Castle Island and why do you need to be there? And why does it involve me?" *This doesn't matter, anyway. It's just an illusion.*

"I don't know how you're involved, really, or why. But I can tell you about Castle Island." He waited for her nod. When he got it, he made a rueful, bitter face, and began. "There once was a prince who thought the world should revolve around him.…" Her blood chilled as he described his home being attacked by a vile sorcerer and his parents casting a massive spell that had saved him and his siblings, yet went awry, binding them to the castle and cursing the kingdom if they failed to return in time. He recited a message from his father's spirit, telling him to wait for a guide, and that when she arrived he needed to be back on Castle Island by the fourth night, to reunite with his siblings and kill the sorcerer. He paused, expression going hollow. "The next thing I knew, I was stuck here in the wolfyn realm, doing my damnedest to make them believe I'd lost my memory in the vortex and keep them from guessing that I was a member of a royal house…and all the while, waiting for my guide to show up. Then, about a week ago, I started having these dreams."

"Dreams," she whispered, body heating suddenly.

He nodded. "I saw you, Reda. Your face. Your eyes. The magic was making sure I would recognize you when you arrived."

She moved restlessly, shifting her legs away from his. "There's no such thing as magic."

"Maybe there isn't in your world. But there is in mine."

Her pulse thudded loudly in her ears. The department shrink had talked about hospitalization but in the end had signed off on an outpatient program with intensive sessions that had started off daily and tapered from there. Now, she wondered whether that had been a mistake, whether she had faked her way through her recovery, fooling even herself, until now. Was she in a hospital room somewhere, staring blankly out a window while her mind roamed free? Panic sparked in her chest as she tried to imagine it but couldn't, tried to connect with her "real" mind trapped somewhere else, but couldn't do that, either. The cave, the man and his story felt entirely real. Which would mean...

"No," she said, pushing herself up to the hunched-over crouch that was all the cave allowed, which made her feel trapped and squirrelly. "This isn't... I'm not your guide. There's been some sort of mistake."

He hadn't moved a muscle, except to follow her with his eyes. "When you first woke up in the cabin, you recognized me. I saw it in your face."

"I..." *dreamed of you, lusted after you, imagined you were all the things I haven't been able to find in a flesh-and-blood guy.* "Okay, maybe there were a couple of dreams, but there wasn't anything about me guiding you anywhere." She didn't mention waking up hot, bothered and alone. Clearly, their dreams had been very different: she had dreamed of finding love; he had dreamed of saving his people. Was that what her subconscious wanted her to see? That she was too wrapped up in her own problems? That one resonated a little too well, making her queasy. Pressing a hand to her stomach, she said, "I need to…you know. Outside."

He touched her free hand briefly in support. "Go out the back and stay close. There's a grove of borer trees on the other side of the stones, and you don't want to mess with borers."

She didn't ask why, didn't intend to find out. "I'll be back in a few minutes. I think I just need some air." And some space without him there to remind her how numb she'd been for too long, just going through the motions, stuck in her own little world.

Outside of the cave, the air was cold, stark and silent, with none of the howling of earlier. The huge moon lit her path as she picked her way over the rocks, getting clear of Dayn's sight as if looking for someplace to relieve herself. Then, with her heart pounding and fear souring the back of her throat, she looped around and headed back downhill, stumbling in her haste to get to the stones and break out of the hallucination before she did something really stupid… Like buy into it.

\* \* \*

With Reda gone, the cave was cooler and far less interesting, drained of the intense, compressed energy that practically shimmered around her. But it was also a whole hell of a lot calmer.

Dayn exhaled slowly, telling himself that it was going to be okay. This was going to work. She finally seemed ready to consider that she wasn't caught in some strange and elaborate dream, and once they got past that, he was sure her memories would resurface and she would be able to guide him. At least he hoped to the Abyss that it would work that way. He was starting to fear it might not, because a human seemed a very strange choice for someone to guide him through the magical realm of Elden. Which made him think that this part of the spell, too, had been damaged by the sorcerer's magic.

Not that *she* was damaged; exactly the opposite, in fact. She might have some human suspicions and disbelief when it came to the magic, and an apparent tendency to go wide-eyed and catatonic under fire, but she drew him, compelled him. Unlike the willowy, aloof wolfyn females he had spent the past two decades with, she was compact and curvy, and her emotions were written so clearly on her heart-shaped face. He had caught himself staring into her eyes, which reminded him of the deep blue skies of home, and basking in her voice, which was sweet, soft and wholly feminine.

Which was why she wasn't the only one who had needed a minute alone. Because he needed to get a grip on himself, needed to regain some perspective. This wasn't about him being a man and her a woman; it was about him getting his ass home and taking care of business there. And after that he would be back to being a prince of the realm, with all that the title implied. Which meant there was no benefit to him noticing how his sweater clung to the curves of her breasts and hips, and that the hitch of her breath when she caught him looking at her told him the attraction wasn't one-sided.

"Priorities," he said to himself, hearing the word echo through the otherwise silent cave, the air empty of wolf howls. The ritual was done, then, and it was time for him and Reda to head back down to the stones. Maybe she wouldn't even need to remember. Maybe her just being there would cause the vortex spell to work for him as it hadn't before.

Rising to the crouched-over crabwalk required by the cave, he eased out and straightened, calling softly, "Reda?"

There was no answer, but she wouldn't have gone far, given that he had mindspoken her to stay close.

Not long after he arrived in the wolfyn realm, he had discovered that his mindspeak powers worked on all females, regardless of what realm they came from. When he had physical contact—as he had just now, touching Reda's hand—he could implant suggestions, even orders. That was how he'd kept Keely from knowing certain things he didn't want her to, and how he'd initially pushed Candida to protect him—until she had figured out what he was doing, and went for his throat. After that, he had told her everything, and instead of killing him, she had decided to help him, instead. And thank the gods for that.

Although the pack's wisewoman hadn't been able to send him home, she had given him the vortex counterspell, and more recently had been working on some new poisons she thought would work on beings of dark magic, like the Blood Sorcerer. More, she had helped him work out the limits of his mindspeaking powers in the wolfyn realm, and they had discovered that while he couldn't make a female do something she was against or prevent her from doing something she really wanted to, he could influence other, less definitive emotions. That was why he hadn't been able to push Reda into opening up to him—she was too set against it. But given her obvious fear of the wolfyn and the fact that she was starting to warm up to him, she would obey his command to stick around. She ought to be right nearby.

Only she wasn't.

Cursing under his breath, growing increasingly anxious when there was no sign of her, he walked all the way out to the edge of the borer grove, where the ground started to go hollow. Then he backtracked and circled around the cave. And he picked up her trail heading back down the incline, beelining straight for the standing stones.

"Son of a *bitch*." He had underestimated her mental strength, her disbelief and her determination to break free of what she thought was an illusion. Scrambling back to the cave, he grabbed his supplies and weapons, hoping to hell he hadn't just made a fatal mistake. Worse, as he pelted downhill, the horizon beyond his tree-hidden cabin started to glow.

His stomach plummeted. He was going to be too damn late.

Standing just inside the stone circle, Moragh threw her head back and laughed with delight as fat blue sparks leaped from one stone to the next and wind stirred her hair, fanning it out around her face.

Raising her voice to carry over the sparks and crackles of power, she called, "Oh, joyous dark gods, I knew it, Nasri! I always knew the Book of Ilth was real."

She had argued with the sorcerer's so-called scholars, who had written the text off as either fiction or a heretical interpretation of the gods and the Abyss. Granted, nothing had happened back then when she had tried the two simplest spells, but she hadn't known that location mattered. It stood to reason, though, that the separation between realms would be thinnest at certain points, the magic connecting them more active. It had taken the lost prince's spell to draw her to the right place at the right time, and the stirring of vortex wind for her to figure out that she needed to try the first of the two spells she had memorized.

It had worked then, and again just now. She was facing the beginnings of a vortex of her own, one she controlled.

"Are we going home now, Mistress Moragh?" Nasri

called from where he stood outside the stones, holding the submission chain of the surviving ettin, which was still stupidly looking around for its brother.

Admittedly, she should have set both of the creatures on the prince and made sure of the kill. But she hadn't realized right away that something in this realm—gods, she was in another *realm*—would dull her connection to his father's spell, making her unable to track him beyond the immediate area of the standing stones. But no matter, she suddenly had new and wondrous options.

"Yes and no," she said in answer to Nasri's question. "I must return home and retrieve the Book of Ilth." Her heart lifted at the thought of wielding the book's power—it didn't contain only realm-travel spells, but also summoning spells more powerful than anything the kingdoms had seen in centuries, power transference spells—the possibilities were nearly limitless. "I will take the ettin with me, so you are not troubled by him, and then I shall seal this portal behind me, so the prince cannot follow." That was the second of the spells she had memorized. Sealing this particular portal might not trap the prince in the wolfyn realm—there were probably other locations where vortices could be made—but it would slow him down, giving her enough time to steal the book from the very scholars who had mocked her for believing it real.

The gnome's eyes widened. "And me, mistress?"

Satisfied that the vortex was well under way, she stepped out of the stones, froze the ettin in place with a three-word command and then turned her attention to Nasri, who had backed away a few paces when he thought she wasn't looking. And even though he had long ago stopped appealing to her, the thought of what she was about to do had her secondary canines descending easily, breaking the skin with that itchy pinch of pain she loved so much, and then gliding into place alongside her lower teeth, just touching the gums with a kiss of the wickedly sharp points.

"I have a special job for you, Nasri."

He blanched at the sight of her fangs, but the compulsion was well rooted. Even as his entire body cringed away from her, he took three jerky steps forward and raised his arm, offering her a wrist dotted with toothmarks in various healing stages.

She surged forward and took his throat instead, biting deep and hanging on as he writhed and the glorious tang of blood flowed down her throat. New connections formed; new magic came to life, and she found his weak little mind with hers. *Now pay attention. This is what I want you to do....*

Reda didn't scream, but that was only because she was paralyzed, stuck flat to the ground beneath a dense clump of underbrush at the edge of the clearing, where she had a perfect view of the dark haired woman *drinking* from the neck of her small, wizened servant, and a clear soundtrack of the vampire's rhythmical sucking noises interspersed with mewls of horror from the victim.

Her gorge rose. This woman—this Moragh—was a vampire. Dear God.

She swallowed again and again in an effort to keep herself from puking at the sight of the little man's body convulsing, his hands fluttering at his sides, as if he wanted to fight her off but couldn't. Just as he had wanted to run the other way before, but had held out his arm instead. *Compulsion. Enthrallment.* First the wolfyn and now this. Was every nonhuman creature in this realm capable of inflicting its will on others? *I have to get out of here,* she thought as the breath sobbed in her lungs. *I just want everything to go back to normal.*

She had to get through that vortex, and she had to do it now, while the vampire was occupied. But she couldn't move.

*Not now,* she begged her body. *Please don't freeze up on me now!* But she couldn't force herself to stand and make a run for the standing stones, couldn't so much as wiggle a toe. She was vapor locked again. Immobile. Useless. All she could do was watch as the vampire let go and the little man swayed on his feet, throat drenched with blood. His eyes were glassy and unfocused, his voice monotone when he said, "I shall find the pack."

He stumbled off, headed on a tangent for the woods, seeming not to care that there was blood streaming down his front.

The vampire watched him go with a small smile playing over her bloodstained lips. "I wouldn't worry. I suspect they'll find you very soon." Moonlight glinted off her fangs as she smiled fully, horribly. Then she turned away, snagged the monster's chain off the ground and led the creature into the stones.

The vortex roared and they disappeared.

The second they were gone, Reda's paralysis snapped and she was on her feet and racing for the stones, her heart pounding as she called up the spell that had gotten her into this mess.

She was only a few steps away when Dayn burst from the trees, shouting, "Reda, *wait!*"

Hesitating, she glanced back. And as she did so, a cracking sound filled the air and the vortex collapsed in on itself and disappeared. Seconds later, there was a brilliant amber flash and the air went utterly dead. "No!" She flew through the stones and raced to the center. "Wait, no! Take me!"

"Reda, stop." He grabbed her by the arms. "Stop. It's over. It's gone."

"No! She's sealing it off. Don't let her seal it off!" Even though she knew in her heart that it was already too late, she beat on his arms, struggling to get free, not just from him, but from this whole awful place, with its werewolves and vampires and three-headed monsters. Then, when that didn't work, she collapsed against him, grabbing his jacket to get in his face and cry, "Did you see her? Did you see—?"

She broke off when his arms shifted, their bodies aligned, and she became suddenly aware that he was hard and aroused, his eyes glazing as they locked on hers. And although it was the entirely wrong time, the entirely wrong place, heat leaped up inside her, flaring through her veins. Breath thinning in her lungs, she pressed against him, arched into him as his lips came down…parted…

And moonlight glinted off the two long, curving canines that hadn't been there before.

# *Chapter 4*

One second Dayn was locked on Reda's mouth with nothing in his head except: *Need. Want. Now.*

In the next, she screamed and jerked away from him, her face ashen with shock, her mouth a round O of horror as she whispered, "No. Dear God, no. You're…"

Startled, he reared back. "Reda, what—" And he felt his lips slide over his secondary canines. His *fully extended* secondary canines. The ones that were a good bit bigger than the witch's, and made for the exact same purpose. "Oh, shit. Wait. I can explain." He took a step toward her, reached for her. "It's not—"

She broke and bolted, scattering like a wild hare into the nearest section of trees, which put her headed away from both the cabin and the cave.

He went after her, but let her get ahead and moved only fast enough to keep her in sight. Not just to give her some room, but to give himself some, too. Because he was suddenly very *not* okay with what had just happened.

He'd seen the female blood drinker feeding from the gnome's neck vein, and he'd damn near lost his mind. Or maybe he *had* lost it there for a few seconds, because that was the only possible explanation for him trying to kiss Reda with his fangs up close and personal. "Wait," he called, lengthening his strides to catch up to her. "Please, just give me a minute to explain."

She threw a panicked look over her shoulder, then at the surrounding forest. And, seeing a lighter spot off to one side, swerved and bolted toward where the normal forest trees gave way to a roughly circular patch of scattered trunks whose roots overlapped and intertwined in intricate patterns.

"Reda, no!" he shouted, accelerating after her. "Stop! Those are borers! The ground isn't safe!"

But she just kept going. Either she didn't believe him, or she didn't think a tree could be worse than a vampire. She plunged into the grove, pounding across the root network, seeming not to notice how her footsteps suddenly echoed hollowly.

Cursing, Dayn followed her in, staying close to the skin-smooth trunks and leaping among the sturdier roots. The surface gave like a mattress beneath his boots and the stink of sulfur wafted up, warning that the grove was fully mature. The roots of the carnivorous trees had pushed aside the earth, creating a hollow to collect their digestive acids.

Too late, she understood. She stopped abruptly near a large parental tree, hands outstretched for balance, and looked back at him with new horror written on her face.

And she fell through.

"No!" He lunged for the ragged hole, stopping on the last sturdy root and coughing against the sulfurous stench that rose up from the torn spot. His gut wrenched. "Reda!"

Then—thank the gods—a wrist-thick root near the edge of the hole shuddered and he heard a low cry of, "Help me!"

"I'm coming." Yanking off his sword belt, he jammed the leather-sheathed short sword into the huge trunk of the main borer, fisting it so hard that the blade sank in, leather and all. Then, hanging on to that anchor, he leaned out as far as he could without falling in himself. Which put him close enough to catch a glimpse of her wide, frightened eyes, but not close enough to grab her. Stretching out his hand, he strained to close the gap. "Move slowly and don't shift your weight when you reach for my hand," he ordered, his voice rasping with the burn of the sulfur vapors. He couldn't see her face anymore, couldn't see anything but her hand reaching up for his. Slowly. Slowly.

The ground sagged and collapsed as the smaller roots gave way, tearing, tearing... And then she screamed, lunged upward and grabbed his wrist as the rootwork around her fell away.

Dayn yanked her up and against him and propelled them both to the main trunk; then he spun them and pinned her against the tree with his body, in case she was still thinking about trying to run. Instead, she burrowed both hands beneath his jacket to wrap her arms around him and grab fistfuls of his sweater as she buried her face in his chest and clung, shaking.

And if things had been entirely wrong in his universe only a few moments earlier, now they suddenly seemed very, very right. She fit seamlessly against him and warmed him where he had been so cold. She was safe. She was unhurt. And she was in his arms.

*She's your guide, dumbass,* snarled a very human-sounding voice of reason. *And you're supposed to be remembering your damn priorities.*

But wasn't his guide a priority? He didn't know what role she was supposed to play in his journey, but was beginning to suspect it wasn't nearly as simple as merely showing him where to go. For now, though, it was enough that she hadn't left him stranded in the wolfyn realm, hadn't fallen to her death.

"Shh," he said against her temple, letting the subtle flowers-and-spice scent of her curly hair fill him with a touch of the feminine whimsy he had gone so long without. "I've got you. You're okay."

She sucked in a shuddering breath. "But you're, you're…"

"Not a threat to you, I promise." He pulled back far

enough to give her an exaggerated smile that included only normal teeth. "See? The spares are all tucked away. I'm not going to bite you, and I can't turn you. The human legends have it wrong, Reda. I swear. I'm just another kind of man."

She shrank back against the tree, though she didn't let go of his sweater. "The woman. Moragh. She…" She shuddered, face plastered with revulsion. "He couldn't pull away. He wanted to, but he couldn't. She was controlling him. And then, after…it was like she was inside his mind."

Damn it. He hesitated, trying to find the right words, because he suddenly wanted—needed—her to understand this part of him. He cursed the bad luck that she'd seen the witch feeding from the throat in a brutal, invasive attack of mind and body rather than the way it should be, as an expression of…well, love, really.

He blew out a breath. "Blood drinking is an inherited trait like any other, but it's magic, too, so it comes with various other, um, characteristics. Most of us are stronger and quicker than average. I can heal fast, especially when I'm in fang mode. Some of us can move things without touching them, and lots of us can mindspeak to one degree or another."

"Mindspeak," she repeated, eyes going white-rimmed. "Brainwashing, you mean. That's what she did to him."

"What you saw just now was something that shouldn't have happened. A blood drinker normally feeds from the wrist or elsewhere, not the throat. There should only be throat action between consenting lovers, usually mates, because it creates a bond between them, makes them aware of each other on a different level." He paused, "Yes, it's possible for a mindspeaker to put a compulsion on someone when they drink from the throat, like you just saw. But it's just…not done. There are codes. Ethics."

It galled him to find one of his kind allied with the Blood Sorcerer, and it disturbed him deeply that seeing her feed had brought out his fangs. That was partly due to how badly Reda had inflamed his senses, but that was no better. He shouldn't be thinking of her in those terms; he couldn't be. Hadn't he learned anything from his past mistakes?

"Did you…can you compel someone like that?"

Though it was tempting to terrorize the wide-eyed human into keeping her distance, he needed her to trust him. So he went with the truth. "I can mindspeak with my blood kin and, in this realm at least, I can compel most females when I'm touching them." Seeing her expression go blank and scared, he said quietly, "Reda. Look at me." He waited until she focused, waited until her eyes truly met his, before he said, "I swear on my honor that I haven't mindspoken you. Though, honestly, not for lack of trying. Maybe it's a realm thing, maybe something to do with my father's spell, but I don't seem to have any effect on you."

He hadn't meant it to come out that way, but a faint rueful spark lit in her shimmering eyes and she unknotted her hands from his sweater and smoothed the wool with her palms. "I wouldn't say that, exactly. But about what happened back there."

"It won't happen again. I didn't even realize I had my secondaries down—it's been a long time since I've been around another blood drinker, never mind one who was feeding like that." He swallowed. "I overloaded on her magic for a few seconds there, and you caught the edge of it. Like I said, it won't happen again, I promise." He paused. "But I want you to promise me something, too. I need to know that you're not going to take off on me again like that. You need to stick with me, and if I say something's dangerous, I need you to believe me. Because the dreams say that we're in this together. And whether or not you believe in all this, I do. And from my perspective—" he nodded to the ragged hole "—you almost just became plant food. So promise me that you'll stick with me and let me do my best to keep you safe."

"I promise," she said immediately, somewhat to his surprise. And then her eyes filled in earnest, welling up and spilling over. Voice quivering, she said, "This is real, isn't it?"

His heart twisted for her, but there was nothing to be gained by lying, so he nodded slowly. She nodded in return, then leaned her forehead against his throat. And burst into tears.

Reda hated crying. It only ever made her feel stupid and sore afterward, not better. And if there was anything she hated more than crying, it was crying in front of someone else.

Now, though, she didn't have a choice. The emotions were too huge and overwhelming, the situation too strange, for her to hold in the tears. They erupted from her in racking, tearing sobs that hurt her throat, burned her eyes and left her helpless to do anything but hang on to the nearest solid object.

She cried over the memories she had turned away from, the beliefs she had lost. Because if this was real, if she was really here, really in another realm where magic worked and werewolves and vampires existed, then her father and the others had been wrong, her maman, right. She sobbed for herself, in fear and reaction. And she wept in anticipation of failure, because she didn't know what to do, how to help Dayn or even if she was really supposed to. She heard the whispered words: "To my sweet Alfreda on her eighth birthday, with the rest of the story to come when you turn sixteen." Maybe she would have known what to do if she had gotten the rest of the story. Now, though, she was lost, adrift.

Not entirely, though. Because she was anchored to a big, solid object.

Dayn was the one with the bigger problems, yet he didn't protest her tears or tell her they needed to hurry. Instead, he molded her against the strong warmth of his body, stroked her hair and was just *there,* in a way nobody had been for her in a long, long time. And when the tears finally subsided, leaving an achy hollowness behind, he waited another minute before he eased away from her. "I'm sorry you got dragged into this. We'll go to Candida—she's the wolfyn's wisewoman—and see if she knows of a way to unlock the standing stones. The witch can't be the only one who knows that trick."

Candida. The wolfyn. "The little man said something about finding the pack."

"They're more than a match for one gnome." But he moved a few steps away, to where the intertwined roots formed a path of sorts. Then he turned back and held out a hand. "Come on. Let's go see the wisewolfyn. She's a friend. She'll help."

Understanding shimmered through Reda on a surge of cold, numbing nerves. Because standing there on the pathway with his hand outstretched, painted monochromatic by the moonlight, he suddenly became one of the last woodcuttings from her book. The scene came after the woodsman had killed the wolf and saved the girl, and brought her back to the edge of the village where she lived. Then, instead of walking away, he held out his hand and asked her to come with him.

In the book, it was the beginning of a new life. Here, it was a moment of truth. A choice between conscience and cowardice.

She took a deep breath. "Do you know the story of *Rutakoppchen?*" When he nodded, she continued, "I had a copy when I was a little girl. My mother told me it was the only one in the world…." She told him the story of her book from her eighth birthday to that afternoon in MacEvoy's shop. And her inner wimp made every word an effort. He had seemed ready to send her home, and now she was buying in deeper.

What the hell was she doing?

When she finished, Dayn cleared his throat. "Thank. The. Gods." His voice was rough with emotion. "The magic brought you and the book back together after all those years because it was time." But then he paused, the light of hope that had taken up residence in his eyes dimming somewhat. "Without you knowing everything your mother would have told you, though, or even how she was related to the realm, it may not be enough."

*He's right,* wimpy logic said. *You should go home, leave him to his quest. You're not prepared for this place, and you're not a save-the-world kind of girl.*

Instead, she said, "There's more. In my book, you're the woodsman."

She hadn't seen him truly surprised before, she realized. "Me?"

"Your perfect likeness, even down to the pattern on your shirt. And you're not the only thing I recognize here—your cabin, this forest, it's all in there...but the standing stones aren't."

He went suddenly fierce. Intent. "There are rumors of vortices showing up in other places. Nothing confirmed, though."

Taking a deep breath, she said in a rush, "The inner back cover was carved with a picture of a huge natural stone archway between two cliffs. There was a river at the base, trees all around it and a waterfall coming down from one side." She was simultaneously terrified and relieved by the look on his face. "You know where it is, don't you?"

He nodded, shoulders easing. "About a day and a half away. Two days, tops. It's called the Meriden Arch." His breath left him in a rush and he closed the distance between them. "Thank the gods." He took her hand, lifted it and kissed her knuckles. "And thank you, for remembering."

But he wasn't really thanking her for remembering, was he? He was acknowledging that she could have held on to her ignorance, refusing to recognize that she knew more than she thought.

She glanced down at their linked hands. "I'm not brave."

"Being brave isn't about being unafraid. It's about functioning through the fear."

"Like I said—not brave. I freeze. I don't mean to, but things happen and I just…stand there."

"If Candida knows the spell to unseal the standing stones, you don't have to come with me. You can go home from here, your duty fulfilled."

It was oh, so tempting. But at what cost? If this was all real, then so was the threat to his homeland and siblings…and to Dayn himself. And although rationality screeched at the thought, she was still drawn to him, even knowing he was a vampire. If there was a chance she could help him, she wanted to try. So she forced the words past logic and reason, saying, "Along the bottom of the picture was carved words that translated to 'Here they can part, each to their own.' Even my maman said it was an odd ending for the story, since the woodcutter and the girl go off together."

He nodded slowly. "It wasn't about them—it was about us. We both need to go there to get back—you to the human realm, me to the kingdoms."

The thought shouldn't have brought a twinge.

She nodded. "I should warn you, though. A good man—my partner, my friend—died a few months ago because I froze at the wrong time. You can't trust a coward like me to have your back."

If he had knee-jerked the "you're not a coward" response, she wouldn't have listened, just as she hadn't to anyone else who had said the words. She knew what she was. But instead, eyes darkening, he brought up his free hand to touch her cheek, as if brushing away a tear she hadn't shed. "Sweet Reda, you've had a time of it, haven't you? Don't worry about having my back. I can take care of us both."

Her heart shuddered at the quiet promise, which was backed up by the implacable determination in his eyes. He had so much riding on him already, yet was stepping up to take more because she needed him to, which made him a better man—vampire or not—than the others in her life, save for the partner she had lost.

Dayn, too, was lost. But he was working to get himself found.

Did she make the move? Did he? She wasn't sure of that, wasn't sure of anything except that their lips were suddenly a breath apart.

This was the moment she should hesitate, she knew,

the time when freezing in place would be the smarter, safer thing to do. Here, in this strange realm, in an almost-embrace with a man who was nothing like her, she should back down, back away. But the heat that raced through her made her feel suddenly alive, when she had been numb for so long that she had mistaken it for living. And they had their endpoint already: the Meriden Arch, forty-eight hours from now.

*Two days,* she thought. *What's the harm?*

So she didn't back down or away, but instead held her ground as he moved in hard and fast. And kissed the hell out of her.

# Chapter 5

$S$oft warmth against his lips. Silky heat on his tongue. *Spice and flowers. Curves.* The sensations rocketed through Dayn. Gone was any hint of reserve or control, leaving him only able to act and react, not think or plan.

Growling low in his throat, he crowded her back against the tree until their bodies were aligned, pressed together, touching from knee to chest. He kept his hands on her face, willing them to stay there with the last threads of his control, knowing that if he touched her– -really *touched* her, the way he was suddenly dying to do—that he would be truly lost. Although in that moment, he couldn't remember why that was a bad thing.

It had been two decades since he had held a woman

out of anything other than necessity, since he felt a burn that went beyond the physical to something more. But now, as their tongues touched and slid, as his body went tight, tense and hard, he wasn't just kissing a woman. He was kissing a dream he hadn't been aware of having.

She thought herself a coward, yet had a core of strength. She had lost someone close to her and blamed herself for it. And she didn't—couldn't—understand how much that hit home for him. He didn't know if the grief and guilt in the kiss was hers or his, but those emotions eased as the heat rose between them. And for the first time in a long, long while, he didn't feel alone.

*Warm skin beneath his palms. Urgent fingers at his waist, his back, his shoulders, sliding into his hair. Heart pounding. Body tightening. A trickle of magic and moonlight, and—*

"Abyss." He broke the kiss, pressed his forehead to hers. "We can't do this right now." *Priorities.*

She was breathing just as heavily as he, and her fingers dug into his wrists, but she nodded. "Yeah." And neither of them mentioned the "right now" or the way it left open the option of "later."

He stepped away, not letting himself reach for her again. "We'll stop at Candida's first. She's got some things I'll want to bring." Like the poison she had designed for the sorcerer, and maybe a trick or two that could help him keep Reda safe. Because while she couldn't be his top priority, she had very definitely become his responsibility.

The thought bumped up against the promises he had

made to his father's spirit, but didn't unsettle them. He was headed where he needed to be going, with the woman who was to guide him. And when he went to Elden, he'd be going alone.

They set off along the track.

The cold, moonlit night had gone quiet, suggesting that the pack had moved on. Reda kept up easily, though she had to take three strides for every two of his. And although he told himself to think about what he needed from Candida, and the route they should take to reach Meriden Arch safely, without running afoul of the packs whose territory they would be traveling through, his thoughts kept circling back to the woman at his side.

As a younger man in Elden, he had gravitated toward the women of the queen's Special Guard and assertive, weapon-savvy guardsmen's daughters, as Twilla had been. And in the wolfyn realm he had spent most of his time with Candida or Keely—both alpha bitches, strong leaders. Not the kind of women who would weep or admit their fears. Reda, on the other hand, wore her emotions out in the open, without subterfuge. Yet, strangely, he hadn't wanted to move away when she cried, hadn't been impatient with her tears. Maybe part of that was because he understood what it felt like to be uprooted and lost, and, more, to have failed a loved one. But another part of it was less easily defined—he had wanted to hold her, comfort her, protect her, kiss her. And now that he knew her taste and the sexy sound she made at the back of her throat when they kissed, he wanted to do all that and more.

At the thought, his skin heated and his gums itched where his secondaries burned to be set free.

The response was even more discomfiting this time around, because his blood drinker's power was threatening to lock on to her, binding him more deeply than he could afford. Or was it just that drinking and sexual arousal had become inextricably linked in his mind? Maybe it was as simple as that.

He willed his secondaries far into hiding and quelled the magic. And he resolved to be on his guard.

After nearly an hour's hike, they turned up the last narrow track leading to Candida's cave, where she lived the lone existence she preferred, close enough to the pack to mediate squabbles and provide the healing and auguring that were her specialties, yet far enough away to discourage drop-in visits.

"Hope she's not out running," he said as they headed up the last ridge, which crested right before where the high hilltop flattened out in front of Candida's cave. "She doesn't go out with the pack every moon time, but will take a run now and then." Aware of Reda's nerves—which were understandable given that she'd been raised on the *Rutakoppchen* version of wolfyn lore—he continued, "She's an inventor, one of the best at figuring out how to take human tech and make it run off magical power cells they use for energy here. In fact—"

He broke off, blood icing as he scented smoke, thick with the rank odors of searing hair and burning flesh. Worse was the prickle of stale, foul magic.

"No!" he shouted. *"Candida!"*

He bolted over the last rise with Reda at his heels.

The entrance to the cave was a churned-up mess, with wisps of dark smoke curling around the top edge of the unlit opening. His heart hammered a sick, awful beat as he ducked inside and hit the lights, bringing up the glows strung throughout the cave and illuminating a scene of utter chaos.

And murder. Because amid the strewn wreckage of the wisewolfyn's supplies and household goods lay a huge mound of gray-buff fur. *"Candida,"* he rasped, crossing to her and going to his knees. "Gods. What did she do to you?"

The wisewolfyn's eyes were a pale, milky white, her throat torn open, her body badly burned, with patches of fur gone and the angry red flesh pitted with deeply charred stripes. A length of sword-stock metal protruded from the dying fire, suggesting the means for that torture. And torture it had been. The witch, Moragh, had hurt her, burned her, no doubt mind-raped her…and most likely all while he and Reda were hiding together in the small cave, waiting for the wolfyn to move on from the standing stones.

Again, he'd been in the wrong place at the wrong time. If he had realized the ettin hadn't stumbled through the vortex accidentally, if he'd been paying attention to the magic fluxes in the air…

"I'm sorry." Reda gripped his shoulder.

Resentment welled up, though he knew it was misplaced. It wasn't her fault they had gotten off to a rocky start; it wasn't anyone's fault. But it all sucked nonetheless.

"She was strong," he grated. "She resisted the mindspeak, tried to hold on to her secrets." Thus, the hot iron. "The magic got to her in the end, though."

"How can you be sure?"

"Her eyes." He gestured stiffly. "The white is a sign that she's been emptied out by mindspeak."

Reda sucked in a quiet breath, but didn't move her hand from his shoulder. Her grip was firm and strong; it said, *I've got your back* and *I'm sorry.* And maybe even *I'm here for you,* which was something he was very unused to.

After a moment, he continued, "The wolfyn normally revert to human form when they die. This says… shit, it says to me that Moragh stripped her all the way down to feral before she died." Which would have been a horrible fall for the proud, highly civilized wolfyn. She would have hated dying in wolf form, would've hated him seeing her like this. And she would have despised knowing that the witch had broken her.

"Should we do something for her?"

It took him a couple of heartbeats to figure out what she was asking, but far less than that to see that it was impossible. "No. We need to get moving." He pulled himself to his feet, hating the necessity. At the question in her eyes, he added, "Moragh sent her servant to tell the pack that I'm a blood drinker. Odds are, they're already on the hunt." He paused. "I'm sorry."

"Why? You didn't do this."

"I didn't stop it, either." He turned for the back of the cave. "Grab what you think you can use."

"Does she have any archery equipment?"

He stopped and turned back with a raised eyebrow.

"I was a junior archery champ three years running. The family rule was that each kid had to get good at a weapon. I think my father wanted to…" She shook her head. "Anyway, I can shoot. And I'm going to need a weapon."

"In that trunk over there," he said, gesturing. "Grab whatever crossbow bolts you can find, too, and another waterskin."

"Got it."

While she rummaged, he took a deep breath and faced the back wall of the cave. Then, tapping into the energy flow that enabled the powers of the wolfyn, he said softly, "Let that which is hidden be revealed."

The rock face shimmered and then disappeared, revealing stacked rows of brightly painted, intricately carved drawers.

Behind him, Reda gasped and something clattered.

"It's okay," he said. "It's just low-level cloaking magic. It's not a big deal."

"It is to someone like me."

Which just reinforced the fact that they came from two completely different worlds that intersected here, in this strange halfway realm. The knowledge tugged at him, but he ignored the tug and focused on the racked drawers trying to figure out which of Candida's tricks he could use to keep himself and Reda alive long enough to get to Meriden Arch, and from there, gods willing, home. And, in his case, to war.

At the thought, he reached first for the small red-capped leather tube that contained a smaller glass flask. An inch of amber syrup clung to the bottom, barely moving when he shook the carrying case.

"What's that?"

"Poison," he said without looking at her. "I'm going to use it to kill the Blood Sorcerer."

Reda didn't let herself dwell on the way the things she found packed away were familiar yet not, knock-offs that were ever so slightly wrong in their details. She didn't let herself dwell on how seeing Dayn do magic had shaken her to her core and, more, how it had aroused her, as if her libido was reacting to a surge of power she hadn't felt anywhere else. But while she was so busy not thinking about all those things as she loaded her rucksack with additional provisions and strapped a dozen arrows on the outside, she had far too much leeway to think about the clash between the pretty bedding and clothes in the trunks that lined the wall...and the wolf carcass that lay nearby.

Only it wasn't just a wolf, was it? It—*she*—had used these blankets, worn these clothes, chosen the now-broken knickknacks. *Candida,* she thought, glancing over at the motionless form, not sure if what she was feeling could be classified as pity, revulsion, confusion or all of those things at once. Probably the latter. She pitied the woman who had hung an abstract slash of color on the wall, yet reviled a species that, even in war, could enthrall, seduce, use and then discard women. *It was a long time ago,* she reminded herself. But still. The potential was there. More, the power was there.

Yet Candida had died trying to protect her blood-drinking friend.

Apparently finished gathering what he wanted, Dayn moved away from the racks to cover Candida's body with a heavy woven robe. He stood for a moment, whispering what she thought was a prayer, or maybe an apology.

Her heart bumped lightly in her chest and a new warmth moved through her, strange and unfamiliar. Tenderness.

*He's a blood drinker,* she reminded herself, but the warning bounced back with a rebuttal that came from deep within her: *perhaps, but he's also a prince.* Those things were both his birthrights, and both were labels that did nothing to describe the man himself. Dayn the blood drinker was dark and sexy; Dayn the prince was driven and determined to fulfill his promises. But at the same time, Dayn the man was very real.

Back home, her friends said she was too picky, that every man came with a mix of good and bad things, that she had to find a mix that worked for her rather than holding out for Mr. Perfect. What they hadn't gotten—what she hadn't been able to make them understand—was that she wasn't looking for a flaw-less man; she wanted one that was larger than himself, who cared about more than his car and flat-screen, and whether or not he got promoted at work. She wanted someone who combined her father's rigid code of ethics and military heroics with her mother's empa-thy, whimsy and lust for adventure.

She wanted the woodcutter, the storybook prince. And she had found one—for the next forty-eight hours, at least.

Finished, he turned to her, caught her watching him, but said only, "You ready?"

Standing, she slung the rucksack over her shoulder, where it joined the unstrung bow. "Did you find what you were looking for?"

He nodded. "I got the poison I wanted—which she didn't finish testing, so I have no idea if it'll work or not—along with a good supply of wolfsleep sap, which is roughly like chewing gum in your world, but also works on wounds. And this could come in handy." He dug into his battered rucksack and held out three small lumps of greenish stuff that had the consistency of putty and an oily sheen.

Reda wrinkled her nose, though any smell they might have had was buried beneath the foul smoky taste that coated her mouth and throat. "What are they?"

"Wolfsbene."

She eyed the stuff with new interest. "A repellant?"

"Not *bane*," he corrected, "*bene*. As in *benefits*. It enhances their human forms, giving them added strength, speed and stamina. It'll work for us, though not to the same degree. Think of it as rocket fuel for human forms." He tipped the lumps into a small envelope made of smooth tree bark, and handed it over. "Keep this on you. I've got more, but I want you to have your own in case we get into a situation where you need it and can't reach me." He paused. "There are side effects, so only use it when you absolutely have to."

She stilled. "What kind of side effects?"

"It doesn't just energize the body—it, ah, dials the other systems up, too."

"What is it with this realm and roofies?" she asked, flushing slightly because her first gut-level response to the idea wasn't nearly as negative as it should have been.

"What's a roofie?"

"Apparently this is." But she pocketed the envelope, because she felt suddenly very tired, as if her body had been waiting for her to notice the ache of fatigue. She didn't know how long she had been in the vortex, didn't know what time her internal clock thought it was, but she could use some rest.

That wasn't in the cards, though. If the pack was after them, they needed to move.

"Oh, and here." He held out a roll of thick laminate that reminded her of the place mats at the waterfront lobster shack back home. "In case something happens." She unrolled it and found herself looking at a map of entirely unfamiliar names and places, with Meriden Arch marked in ink and a couple of notes about trails and things to avoid. He said, "Basically, just head west, cross the canyon at the bridge and then angle almost due northwest from there at another day's hard march. The landmarks and stuff are on there."

A lump gathered in her throat, but she nodded and managed, "Thanks."

Although she tried not to think about making the trip alone, it nagged at her as they retraced their route down from the wisewolfyn's cave. She kept thinking of the furry gray body and the dead, staring white eyes, which started whispering in her mind, *It could happen to you, too.*

More, as they turned from a main road onto a narrower path that forced them to walk single file, with her following his rangy, seemingly tireless form, nerves tingled to life within her, tightening her stomach and making her want to curl up and hide.

*Breathe,* she told herself, hating the misfiring instincts that poured adrenaline into her bloodstream, making her too jittery to fight, to flee, to do something, anything!

The moon seemed too big, the crater shadows too irregular, the trees on either side of the trail too smooth, their joints too regular. The night crowded in on her, pressed on her.

*Breathe, damn it.* She focused on the trees and the darkness, the feeling of the bow on her back and the arrows she'd stuck in easy reach. *You're okay. You're doing this to yourself. You're—*

Brush crackled suddenly on either side of her and

huge shapes emerged, furred, fanged and growling. *Wolfyn!*

"Run!" Dayn shouted to her. *"Go!"*

Reda gasped and whirled to bolt, but there was already one behind her, then another and another. Within seconds, she and Dayn were surrounded by more than forty of the creatures, all with their heads down menacingly and golden fur spiked down their spines.

She fell back, gaping at the terrifying beauty of them. Candida's inert body hadn't prepared her for the shifters' sheer *presence.* The wolfyns' shoulders came up past her waist and their bodies stretched out, looking almost more like those of huge lions than wolves. Their coats had saddle marks that glowed reddish even in the moonlight; their heads were narrow triangles that made her think of wide-open spaces rather than dog parks, and their eyes were a vivid, vibrant amber.

A huge male stepped up to face her. He was the biggest among them, had the brightest markings and thickest fur. His forehead was broad, his eyes wise; they seemed to look into her and whisper, *Come to me. I can protect you, cherish you, adore you.*

Heat flared through her as she stared, transfixed. *Come to me.*

She took a step toward the gorgeous creature. Reached out her hand to touch the thick, luxurious fur.

And all hell broke loose.

# Chapter 6

"*No!*" Dayn broke free from the betas surrounding him, grabbed Reda and jerked her behind him. Then he got right in Kenar's face and shouted, "She's a *guest!* By rights and tradition, *back off!*"

The pack surged forward, but then subsided, growling as Kenar snarled a full-throated roar and sank back onto his haunches and then sprang erect, his form blurring as he changed. When the magic cleared, he stood there in his human form—slightly shorter than Dayn, bullnecked and square-featured, with heavy, powerful muscles and boxing-glove hands. His face was flushed, his eyes narrow with hatred. "She doesn't have any rights if she's traveling with a fucking bloodsucker—

and, more, a Forestal murderer. Because that's what you are, isn't it, *Prince* Dayn?"

And, just like that, twenty years of peaceful coexistence were nullified by the crimes of a long-ago war. The wolfyn surrounding him growled and scuffled, their canine faces wrinkled with hatred. They weren't just there because their alpha had led them; they truly wanted him dead. He didn't see Keely, didn't know what that meant. As for Kenar, there was hatred in his eyes, but calculation, too. He was using this somehow, or planning to.

Fumbling a little in his haste, Dayn palmed two blobs of wolfsbene from his pack and jammed one into Reda's unresisting hand.

"Did the witch's messenger tell you that she's a blood drinker herself?" he demanded solely to buy time. Pretending to scrub his face, he gulped the wolfsbene, which was slimy going down, with an aftertaste somewhere between mint and mud. He grimaced but continued. "Or that she tortured and killed Candida?"

He heard Reda cough, hoped that meant she had taken her dose.

The pack members shifted restlessly, some whining at the news. But Kenar bared his teeth. "We killed her servant, which makes us even, claw for claw. More, he was loyal, which was more than I can say for the wisebitch. How long had she known about you?"

The first shimmers of heat and power filtered into Dayn's bloodstream, which was good, because the pack was closing in, shifting tighter, backing him and Reda into each other. Talking fast now, he said, "You're believing the witch's messenger over Candida? Did he give you any proof, anything more than a good story?"

"Yes!" Kenar roared, and the sound was echoed by his betas. "Yes, he offered proof. He used a spell to show Keely the sick, twisted things you made her forget! She was your *lover*. How could you feed from your lover? Oh, right," the alpha sneered. "Because you're a prince of the realm and you could make her think whatever you wanted. Fucking bloodsucker, disgracing my sister like that. *Using* her."

*Oh. Shit.* Reda's gasp had Dayn's heart dropping, even as guilt knotted tight and sharp in his gut over what he'd done to Keely. Not just because of the feeding and the cover-up, but because he saw the politics now. "You son of a bitch. You're going to use this to boot her out, aren't you? I bet you've just been waiting for a good excuse."

The wolfsbene was flowing hard and fast in his veins now, but there was nowhere to run. He went for his crossbow, bringing it up.

Kenar's eyes lit with vicious fury. He signaled the pack forward and shouted, "By Right of Threat—*kill them!*"

Dayn nailed the closest beta in the haunch, aiming to wound but not disable. As the male went down howling and snapping at the bolt, Dayn grabbed Reda's hand. "Come on!"

They made it only a short way before the ranks closed again. Reda had his back, fending off the creatures with sweeps of her unstrung bow as he sent two more bolts into the crowd. And over his shoulder, he said, "I'm sorry, Reda."

But apologies didn't fix anything, did they? Never had.

Grief and guilt rose up within him like old friends as he pulled his short sword. "I'm going to try to make a hole. Be ready to run and hang on to that map." Because she would be running without him. There was no way Kenar would let him live now.

"Dayn." Reda's voice was choked, but that was all. And he didn't blame her for not knowing what else to say.

Roaring, he swung the weapon in a glittering arc and surged forward with her right behind him. He made it through the first rank, knocked aside a big beta in the second, and—

Without warning, an arrow seared so close that he felt the vibration on his skin as it passed him and carved a nasty furrow across the next animal's back.

"'Ware the woods!" Kenar yelled as another arrow sang past and glanced off the shoulder of an older wolfyn in the outer rank.

Not stopping to question the rescue, Dayn grabbed Reda's hand and hauled her toward the gap that had just been punched in the line. "Come on!"

They flew across a section of open road, then across to where a huge rock face rose up thirty or so feet to a sloping plateau. With the wolfsbane flowing through his veins and the entire Scratch-Eye pack lunging after him, Dayn made it up the sheer stone face in two big bounds, dragging Reda with him.

They crested the top and charged along the downslope, which put them on a narrow ridgeline with dense scrub on either side, forcing the pursuing wolfyn to run parallel to them, howling and barking in challenge, anger and threat. But Dayn's heart pounded and his muscles burned, propelling him faster than any human, faster even than most of the wolfyn. And Reda matched him stride for stride.

They soon outdistanced the bulk of the pack, until only a few of the fastest wolfyn were keeping pace where the ridge swept lower to flat ground and the scrub thinned along a narrow plateau that ended in the canyon: a wide chasm that was spanned right at this point by a narrow rope bridge.

As they charged down the steep incline and their pursuers closed on either side, Dayn said, "Stay behind me, but keep up. If we can make it across that bridge, we can pull the pins from the other side." There were other ways across, but they involved a half day's detour. She made a noise that might have been assent, might have been a whimper, but there was no time to stop and discuss options.

And there weren't any other options.

Dayn's pulse throbbed, thudding in his head and beneath his skin, and power seared in his veins, urging him on. When they broke from the last of the trees to the flat plateau that led to the bridge, there were only two wolfyn still following. Those two, though, closed in *fast*. Then, as if choreographed, they split and attacked, one from each side.

As they leaped, Dayn shouted, *"Down!"*

He and Reda hit the dirt and the wolfyn actually *collided* in midair. The larger one drove the smaller back and down; they landed hard a few feet away and scuffled.

Dayn dragged Reda up, ready to run again, then stopped dead as he saw that the two wolfyn weren't struggling to get up and continue the chase. They were fighting.

And one of them was Keely.

The battle was short but vicious; within seconds, she rose to her feet, leaving the other lying stunned and still. Then she shimmered and changed, becoming her familiar self. Except that she suddenly looked entirely unfamiliar—still tall, gorgeous and stacked, but...he didn't know what the "but" was, actually. It was there, though.

She looked at Reda. "You're his guide?"

"So he tells me." The women shared a look that excluded him, left him baffled.

"You knew?" he demanded of Keely. "How?" Then, because there was only one possible answer, he said, "Candida told you."

"She wanted someone else to know, in case anything happened to her. When the witch's servant came, I pretended I didn't know, and tried to think of a way to get a message to you, warn you of what was going on, but I couldn't."

The guilt was a raw ache inside him. "I'm sorry. I would have told you everything, but…Kenar."

"Kenar," she agreed. And there was something in her voice that hadn't been there before. Anger, maybe, or defiance. He wondered whether that was new or if, like her collusion with Candida, there were layers to her that he hadn't seen.

"Thanks for helping us get away," he said, knowing that must have been her. His eyes went to the still form of the unconscious wolfyn. "Will you get in trouble?"

"I'll blame it on you." She glanced back along the ridgeline, where growing howls warned that the rest of the pack was regathering. "You should get across the bridge and pull the pins."

"That's the plan."

"Which way are you headed?"

"Northwest," he said without hesitation, giving her his full trust, though far too late. "To Meriden Arch."

She nodded. "I'll tell them you went south, then. We'll head for the log crossing down by Candle Pass."

That would put the pack a solid half day behind them. "I'll owe you one. Hell, I owe you, period." He paused. "Keels, I'm sorry about the mindspeaking. I just…I had to feed."

She shrugged, and her voice held only wolfyn practicality when she said, "I was pretty freaked out when Candida first told me, but she helped me get over it. And in the long run, it was a fair trade—I used you for sex, you used me for blood. That's what people like us do—use each other."

It was a hell of an indictment. And he couldn't deny it.

He swallowed hard, very aware that Reda had drawn away from him; her arms were wrapped around her body as if she was freezing and she stared out over the chasm as if she couldn't look at him. He wanted to pull her aside and tell her that wasn't how it had been between him and Keely. Except that it was exactly like that—she had nailed it. They had used each other, and each been content with the deal. Now, though, with the wolfsbene running in his veins and Reda in the picture, the arrangement echoed cold and bloodless.

He didn't have the luxury of time to pull her aside, though, or even try to reason through the sudden change inside him. They needed to move now, talk later.

To Keely, he said, "Be careful, okay? And be happy."

"Go." Her amber eyes went from him to Reda and back. "And hey…you be happy, too, okay?"

He didn't know how to answer that, so he just nodded. "Thanks for everything. Business deal or not, you helped make the past twenty years bearable." He didn't kiss her goodbye, just as he had rarely kissed her hello. Theirs had never been that sort of a relationship. Instead, he nudged Reda toward where a low line of trees hid the edge of the canyon. "Come on. Keely will buy us as much time as she can, but we need to get across the bridge and drop it from the other side before the pack gets here."

She didn't say a word as they jogged toward the trees, but he didn't know for certain if that was because she was shell-shocked by the wolfyn attack, upset over the Keely thing, or something else. Or all of the above.

But he did know for certain that his arrangement with Keely had nothing to do with his feelings for Reda. One had been business and practicality, while the other was entirely impractical and ill-advised. Yet even knowing that, he couldn't keep his eyes off Reda. Part of it was the wolfsbene, yes. But most of it was her.

He wanted to crowd her, nip her, hurry her along. Instead, he stayed by her side, pacing her and guarding her flank as they reached the chasm's edge and headed for the bridge. There were enough trees that they didn't get a clear look at the spindly structure until they were nearly on top of it.

Reda stopped dead, her face going stark in the moonlight as she said, "Oh, hell, no."

"It's safe, I promise." But, admittedly, it wasn't the most inspiring sight. Four long ropes were strung from one side to the other: two suspending a sparse walkway of wooden planks that glowed nearly white in the moonlight, and two more lines at shoulder height for balance. Shorter lengths tied at gallop-stride intervals supported the fluid structure, which moved and rippled in the air currents that convected up from the depths. He nudged her forward. "You can do this. I'll be right behind you."

"No." She backed up until she bumped into him, her back to his front, stirring heat and echoes of the earlier kiss he was trying to keep at the edges of his mind. "There's got to be another way."

"There isn't."

"What if—"

Hearing the first ominous hunting howl behind them, he came around in front of her and cupped her face in her hands. "We need to keep going forward, Reda. It's the only way."

He had meant only to take her attention off the bridge, but when he touched the soft skin of her jaw, heat washed through him, and something deep inside said, *Mine.* And when her eyes came up to meet his, need tightened to a fist in his chest, and that same something said, *Now.* He didn't fight the urges, though maybe he should have. Instead, he crushed his lips to hers, swallowed her gasp and took them both under in a kiss that shouldn't have been pure perfection. But was.

One second Reda was terror-stricken, and the next she was on fire.

There was no transition, no warning, nothing but the sudden press of a hard male body and the demanding shape of his lips and tongue against hers. She should have yanked away, but couldn't find those synapses amid the heat and needy, greedy desire that flared instantly through her.

*Oh,* she thought, as fear melted beneath the onslaught. *Oh, yes.* Was it from the wolfsbene, whose power she could feel floating in her veins? Possibly. Probably. But she suddenly didn't care.

He slanted his mouth across hers, taking the kiss deeper, and fire kindled in her blood. Something fierce and possessive welled up in her—a sharp-edged need to dig into him and leave a mark—and that had her pouring herself into the kiss, into the moment and the man. He jerked against her, his fingers at her nape and hip, hers fisted in his shirt. And in that moment, there was only the two of them and a kiss that made her heart shudder in her chest and her entire conscious self say, *Yes, this.*

*This* was what she had been missing with the other men she had dated, the ones she had tried to convince herself were Mr. Right, Mr. Good Enough or Mr. Prince Charming Is a Fairy Tale So Get Real. *This* was what she had been searching for: the wrenching burn of lust, the grasping inner greed that said she had to touch him, kiss him, have him. And more, *this* was the gut-deep knowledge that it was mutual, that he was going crazy with the need to touch her, as well.

*"Gods."* He tore away from her and stood for a heartbeat with his chest heaving and his eyes fierce and wild. Then he grabbed her by the waist, spun her off her feet and deposited her on the first of the moon-silvered wooden slats.

She gasped and grabbed for the handhold ropes, panic sparking as the whole assembly dipped and swayed and pebbles skipped off the edge of the precipice and didn't make any sound of hitting bottom. She lurched back, but slammed into a yielding wall that was as immovable as a cliff, yet warm and muscular. And she could feel his heartbeat, quick and aroused, and echoing into her where it settled in a throb of liquid need.

"Go on, you can do it," he whispered in her ear, his voice deep and sensual. Then he shocked her by nipping her neck hard enough to bring a pinch of pain that took her mind off the yawning chasm below them. He crowded her with his body, bracketing her with his arms and legs. "One foot in front of the other."

Thrown off balance when his knee nudged the back of one braced leg, she took a stumbling step forward, then another when he repeated the move on the other side. "Stop it."

His only reply was a low growl as he nipped her neck again and crowded her more, herding her along the narrow bridge.

Heart hammering, she let herself be driven. The little bites sparked an atavistic heat that stripped her of her civilized outer shell and left only her primal brain behind. And that part of her reveled in the way he was dominating her, pushing her past her comfort zone and into uncharted territory.

She was aware of the yawning drop beneath her feet, the warm updrafts that came from below and the way the bridge swayed even though he steadied it by stretching his arms and legs as wide as he could against the taut ropes. But those inputs were secondary to the pounding heat that flared through her veins, carrying a brilliant, throbbing power that came only partly from the aphrodisiac side effects of the wolfsbene.

The rest of it was him.

"Go," he urged, his voice a low growl that spoke of things other than crossing a bridge. "Faster, Reda. Hurry!"

Her head spun with vertigo, magic and the heat of the man at her back as she took a step. Felt the bridge sway. Took another. And another. The breath backed up in her lungs as the throb of fear became a hard, hot churn of excitement, then a building sense of euphoria when her feet sped up and her body started compensating for the sway.

Behind them, fresh baying broke out, becoming suddenly sharp on the night air, closing fast. The wolfyn were coming!

"Hurry," Dayn urged, but she didn't need to be told.

She flew along the rest of the bridge, her heart tapping a rapid, excited beat as they neared the far side and her strides lengthened until she was hitting every second slat, then every third. And she was across!

Solid ground felt strange and static, but she bounced on her toes as she spun back to see Dayn getting to work on the pins securing the handrail ropes to the edge. One gave, then the next.

Crouching opposite him, she copied his moves, loosening the third pin and then pulling it out. One side of the bridge sagged and the whole thing twisted in the moonlight. Her stomach dipped at the sight of the structure they had just trusted their lives to coming unraveled so easily, so thoroughly. Then he gave a hard yank, the last pin came free and the bridge sagged and fell, the moon-brightened planks making it look like a dwindling dotted line. Then it was gone.

Shadows moved on the other side as the first of the wolfyn broke out into the open, moving fast and silent.

"Follow me," Dayn said, and moved off, headed south.

She fell into step beside him without comment. And was surprised to realize that she trusted him as her leader, her alpha. She wasn't second-guessing everything he said, wasn't trying to understand it within her old framework. Instead, she was following where he led.

*Be careful. You've only known him a few hours, half a day at most,* argued her rational, practical, logical, *boring* self, projecting a warning that was quickly lost to the joy of running beside Dayn as he sped up. The wolfsbene power flowed higher again, as if called by the sheer relief of being free to run as they chose, with their pursuers left far behind.

He plunged into a loose thatch of trees and immediately veered in the opposite direction, heading them back north after making a fake to the south, to lead the wolfyn toward the southern crossing as he and Keely had planned.

The memory soured some of the relief. *I used you, you used me. That's what people like us do.* The bitch's words haunted Reda, because they were so unlike the man who jogged beside her…and yet, the wolfyn had known him for two decades, Reda for six hours or so.

The trail they were on widened, giving her room to

move up and run shoulder-to-shoulder with him. But where before her blood had throbbed in time with their strides, now she felt like they were subtly out of sync, thrown off-rhythm by the questions circling around in her head.

He glanced over. "Go ahead. Ask." His expression was cloaked in shadows.

A chill tightened her skin. "Are you reading my mind?"

"I told you, I can't connect with you."

There was no reason for that to sting, yet it did. Which was proof positive that she needed to get a grip on herself. "Then what is it you think I should be asking?"

"Whether I drank from Keely and made her forget about it. Yeah, I did. Wolfyn blood is powerful stuff for my kind. I needed a hit once per year, just as she needed a mate one night a year, so she could have a satisfying run during the blood moon without jeopardizing her brother's leadership."

Reda's stomach gave a slow roll, not just at the idea of him drinking the wolfyn's blood—with or without her knowledge—but also because he had so easily walked away from his long-time lover without so much as a backward glance. And only a few minutes later had been kissing her, Reda, and making her feel needed. Special. Powerful.

*Don't go there.*

Dayn slowed to a ground-eating walk, shifting his rucksack. "I know it looks bad. Abyss, it *is* bad. Keely and I traded sex, but then I stole her blood, which makes us far from even."

Reda didn't know what to say, or even what more he could say that would ease the tightness in her chest, so she let it go. And after a while, the tightness eased on its own, and she thought that maybe that was part of being brave, too—letting things go.

They kept traveling for an hour. Two. The forest closed in on the road they were using, and she became very aware of the dark wall of trees on either side of them, the occasional rustles and crashes of startled creatures.

At the sound of a not-too-distant howl, she stiffened. "Is that the pack?"

"Just a loner looking for trouble," Dayn said, voice slightly rusty from disuse. At her look, he elaborated, "A male can get kicked out of his pack if he challenges the alpha and loses, or if the alpha thinks he's likely to challenge and wants to avoid the fight. Sometimes he can join another pack, but unless he can really suck it up and play beta, there's usually the same problem there, too. Which means he ends up on his own, except during the moon time."

Sliding cautiously into the conversation, she said, "Why then?"

"Because those are the only three days that tradition allows a wolfyn male to claim the Right of Challenge, which is the ability to fight the pack's leader for the right to rule. That's also when disputes are settled, punishments are decided, matings are formed or broken.

The wolfyn have boiled most of the family stuff and politics down to these three days, leaving the rest of the year essentially peaceful."

"Does it work?"

"It seems to."

"Civilized." She frowned, trying to put that into the context of what she'd just seen of the wolfyn. "That male back there."

"Kenar. Keely's brother."

"He tried to enthrall me, but you stopped him."

"Yes."

She shook her head, trying to dislodge those few seconds when she had been utterly under the big creature's amber-eyed spell. "I thought you said they wouldn't try that in their home realm."

"Kenar is…" He paused, as if searching for the words. "Keely and I might have used each other one night a year, but Kenar uses everyone all the time. But he's smart. He makes it seem as though he's following the traditions to the letter, when he's really bending them to suit his needs. And because he's the alpha and he's kicked out the very few males who stood up to him, he can control his pack almost absolutely."

"It sounded like Candida and Keely weren't as firmly under his control as he thought."

His lips tightened and he glanced back southward. "I hope she knows what she's doing. Kenar is charming enough when he gets his own way. But he doesn't take it lightly when he's crossed."

Reda nodded. "I know men like that. Saw too many of them on the job."

He cut her a look. "What job?"

"I…" She hadn't meant to go there, didn't know how they had even come to be talking like this, like they were normal friends out for a normal walk. Or a normal first date or something.

"It's okay if you don't want to talk about it," he said. But in her heart, it jarred, made her think he was too often ready to move forward and not look back, just like the major.

"I was a cop," she said.

"A guardswoman," he said with a strange note in his voice. When she glanced over, though, he shook his head. "It's nothing. You said 'was.' What happened? This is about your partner?"

"I froze." She crossed her arms, caught herself doing it and jammed her hands in her pockets instead. "You're shocked, I'm sure. And yes, that was sarcasm." When he didn't say anything, she told herself to leave it alone, let it lie. Instead, she found herself saying, "We just went in for coffee, that's all. Benz didn't even want to—but I was cold, tired and cranky, and our shift was going to run over because a couple of guys had called in sick, so he stopped and went in for me. And he didn't come back out."

Maybe it was the wolfshene, maybe the crazy reality out of reality she found herself in, but suddenly the memory was right there in front of her, where before she hadn't been able to remember any of it clearly.

# Chapter 7

"Seriously, Benz, what is taking so long?" Reda killed the cruiser's engine, pocketed the keys and climbed out, slamming the door harder than she really needed to. "Did you have to grow the coffee beans or milk the half-and-half cow yourself?"

More likely he was chatting up the pretty brunette who worked the counter at the Porthole Packie. Normally, it didn't bother Reda when her good-looking, easygoing partner went into casual-flirt mode, even when the flirtee was a good ten years younger than him and a coed at the nearby state college. Tonight, though, the thought set her teeth on edge. She might not have been all that into the guy who had just "it's not you, it's me"'d her, but being newly dumped—again—really *ought to earn her some priority in the coffee department. Maybe even a bonus Snickers.*

*Which, apparently, she was going to have to get for herself. Muttering under her breath and ignoring the curious looks of a couple of passersby—what, never seen a girl cop wearing a uniform and a mood before?— she pushed through the portholed door and into the liquor store, which, like so many of the local places, had recently been forced to diversify to stay afloat, putting in a general store section that boasted damn good serve-yourself coffee.*

*As she came through the door, she automatically glanced up at the curved overhead mirror, which was angled toward the register area and backed up by video surveillance.*

*She froze at the sight of Benz standing on the wrong side of the counter with his hands up, a gun in his face and the coed cowering behind him with her eyes closed and her hands covering her ears. Then Reda looked from the mirror to the register, and saw it was for real.*

*In the nanosecond it took for the perp to look over, go white-eyed and start screaming for her to toss Reda's gun and lie on the floor, her brain snapshotted the scene—assessed the lines of sight, possible cover and the positions of the three other people in the store. She instantly saw herself pretending to follow orders but instead launching herself into a nearby display, saw it fall into the gunman, saw Benz come over the counter and take the guy down. It was training, planning and instinct all wrapped into one. And it didn't happen anywhere but in her mind.*

*In reality, she just stood there.*

*"Get down!" The perp jumped back a step and shifted his gun from Benz to her. She saw the panic in his eyes and knew she had to react, had to get the hell out of the line of fire, but she freaking* couldn't. *Her brain wouldn't work; her body wouldn't move.*

*The guy's eyes changed. And Reda saw her own death.*

*"No!" Benz lunged over the counter and went for the guy, just as she had pictured, but she hadn't provided a distraction, hadn't done anything.*

*The perp spun back and fired as Benz hit him. The .38's sharp report jolted her from her paralysis as the men went down together, but she was too slow in fumbling her weapon from its holster. The gunman got up, scrambling out from underneath Benz and bolting for the back exit.*

*"Stop!" she yelled. "Freeze, police!" Which just wasted time.*

*Besides, he was already gone, the door swinging into place behind him.*

*She hesitated another gutless moment—chase or stay? One look back at Benz made the decision for her. Blood pooled dark ruby red on the hardwood floor. She grabbed her radio and called in an officer down, assistance and an ambulance needed, then crouched beside him, skidding in his blood and seeing the ragged tear in his neck.*

*She clapped a hand over the wound, putting on pressure like crazy, telling him to hang on, that help was on its way.*

*None of it mattered, though, because like the man who had killed him, Benz was long gone.*

"And when the detectives started asking me about the perp, I couldn't remember a damn thing," she finished, oblivious now to the dark forest pressing in on either side of them, seeing only the liquor store, the blood, the expressions on the faces of the other cops afterward. "The other wits hadn't seen his face and the video was useless. If I could have given them something…but, no. It was all gone, *pfft,* total fog, like my mind had locked up along with my body. I couldn't even help that way. I was deadweight. Useless." She glanced over at Dayn. "Just like I have been pretty much since I got here."

He met her eyes, though his expression was lost in the darkness of the predawn that had started lightening the horizon to a deep, rich blue. "You're expecting me to say it wasn't your fault."

Her stomach gave an ugly-feeling lurch. "You think it was."

"I think it won't matter worth a damn what I think. You've got to work it out for yourself and find a way to make peace. Or not." But although his words put up barriers, the soft rasp of regret in his voice went right through them, and reminded her who she was talking to and what he'd been through. He hadn't just lost a partner; he'd lost his family, his life, his heritage.

"Sorry," she said, blush coming on hard and fast. "You were just asking to be nice, and I rambled on, and—"

He reached over and took her hand. "Reda, stop. That's not what I meant."

She swallowed, trying not to cling too hard to his hand. "Sorry. I'm not good at reading cues. My brothers say it's because I spend too much time by myself." Or they had before they moved away to start new jobs, new families, leaving her behind.

"I'm familiar with the concept." He let go of her hand, but they were walking closer than before, their shoulders and arms brushing in rhythm as he said, "I've spent twenty years dying to get back to Elden, reconnect with my brothers and sister and kick the Blood Sorcerer's ass, not necessarily in that order. But I've also spent most of that time blaming myself for not being in the castle when the attack came."

"You wouldn't have been able to," she trailed off, getting it.

"Exactly. Right or wrong, what matters is that I feel responsible." He paused. "There was a girl, Twilla. She was a guardsman's daughter, and planned to train for the queen's guard."

"Oh." It was ridiculous to feel a twinge. But she did.

"My parents didn't approve because she was common-born and they had plans for me. We argued and I stormed out, and was gone when the castle fell. Worse, the last things between us in their lifetime were angry words and accusations." He spread his hands; the gesture was visible now in the pink light of a new day. "I'm not proud of myself. I wish I had been a better man, a better son. Hell, a better prince. But I can't go back and change that. All I can do is be better the next time, whatever form that next time takes."

"Oh," she said again, only this time it was a softer noise, one of understanding that was what he meant when he talked about moving forward and looking ahead. He wasn't trying to get away from the past, or ignore it. He was trying to fix the future.

And in that, he was nothing like her father and brothers, who spent so much time looking ahead of themselves that they couldn't see what was right in front of them.

Her opinion of him, which was already dangerously high, notched up again. And that, combined with the wolfsbene, made her far too aware of the way their arms brushed now and then as they walked. The contact was almost undetectable through the layers of sweaters and leather, but she knew. She knew.

Yet even though the heat of arousal stayed high in her bloodstream, her energy—at least for hiking—was rapidly fading. She didn't say anything, though, just pushed onward until Dayn nudged her with his elbow and pointed to a narrow game trail leading away from the main track. "There. That's what I was looking for. It leads to a hunting cabin about a mile in." His teeth flashed. "It's Kenar's, and we know for a fact that he's way behind us. The pack will need to rest, so we should be safe. I brought a couple of wards. I'll set one down here to warn us if someone's coming up the trail, then set the other to surround the cabin."

She nodded and said, "Okay." But what she really meant was, *Thank God.*

The sun was coming up over the horizon, signaling the end of a nearly interminable night, but she didn't look around, didn't care where they were or what it looked like in the light of day. Her focus narrowed to the few feet in front of her as she followed Dayn up an incline that at times turned so steep that they were going almost vertical, using roots and rocky outcroppings as hand and footholds.

Then, finally, he crested the climb and turned back to her. "Come on. We're here."

She gave him her hand, trusting his strong grip to pull her up onto what proved to be a wide ledge at the base of a rock-strewn mountain face. Near the back, snugged up against the rock ledge, a small log cabin was nearly hidden among squat, scrubby pine trees that looked short, proportion-wise, but towered over the small structure.

Barely even registering that reminder that she wasn't in Kansas anymore, she followed Dayn to the cabin and obediently hung back at his gesture, too tired to insist on helping him scout the area and set the wards. As he rejoined her, he was mixing some sort of powder into the contents of the waterskin he'd carried over his shoulder.

As he reached her side, he tipped his head back and drank deeply.

Reda's attention was caught far too thoroughly by the way his throat worked, her eyes locking on a rivulet that escaped and tracked down. She felt the tickle against her own flesh, and the sensation reached inside her to stroke the kernel of heat that was all that was left of the wolfsbene's power.

She quivered slightly as he lowered the waterskin and offered it to her. "It's a mild stimulant. It'll clear the fog and keep you from going so deeply unconscious that you can't run if we need to."

As she took the potion, the quiver grew claws, dug in and spread through her body—a potent combination of fear and arousal that instead of freezing her in place made her want to move into him, curl against him. She didn't let her hand shake, but as she downed the mixture, which had a mellow citrus flavor but the aftertaste of too-strong black tea, she was entirely aware of Dayn staring at her, watching her as she had watched him.

She wondered whether he was feeling the afterburn, whether his skin felt singed as hers did, gone suddenly prickly and sensitive beneath her clothing.

Lowering the waterskin, she deliberately met his gaze. And was nearly scorched by it. His pupils were dilated, his body tense and somehow seeming larger than it had only moments before, as if he had puffed up with the same atavistic mating urge that suddenly surged within her.

Her face fired with an intense flush that quickly washed down her throat to heat the skin of her upper chest, then her breasts. Her nipples crinkled in an excitement that was echoed in her core, until her entire body thrummed with sensual awareness.

*It's just the drug,* that lame-ass, cautious part of her said, but only weakly because the reality was that it was Dayn. And she was so damn tired of being rational, practical or logical.

He wasn't the woodsman, wasn't the lover she had seen in her dreams. But that hadn't stopped her from wanting him from the first moment she had awakened and looked into his eyes. More, as they stood there on a hidden rock ledge, as safe as they could be under the circumstances, rebellion rose up within her. Greed. And, oddly, logic.

She might not be stuck in a dream, but this sure as hell wasn't her real life. And given that, as long as she guided her prince to the archway on time, what was the harm in taking what she wanted for the next forty-eight hours?

Dayn saw the change in her eyes, saw awareness followed by understanding, then determination, and knew she was going to be the smarter of the two of them, and back away. Which was probably a good thing, because now he was the one who found himself paralyzed, locked in place not by fear, but by desire. Perhaps there was some fear in there, too, brought by the knowledge that this wasn't just about the potions, at least not for him.

Yes, lust pounded through him, throbbing beneath his skin, hardening his flesh and making him want to close the distance between them and take her mouth, her body, her sex. But there was also the tenderness and respect that had come to life through the night as he watched her struggle to deal with the situation she had found herself in.

She thought herself a coward, but he saw a survivor who had been forced to rebuild her life too many times alone and had stopped believing—in herself, in luck, in faith. And that part of her reached out to the same part of him and made him feel, for the moment at least, a little less alone.

She was his guide. But she was also a woman in her own right…and that woman drew him, compelled him, made him want. And that, combined with the potions, meant that she would have to be the one to walk away.

Instead, she took a step toward him.

The breath stilled in his lungs. "Reda." That was all he could get out. Just her name.

Her lips curved; her eyes darkened to the gorgeous blue he had seen in his dreams. "Dayn."

And she took another step. One more and she could be touching him.

Even his heartbeat seemed to hesitate, and in that moment, it was like he was back in Elden woods, lying in wait for a fierce and dangerous creature that at the same time was beautiful and oddly timid. There was that same hum of anticipation in his bloodstream, that same sense of dawning wonder and the inner whisper of, *Yes, that's it. Another step or two, my beauty, and I'll have you.*

"The drug," he began, then fell silent when she took that last step, putting them face-to-face, not touching but close enough to touch. To kiss. To do more. Even through the heavy layers of his clothing and coat, he was aware of her body, her warmth.

She pressed a finger to his lips. "It's not just the drug for me. And even if it is, I don't care." Her eyes flashed. "I've been stuck in a rut, not just because of what happened to Benz, but because I haven't found what I want—in a man, a job or a life. It wasn't all bad, but I keep thinking it could be better. And now—" She broke off, pressing her lips together for a second before she said, "What matters is that, right now, I feel *alive*."

*Yes,* he thought. *Alive.* That was the word for the awareness that raced through him, making everything seem fresh and bright as the sun crested the horizon and a single songbird trilled from the trees surrounding the cabin. Had he spent the past twenty years sleepwalking through life, only half living because he had been waiting for her?

He thought so. Now, though, he was awake. Gods and the Abyss, he was awake.

Then, suddenly, he could move again. He wanted to rush, to wrap her around him and plunge. Because of that, and because of the way he felt his temper slip and fray, he made himself go slowly.

Achingly, sweetly, slowly.

Framing her face in his hands, he leaned in and touched his lips to hers. He lingered there, drinking in the feel of her soft skin and the way it went from cool to warm against him, hearing the faint catch of her breath, tasting magic and smelling flowers and spice.

The rising heat washed through his body and soul, making the skin at his gums itch. *No,* he said to the magic, *not now. Not with her.* The thought brought a tug because he didn't know where he would be when he next fed, or even if he would get that chance. But he knew he wouldn't be with her, because when they reached Meriden Arch, they would go their separate ways.

"Listen," he began, needing to say something but not entirely sure what. "When we get to Meriden—"

"I don't want to think about that now." She brushed her mouth across his and moved past him toward the cabin, then turned back and held out her hand. "I'd rather think about you."

Heat and need lashed through him as the sunlight brightened from dawn to day and he saw her in living color for the first time: her wild copper riot of hair catching the sunlight, her full lips soft from his own and a flush of desire on her skin.

More, her words moved through him, echoed inside him in a stark reminder that he had been many things— a son, a prince, a sibling, a hunter, a guest—but rarely himself. There were other sons, other princes, other siblings, hunters and guests. But Reda was looking at him, reaching out to him, desiring him alone.

He reached out in return. Their fingers met. Curled. Clung.

And he followed her to the cabin, feeling as if his entire existence had just shifted on its axis.

# Chapter 8

As Reda stepped into the cabin, her mind recorded the scene. The main room was maybe ten by fifteen, and had a soot-stained brick hearth at one end. A queen-size bed took up a raised platform nearby, with a big chest at the foot of the stripped mattress promising blankets against the cold. The remainder of the main space was open, save for a tall cupboard in the corner, where she guessed nonperishables were stored, maybe even an appliance or two.

All of that pretty much fit with her idea of a hunting cabin. The surprise, though, was the door on the wall opposite the fireplace, leading to what looked like a fully plumbed bathroom, including a large, multinozzle shower tiled in strange, smooth gray blocks. "What the heck?"

"Kenar had it installed a few years ago," Dayn said from behind her. "His idea of roughing it."

"A pointed reminder that I'm not in Kansas anymore." She hadn't seen a cistern, pump or solar panels, suggesting that this was another of those places where magic and science intersected.

"Kansas?"

She swallowed a laugh that threatened to turn hysterical. "Never mind," she began as she turned toward him. "I..." She trailed off at the sight of him standing backlit by a window, the yellow light of day throwing him into reddish shadows rather than the blue-white of the moon.

He had dumped his bag in the corner and shucked off his bomber and sweater, though the air inside the cabin wasn't much warmer than that outside. That left him in his shirtsleeves, standing near the doorway staring at her with eyes that seemed to see straight into her.

"'I' what?" he prompted, closing the distance between them, his eyes going very dark as he looked down at her.

"I forget," she said huskily, while her inner self said, *I'm a sucker for the woodsman.* And at the thought, new sparks raced through her, tightening her skin and making her elementally aware of the cabin around them, the bed behind them.

Shrugging her bow and rucksack strap off her shoulder, she let them fall to the floor, then brought her hands up to touch his waist, pressing her palms against the warm material of his shirt and feeling the hard strength of the man beneath.

He cupped her face in his palms in what she was coming to recognize as a habitual gesture for him—or maybe just between the two of them. Then he leaned in and kissed first one of her cheeks and then the other, then the corners of each of her eyes, which fluttered shut. She brought her hands up to grip his wrists, cuffing him in place as his lips skimmed over her face, teasing her, drawing out the anticipation of a kiss. Her blood heated sweetly, carrying a dangerous something that went deeper than lust. But at the same time, the churning desires brought by the dreams, the danger, the potions and the man himself were all mixed together now, becoming a single mating urge, a raw longing that knotted her inner muscles and brought moisture to dampen her skin.

Where only seconds before she had been cold with the realm's sharp air, now she was overheated and tingling. Though he had said he couldn't read her mind— and thank God for that—he shifted to ease her out of her leather bomber, freeing one shoulder at a time first, then sliding it down her arms, moving slowly and somehow mimicking the actions in his kiss.

Caught up in each individual sensation, she could only sway against him and make love to his mouth as he worked her out of her borrowed sweater and then her shirt, then conquered the clasp of her bra with only a brief fumble to betray the difference in technology. Then her breasts were bare to his touch, burning for it.

And they were really doing this. At the back of her brain there was a spark of shock, another of joy and an inner whisper of, *Oh, yes.*

She gasped at the first brush of a fingertip along the side of one breast, then the other. Suddenly craving the glory of skin on skin, she tugged his shirttails free and went to work on the buttons with fingers that trembled as he traced a tightening circle around one nipple and his touch ignited tiny detonations within her. Then his wide palms were covering her nipples, his long fingers shaping her breasts, and she moaned into his mouth at the hard, hot peaks of sensation that brought.

He growled something—maybe an oath, maybe her name—and kissed her again. And where before his kisses had been soft and restrained, a sort of gauzy and romantic foreplay, now his lips were hard on hers, his tongue demanding. And her body lit wildfire-bright in response.

*This,* she thought, *yes.* The past and future stopped mattering, stopped even existing as she kissed him back, throwing herself into the moment, into the man. Her hands shook as she got his shirt off his shoulders, his arms and sent it sailing to the floor atop their dropped bags. And then he urged her up against his body and they were suddenly, shockingly, skin on skin. His light furring of masculine hair feathered her senses as they twined together, kissing deeply, carnally.

"Gods and the Abyss," he groaned against her mouth. *"Reda."*

The raw need in his voice tugged at her, brought a prickle of tears that she willed away, focusing instead on the way her entire body throbbed in time with her heartbeat as she strained up against him, trying to increase the contact, only to be frustrated by their differences in height.

Again sensing what she couldn't make herself say, he looped an arm around her waist and lifted her up against his body. She moaned as she brought her legs up around his waist to rub herself along the ridge of iron-hard cock hidden behind the barriers of his clothing, then again when he pressed her back against a nearby wall and pinned her there, kissing her deeply as he shaped her breasts with his big, gentle-rough hands and surged his hips against her in a rhythm that should have been familiar, but felt like nothing she had ever experienced before.

She touched his bare back and found parallel scar ridges that could only be claw marks, ran her hands up the lean, cable-tough muscles of his arms to his shoulders and felt him quiver beneath her touch, history and need melding together into a man who wasn't like anyone she had ever met before, or ever would.

Tangling her fingers in his thick, rich mane of dark, wavy hair, she softened against him. *Yes,* she urged him inwardly. *Yes.*

As if he had heard her, he broke their kiss, pressed

his cheek to hers and breathed, "Ah, sweet Reda. Sweet, sweet Reda. Come to bed with me?"

Her heart ached with his husky tone, her core with the need to have him buried deep within her. But she tipped her head toward the bathroom. "How about we wash off some of this road grime first?"

His eyes clouded, then cleared. "Really?" He glanced into the bathroom.

And there it was again, that gap between his life and hers. This time, though, instead of discomfort, it brought a new skim of heat and an added tug of desire. She leaned in, nipped his jaw and then touched her tongue to the spot she had just bitten. When his hands tightened rhythmically on her hips, kneading her against him, she whispered against his ear, "Then this will be a first for you, won't it?" And a memory for him to take through the Meriden Arch when they parted.

Refusing to let the heat turn bittersweet, she caught his earlobe between her teeth, then teased him with soft kisses and light tugs as he swung them away from the wall and carried her into the bathroom. There, he let her down and, when she turned to the not-quite-familiar controls, he came around behind her, cupped her breasts in his hands and bent to kiss her neck, her ear, the side of her jaw.

She closed her eyes and swayed against him as the water came on and the streams from four nozzles intersected in the center of the glassed-in shower cube, filling the room with the roar of the spray and an unexpected fragrance that was part pine, part citrus and wholly enticing. Perhaps it was yet another type of wolfyn stimulant, because as the water heated and the glass started to fog, she felt an echo of the wolfsbene's heat radiate from her to him and back again.

He crossed an arm between her breasts, gently holding her still as he slid his free hand down her body to toy with the snap of her jeans, all the while kissing her neck, driving her to a frenzy that was only increased by the fact that she couldn't really touch him, not the way she wanted to.

"Let me," he rasped against her throat, and for a second she stiffened, thinking she felt the sharp point of a tooth and, worse, knowing that if that was what he was asking, in that moment she wouldn't have been able to deny him. But then her pants loosened and fell away, followed by her panties, and then he slid a hand down to cover her mound, hesitating when he found her entirely bare, waxed out of habit because she hadn't wanted to admit there was no point, hadn't been in a long time.

Now, though, that habit wrung an approving groan from him as he tightened his grip on her, pinning her against him. She moaned, her head falling back as he touched her, exploring and then pressing her back, so she could feel the shape of his hard ridge against her buttocks. She was wet for him, dying for him, yet he held her in front of him and stroked her mercilessly, gloriously, in and then not, his fingers sliding slickly against her hot, swollen folds.

She tried to curl around the sensation but he held her back against his chest so she felt every stroke of his clever, clever fingers. "Dayn," she gasped, breath nearly sobbing in her lungs as her body tightened, coiling with the breathless anticipation that presaged orgasm. "I need… God, I want…"

"Let me," he whispered again. "Let go." And he slid two fingers deeply into her, then started thrusting with an increasing rhythm that had her arching into him and clamping around him with growing intensity.

"Oh. Oh, Dayn, I—" She broke off with a low, vibrant cry, shuddering against him as heat and pleasure washed through her, coalescing to the point where he was touching her, working her.

The world seemed to draw in on itself, seemed to hold its breath and go very still for…a…single…moment…and then she went over, clenching around his fingers with a strangled moan. Then she was coming, saying his name over and over as the raw, rhythmical waves suffused her, completed her…and then ebbed, leaving her limp and boneless.

She was so boneless, in fact, that she was almost unable to support herself when he angled her into the shower stall and put her beneath the spray, but then stepped outside the bathroom for a few minutes—long enough for her to wonder where he had gone, what he was doing.

The hot water hit her with sharp enticement, bringing her all the way back as Dayn returned to the bathroom, paused to shuck off his boots and pants and then came into the shower with her.

Without speaking, he drew her up onto her toes for a raw, powerful kiss that said they weren't done. Not even close.

Her blood heated anew at the kiss and the feel of his body going wet and slick against hers as the shower spray sluiced them both. Naked, he was a dream of wide bone structure, lean, rangy muscles and an almost inhuman grace, as if he were the wolfyn-turned-man, not the others. But he was all man where she cupped him, then slid her fingers along his considerable length, very aware that her fingers couldn't completely surround him.

He groaned, pressing into her touch, at first trying to kiss her and touch her in return, but then simply leaning canted into the spray with one hand on her hip, the other bracing his big body against the wall. And while her first thought had been to pick up right where they had left off out in the other room, now that sharp heat mellowed to a softer, more gentle urge.

She wanted to touch him, wanted to make him feel good.

A small shelf within the shower stall yielded a foamy, woodsy-smelling cleansing lotion that felt cool when she first rubbed it between her palms, but then heated as if coming to life.

When she moved around him, he shifted as if to follow, but she pressed him back to where he was, and said simply, "Let me."

He subsided, leaning on his braced arms so his head was beneath one of the showerheads, directly in line with the pounding spray, and closed his eyes.

The simple act of trust fisted an ache beneath her heart. And when a shudder ran through him at the first slide of her slickened hands along the line of the claw scars, it tightened that ache even further. How long had it been since he'd been touched for the sake of touching, not as part of a transaction, but simply because the other person wanted to?

*Twenty years,* logic said. And for a change there was no dissenting vote. He had been in this realm for almost as long as her mother had been gone, and he had been essentially alone that entire time, forced to hide his true nature from all but Candida, who had been a loner in her own right.

Reda's heart ached as she laved his broad shoulders and arms, the back of his neck and then down again to the tight muscles of his buttocks, which clenched rhythmically as she worked on him, and then as she moved lower to his thighs and calves.

He was breathing fast, taking great, deep drafts of air that went off-rhythm when she angled one of the nozzles to rinse him, then slicked her hands down his body once more to chase the suds away.

Done with the back of him, she moved around to his front again, thinking to repeat the process, maybe steal a kiss. But he straightened away from the wall, catching her against him with one hand on her lower back, the other at her nape. His eyes, when he looked down at her, were deep and dark with emotion. "Gods. Reda." Dropping his head to press his forehead to hers, he inhaled as if to say something, but then let out a sigh and whispered simply, "Thank you."

They flowed into the kiss as naturally as breathing, and this time there wasn't just heat and desire; there was a new give-and-take, a sense that he wasn't solely trying to give her pleasure, he was taking some for himself, as well. One kiss turned to the next and the next, and then he was fumbling with the shower controls to turn off the water and bring up a strange, soft light that surrounded them on all sides.

"What— Oh!" A tingle ran over her skin from head to toe. When it was gone, she was dry. Even her hair was merely damp, and the usually unruly waves were tame and soft to the touch. "Magic," she whispered, her voice catching on the word.

"The wolfyn have some redeeming qualities," he said huskily, and scooped her up in his arms, so she was cradled against his chest.

She squeaked and struggled a little, but then subsided to nibble her way up his neck as he carried her into the main room. And she gave another small, "Oh," at the sight of thick blankets piled on the bed and a fire in the hearth. The room was warm and suddenly cheery, and the sight made her throat tighten, because he had done this for her. Even in the heat of things, he had wanted her to be comfortable.

She swallowed past the lump of emotion. "You're a prince."

"I was, once."

Hating the hollowness in his voice, she said, "You will be again. When we—"

He kissed her, cutting her off. Then, still kissing her, he lowered them both to the wide mattress, so she lay beneath him with her legs alongside his, his thighs between hers and the long length of his erection pressing against her stomach, pulsing with an inner beat that resonated deep within her.

Desire washed through her like a friend she'd only just met, feeling so much sharper and more important than ever before, building higher and higher still as they kissed and he notched one thigh between hers, creating intimate pressure as he stroked a hand from her rib cage to her knee and back again in a feather-soft caress that seared her skin and made her want to beg.

New wetness gathered, new aches sprang to life, as he shaped her, touched her, but also arched into her touch, and paused to absorb the sensations as she licked his throat, then pushed on his shoulders to roll him onto his back so she could move lower, then lower still.

"Wait, Reda. I— Ahh." He gave a full-body shudder at the first touch of her tongue along the distended vein on the underside of his shaft. *"Gods."*

He made a move to touch her, but then she took another stroke with her tongue, a long lap from base to tip, and he fisted his hands in the soft, heavy bedding instead, then groaned when she did it again, finding the places where the textures changed and he was particularly sensitive. Where in the past she had been take it or leave it on oral sex, now she reveled in it, storing up his responses and glorying in the way he was submitting to her.

Soon his body was strung tight, his hands working in the bedding, his heavy length jerking in her mouth in movements that spurred new heat inside her.

He said her name, caught her hand, urged her up his body, and then, when they were chest to chest, rolled them so he was in charge once more, pressing her into the bedding with his good, solid weight. Both of their bodies were damp with excitement, slippery with passion, and as he settled between her thighs, his slick, hard length slid naturally into position, poised for entry.

Reda shifted against him, teasing them both with the slide of his blunt head through her slick folds. But then she stiffened. "Wait," she said, almost too late remembering that this might not be her reality, but it wasn't a dream, either. "Do we need something?"

He struggled to focus through eyes gone nearly glassy. "Something?"

"Protection? For, um, diseases and other things." *Please don't make me explain this.*

"Oh." His expression cleared, turned rueful and maybe a touch sad. "No diseases for my kind, to give or get. As for the 'other things,' because of the way my mindspeak works, I must feed from my mate's throat before a child can be made." She wanted to ask, but didn't. It must have shown in her eyes, though, because he shook his head slightly. "No. Never."

Guilty at the surge of a relief she had no right to

feel, she reached up to soothe the hollow echo in his voice with a kiss that started soft and almost drowsy, and shifted something inside her. The softness gained an edge, the drowsiness fled to a demand and the guilt turned to greed, and the desire not just to have him inside her, but to *have* him, to belong to him and him to her.

But knowing that was impossible, she broke the kiss, pressed her wet cheek to the faint rasp of stubble along his jaw and whispered, "Now. Please, now."

She closed her eyes, shutting out the daylight, the strange surroundings and the danger beyond, determined to be there, in that moment, with him. Then he growled low in his throat, and thrust home. And as he slid into her—stretching her, filling her and bringing a surge of emotion that she didn't dare acknowledge—she didn't need to shut out the larger world, because he did it for her. The feel of him, the perfection of the fit, eclipsed everything else in that moment.

Her mouth went round in a voiceless O of pleasure. She dug her fingers into the heavy muscles of his shoulders as he rose above her, poised there for a breathless second of anticipation...and then began to move.

It was gentle at first, the tempo slow, as if he, too, wanted to store up each individual sensation. She rocked with him naturally, the moves more instinct than volition because she wasn't thinking, wasn't planning; she was *experiencing.* She reveled in the liquid surge of his body against hers, the fullness between her legs, the way the pleasure ramped with each thrust, and the vibration of his groan as her hands dragged to his hips, dug in and urged him on.

As things sped up, there was no difference between vampire or human anymore, or between a fairy-tale prince and a disgraced cop; there were only two lost souls filling in the empty spaces for each other, no longer alone. At least for now.

Needs piled atop greed within her as the pleasure found a purchase, took root and began to grow. And where before her orgasm had been sharp and brilliant, all inner fireworks and satisfying heat, the tension that gripped her this time was deeper and more consuming, tightening her inner muscles, overtaking her senses and suddenly making the moment far more important than it was supposed to be.

*This is it,* her body seemed to be saying. *This is what you've been waiting for.*

Turning away from that danger, she buried her face against his neck and moved beneath him. The move wrung a groan from him, then a reverent whisper of, "Reda."

Her name had never sounded like magic before.

Willing away the tears that prickled her eyes, she kissed his throat openmouthed as he rode her, bucked against her and drove the coiling pleasure higher and higher still.

She tasted the faint salty tang of his skin, felt the throb of his pulse against her lips. It pounded in tempo with him, with the pulse of needs that drew tighter within her with each thrust, where he pressed into her inside and out, and hit that spot there, oh, yes, there.

From deep within her came the urge to bite down, to take his essence within her and bind them together. Ignoring the faint itch of disquiet, she grazed her teeth along the vein that angled along the side of his throat, nipped lightly.

He hissed, his fingers suddenly digging into her as he slammed home, setting off new sensations that carried a raw power that tempted her to shy away.

She felt him struggle for control, felt herself hesitate, tempted to duck the intensity and the possibilities. Then, because she refused to be a coward with him, right now in this moment, she found his vein again. And bit down hard. She didn't draw blood, but it was a near thing.

The last remnants of Dayn's control snapped almost audibly. He flung back his head and then bowed into her, wrapping his arms around her to anchor her body against his thrusts, which rocketed up in tempo and swing, driving them both onward.

His hold was powerful, inexorable, and Reda reveled in it. She loved his strength and intensity, loved feeling small, feminine and overwhelmed—at least here, with him. She loved the way he pressed his jaw to her temple, a kiss to her brow and whispered her name as both their bodies went tight and tense, and the pleasure gathered inside her, waiting, waiting....

He turned his head, softly grazed the side of her throat with a wickedly sharp canine, and whispered her name. Fear and pleasure were suddenly the same, sharp and brilliant, and she gasped and came for him.

Pleasure lashed through her, as keen and sharp as a sword that cut through the loneliness and apprehension and left behind strength and wonder. She arched beneath him, breath sobbing, mouth shaping his name as the waves kept coming. Then he locked himself against her, hips working as he groaned long and low in a mix of words—her name, praise, pleas—and emptied himself into her.

She imagined she felt heat warmer than her own blooming inside, caressed by her inner muscles as they pulsed, milking him of his seed. And she, who had always had a slow-ticking biological clock if at all, felt a small, wistful wish that this one could have counted that way, that they could truly be mated.

And for a change, logic and reason didn't have a damn thing to say.

He stayed locked against her while the pleasure leveled off and then faded, and the world around them started to come back into focus. She heard the *hiss-pop* of the fire, saw the brightness of the sunny day outside through her closed lids and felt the shift of the mattress when he levered up onto his elbows, taking his weight off her.

Though she would have liked to linger a moment more, she opened her eyes and met his emerald gaze. And for the first time since meeting him—and she didn't for a second want to count the hours, considering what had just passed between them—his expression was open and unshadowed. It made him look younger and a little naughty, bringing to mind the kind of man who would go for a gallop to blow off some steam, little knowing that the morning would change his life forever.

She, too, felt changed, but she didn't want to look at it too closely. Not now. Maybe not ever.

He cleared his throat. "I, uh, feel like I should say something. But I haven't a clue what."

A tension she hadn't even been aware of melted away, easing her neck and shoulders. "Me, too, and me, neither. So how about we say 'thank you' and set it aside for now?"

His face softened. "Then I thank you, dear sweet Reda, for teaching me about showers, for taking me into your bed, for touching me and for sharing your lovely, lovely body with me."

Her heart shuddered in her chest, her eyes threatened to fill, her throat to lock, and she knew she didn't dare say anything now; that if she did, she would make an idiot out of herself and make them both supremely uncomfortable. So, although it made her the coward, she just nodded jerkily and reached up to kiss his cheek.

Dayn, bless his noble heart, seemed to understand. He brushed his fingers over her cheeks as if brushing away the tears she hadn't let herself shed, then said, "Stay here and see if you can sleep. I'm going to double-check the wards."

She nodded, feeling a blush form at the strange intimacy of the moment, with the two of them strangers except in their dreams. He rose from the bed and padded, gloriously naked, to the bathroom, where he pulled on his pants and boots, then threw on his shirt without buttoning it. When he came back over to her, he had one of his short swords tucked in his belt.

That shouldn't have made him even more appealing than before. She was a modern woman, an evolved human being. But apparently that modern, evolved woman liked men with swords.

*Not men,* she thought, *just Dayn.* And that wasn't logic, reason or practicality talking. It was a fact. And if that put her on the fast track to heartache, maybe that wasn't the worst thing that could happen to her. Because at least she wouldn't be sleepwalking through life anymore.

He snagged one of the waterskins as he returned to the main room, and crossed to the bed and offered it to her first. "Thirsty?"

"Parched." The act of accepting water from him shouldn't have felt profound, just as the satisfied look in his eyes as he watched her drink shouldn't have kindled new sparks of arousal. Flustered, she handed it back. "Thank you."

"Rest. I'll be back in a few minutes."

Nodding, she lay back and curled onto her side with her back to the fire. With her eyes closed, the noises around her seemed amplified. She tracked Dayn's movements by the thud of his boots, the close of the door at his back, the crunch of gravel outside and the annoyed call of a bird disturbed by his circuit of the cabin.

He returned within a few minutes, as promised, and his clothing rustled and boots thudded as he stripped back down before sliding into the bed with her. He curled around her, his front to her back, and folded their hands together over her heart.

And as she drifted off to sleep with his warmth surrounding her, she found herself doubly grateful that he wasn't a wolfyn. Because if he was, she would surely be enthralled.

Dayn awoke near noon, when his internal clock warned that they didn't dare rest much longer, in case their pursuers were still on the road.

In her sleep, Reda had turned toward him. Now, she was nestled close to his side, her head pillowed on the arm he had curled around her. Her breath was warm on his skin, tightening his nipples and sending tendrils of reaction lower down in his body. But those physical responses were tiny trickles compared to the deep wellspring of emotion that even now threatened to fill him up and spill over.

Affection, gratitude, relief, disquiet—there was all of that and more, a complicated mix that said he probably shouldn't have made love with her, and definitely not as intensely as things had wound up getting…but at the same time he couldn't regret the decision, or his eventual loss of control.

They had well and thoroughly loved each other with

no pretenses, no expectations and the knowledge that they would go their separate ways at the arch, taking with them only good memories. And if that thought brought a twinge, he ignored it and focused on how damn good he felt suddenly—refreshed and recharged, and ready to take on the world.

Or to take on a pissed-off pack and a countdown to the night after tomorrow—the fourth night—as the case might be.

At that sobering reminder, he touched her shoulder. "Come, my sleeping beauty. It's time to waken."

He halfway expected her to jolt awake and panic at finding them in bed together. As responsive and exciting as his sweet Reda had been, he doubted she'd ever before taken a lover mere hours after meeting him, doubted she was accustomed to waking in a near-stranger's arms. Their relationship, though, had perforce been compressed, accelerated.

She must have been closer to waking than he had thought, though, because she didn't gasp or jump away from him. Instead, she smiled, eyes still closed, and said, "If I'm Sleeping Beauty, then my Prince Charming should wake me with a kiss."

"You think I'm charming, then?" Without waiting for an answer, he leaned in and touched his lips to hers, a chaste press at first, then going deeper when her lips softened and parted beneath his.

Murmuring, she shifted closer to him and slid her arms around his neck, capturing him against her. The move tugged at him, reaching inside and filling a place he hadn't even known was empty. Fierce joy raced through him as he moved over her, into her, pressing her into the mattress as he kissed her thoroughly, his body awakening to the reality of a lover, *his* lover.

Her soft moan made him want to pull her up and dance her in a mad whirl around the cabin; the gentle tug of her fingers in his hair made him want to sing at the top of his lungs, though he couldn't hold a tune; and the feeling of her beneath him, her thighs cradling him as he swelled and hardened almost instantly despite having come inside her only a few hours before made him want to race out into the forest to hunt the most dangerous foe, solely so he could bring her a talisman of the kill. Though from what he'd heard, humans could be squeamish about such things. So maybe he would pick her wildflowers instead.

The sheer ridiculousness of it was suddenly very appealing. As was the thought of slipping inside her once more and rocking them both to oblivion. He could feel the slick wetness of her cleft against him and the excited race of her pulse beneath her soft, feminine skin. And although they needed to leave the cabin, he was dying to lose himself in her, with her.

Then, suddenly, her fingers were wrapped around him, guiding him. He stiffened, broke the kiss and groaned as she teased the tip of his hard shaft along her wet folds.

Pulling his head from hers, he looked down at the spread of her coppery curls and the glint of her blue eyes. "Gods, Reda. We don't have much time."

"I know." She reached up and kissed his cheek. "So be quick." And she curled a leg around his hips, and urged him home.

Groaning, he plunged into her, then hissed with pleasure as her heated wetness snugged around him, urging him on. He was already teetering at the edge of control when she arched up to meet him, and the liquid, heated friction snapped those last thin threads that said he needed to see to her pleasure before his own.

Grating her name, he caught her by the shoulder and hip, anchoring her as he thrust heavily—once, twice, a third time was all it took before he felt the tingling, tightening sensation that presaged a climax. He didn't try to fight it, but rode it instead, pistoning twice more before the tingles became a roar of heat, the need to cut loose, and he bowed against her, thrust as deep as he could and releasing himself into her with a shattering groan.

He went blind and deaf, insensate to anything but the pleasure of coming inside her as his orgasm went on and on, seeming to last longer than the sex itself.

Slowly, he became aware of sharp prickles where her fingernails dug into his shoulders, the press of her heels into the backs of his thighs, where she had locked her ankles. And the fact that he was probably crushing her.

"Gods." He levered himself up on arms that wobbled like the legs of a newborn beast-chaser foal, and looked down at her, expecting to see…hell, he didn't know what he expected. But it wasn't wide-eyed wonder tinged with fear.

But then again, he realized after a moment, that pretty much summed it up.

"It wasn't just the drug, was it?" she asked softly.

"No." He shook his head. "This is us, sweet Reda." He wanted to ask her if she had come, but couldn't bring himself to admit that he had been that far lost within himself. So instead he resolved that when they stopped next to rest, he would even things up. The thought put a burn of anticipation in his gut and made him look forward to that break and the next, and however many it took them to reach the Meriden Arch.

And after that…damn it, he didn't know what came after that, except that he had a vow to keep and responsibilities to fulfill. He only hoped to hell he could do all that and do right by Reda, too.

Somehow.

# Chapter 9

For Reda, the next two days passed in a blur, yet at the same time there were moments that were imprinted so sharply in her mind that she knew she would remember them forever.

There had been alien fairy-tale moments: like when she watched a hawk skim over the treetops, only to have it grow larger and larger as it approached, then belch smoky flame from a crocodilian head before it screeched and veered off; or when the thunder of hoofbeats called their attention to a herd moving on the other side of a low hill and, just as she turned to ask Dayn why the wolfyn and their guests didn't ride the horses, they crested to see two-dozen massive equids with coal-black coats, ember-red eyes and wickedly sharp unicorn horns that glinted in the sun.

Those moments had grown more alien still when he had told her that the demidragons were nothing compared to the true dragons of Elden legends, like the vicious Feiynd, with its black-pearl scales and assassin's instincts. Or how the wolfyn and unicorns were uneasy allies, their peace treaty based on mutual dislike, and that he—a horse lover since childhood—had tried to learn the unicorn's language, only to find that while wolfyn tongues could speak it, human forms couldn't.

There had been hauntingly beautiful moments, like the sight of a wolfyn pack gathered on a faraway hill, silhouetted against the fat, full moon as they howled in a spine-tingling descant; and how, when they had crested the jagged ridge that separated the territories of two packs—the Nose-Claws and the Bite-Tails, both of whom they had managed to avoid by staying near concealment—a grassy green plain had spread out before them, forming a bowl-shaped crater with a nearly circular lake at its center, reflecting the pale sky and the shape of a round cloud overhead.

And then there was Dayn. He was in all of those memories and so many others from those precious two days. He was her woodsman, her prince, her lover, and in that short, precious, unselfconscious space of time, she had come to know him intimately. She knew how he moved, how he tasted, what it took to make him sigh and how far she could tease before his control snapped and his fangs came out. Literally.

His vampire heritage didn't scare her anymore; he was just a man like any other, albeit one with the powers of his realm and his heritage. He was stubborn at times, and was inexplicably fond of chewing on wolfsleep sap, which she found tasteless, with a weird consistency. But those were insignificant quirks when measured against the whole.

They hadn't used the wolfsbene again, but instead hiked under their own power, with occasional hits of the stimulant potion, which seemed to be the local equivalent of coffee, or maybe an energy drink. They had traveled steadily, talking quietly or walking in companionable silence, stopping every six or eight hours to rest…and make love. And at times she'd had to pinch herself to be sure she really wasn't dreaming, after all.

But, like a dream, the journey couldn't go on forever, and they were nearing the end of theirs.

"Ready to roll?" Dayn asked, coming out of a section of woods that ran almost all the way up to the road's edge. He carried only a single rucksack now, along with his crossbow and short swords; she was wearing the other rucksack along with the bow and arrows she probably wouldn't ever use. It was warmer today than it had been, and he was down to his shirtsleeves, with his jacket and sweater packed away.

The sight of him in his plaid shirt, pants and boots— so like the woodcuttings that had brought her to him— made her heart turn over in her chest and put a wistful lump in her throat. *If only*…she thought, but didn't bother even completing the wish.

"Let's do this," she said, pushing to her feet. By his estimation, they would reach the arch in an hour or two, well before sunset. They hadn't really talked about what they would do when they got there, but she harbored a secret hope that they could steal one last time together, maybe right beside the waterfall.

She wanted that to be the memory she rekindled when she looked at the final page of the book. Lovemaking, not loss. She'd had the joy; she would take the pain that came at the end of this strange magical adventure.

Still, though, her throat went tight as she came even with him on the trail. She flattened her palm on his chest and reached up on her tiptoes to kiss the side of his neck, where the blood vessels ran, and where she was oddly proud to have given him a hickey. He covered her hand with his and squeezed, but when she moved to pull away, he held on to her, trapping her hand against his heart for a moment longer before letting her go.

They started down the road together, shoulder to shoulder, in a silence broken only by the calls of different creatures. She knew them now: the deep roar of the demidragon, the high, clarion cry of the bugle beast, the deceptively sweet trill of the mudhump, which was truly repulsive in both looks and smell.

On one level, she hated the thought of leaving the magic behind, even hated the thought of leaving this strange wolfyn realm. Yet at the same time, she yearned to be back in her safe apartment, in a world where she knew how things worked and she didn't need to be looking over her shoulder all the time, didn't need to remember to be brave.

# YOUR PARTICIPATION IS REQUESTED!

Dear Reader,

Since you are a lover of paranormal romance fiction – we would like to get to know you!

Inside you will find a short Reader's Survey. Sharing your answers with us will help our editorial staff understand who you are and what activities you enjoy.

To thank you for your participation, we would like to send you 2 books and 2 gifts – **ABSOLUTELY FREE!**

Enjoy your gifts with our appreciation,

*Pam Powers*

**SEE INSIDE FOR READER'S SURVEY**

# YOUR READER'S SURVEY "THANK YOU" FREE GIFTS INCLUDE:

▶ 2 Paranormal Romance books
▶ 2 lovely surprise gifts

## PLEASE FILL IN THE CIRCLES COMPLETELY TO RESPOND

**1)** What type of fiction books do you enjoy reading? (Check all that apply)
- ○ Suspense/Thrillers   ○ Action/Adventure   ○ Modern-day Romances
- ○ Historical Romance   ○ Humour   ○ Paranormal Romance

**2)** What attracted you most to the last fiction book you purchased on impulse?
- ○ The Title   ○ The Cover   ○ The Author   ○ The Story

**3)** What is usually the greatest influencer when you <u>plan</u> to buy a book?
- ○ Advertising   ○ Referral   ○ Book Review

**4)** How often do you access the internet?
- ○ Daily   ○ Weekly   ○ Monthly   ○ Rarely or never.

**5)** How many NEW paperback fiction novels have you purchased in the past 3 months?
- ○ 0 - 2   ○ 3 - 6   ○ 7 or more

# YES! I have completed the Reader's Survey. Please send me the 2 FREE books and 2 FREE gifts (gifts are worth about $10) for which I qualify. I understand that I am under no obligation to purchase any books, as explained on the back of this card.

## 237/337 HDL FH9E

FIRST NAME                          LAST NAME

ADDRESS

APT.#                          CITY

STATE/PROV.                          ZIP/POSTAL CODE

## The Reader Service — Here's How It Works:

If offer card is missing write to: The Reader Service, P.O. Box 1867, Buffalo, NY 14240-1867 or visit: www.ReaderService.com

BUSINESS REPLY MAIL
FIRST-CLASS MAIL    PERMIT NO. 717    BUFFALO, NY

POSTAGE WILL BE PAID BY ADDRESSEE

THE READER SERVICE
PO BOX 1341
BUFFALO NY 14240-8571

NO POSTAGE
NECESSARY
IF MAILED
IN THE
UNITED STATES

About an hour into this last leg of their journey, as they marched up the long incline of a rolling hill, Dayn spat his last piece of wolfsleep gum into the bushes, rinsed his mouth with a few sips from the waterskin they had refilled just that morning and wordlessly offered it to her.

"No, thanks, I'm good." Her voice felt rusty, her throat tight.

He tucked the skin back in his rucksack and adjusted the strap an extra time, then fiddled with his sword belt. Shrugged inside his shirt.

She glanced over and raised an eyebrow. "Are you okay?"

"Yeah." His voice, too, was husky. "It's just...we'll be able to see the arch from the top of this hill." He didn't meet her eyes as he said it.

"Oh." *Oh, God.* Her newly reawakened libido tugged at the thought of making love at the edge of the waterfall, but that pleasant flutter was quickly submerged by the thought of what would follow. Aware that her steps had slowed, she made herself speed back up. *One foot in front of the other.* "Well. I guess we made it."

He unslung his rucksack, pulled out his jacket and shrugged into it, only to yank it off seconds later with a frustrated noise. "I hate this. I hate..." He trailed off, staring at his hands. "Oh, gods. This isn't coming from me. It's the magic. The vortex is already starting up."

*"No."* She spun toward the crest of the hill, but didn't see anything strange about the sky or trees, nothing to

say there was magic beyond. There was no glow, no noise. She couldn't even hear the waterfall.

Dayn knew magic, though. He *was* magic.

"Come on!" He tucked a piece of wolfsbene in her hand, and downed his own in a single gulp. "We'll make a run for it!"

She gulped the gritty lump, forcing it past the tightness in her throat and the pressure that made her want to cry out that it wasn't fair, that she needed more time with him. Just another hour, that was all. Though in her heart of hearts she knew even that wouldn't have been enough, and maybe it was better this way. Swallowing, she nodded. "Let's go."

They charged up the rest of the incline together, strides lengthening from moment to moment as the drug kicked in. Power raced through her veins, lighting her up and making her feel mighty, invincible...and even hotter for Dayn's body than she had been moments before. She wanted to trip him and follow him down, cover his body with hers and ride him until they were both wrung limp. She wanted to kiss him, touch him, own him, belong to him.

Instead, she concentrated on putting one foot in front of the other as they crested the top of the hill. The sound of the waterfall hit her first and then the valley opened up in front of them and she stumbled to a halt as she saw it: Meriden Arch.

Dayn stopped beside her, standing so their arms touched.

Even from the half-mile distance, she could see that

it was a match to the woodcutting: a high stone archway capped the top of a waterfall that crashed halfway down an interrupted cliff face to fall in a tumbled pool that gushed to a river leading away. Heavy foliage flanked the waterway and the cliff faces, then thinned to a rolling green valley. All that was the same.

The shimmering in the air below the arch, though, was new.

He was right. The vortex was already forming.

"We need to go." His voice broke on the last word.

"I know." She reached out and took his hand. Their fingers twined together. And they ran down the hill together, shoulder to shoulder, as if they were mated, though that was only a dream.

Her eyes were burning by the time they hit the flatlands, her throat by the time they reached the edge of the pool, pausing near where a wide trail zigzagged up the cliff and led to the archway, where lightning arcs leaped from stone to stone. The air sparkled and swirled but hadn't yet begun to rotate.

They had a little time, then, to say their goodbyes. She wasn't sure if that was a good thing or not. She lifted their joined hands to her lips and kissed his knuckles, grazing the skin with her teeth and making him shudder.

"Sweet Reda." He cupped her face in his hands and bent to kiss her.

She leaned into his touch, into his kiss, feeling a poignant ache grow along with the now-familiar heat, which was made sharper by the burn of the wolfsbene in her blood. She gripped his wrists, held on to him, tried to imprint the moment on her soul.

He drew away before she was ready to let him go. But his eyes were very intent on hers, searching her face as he said, "Come with me. Come to Elden."

"Oh," she whispered as a full-body shiver ran through her; and her blood ran hot and then cold, then hot again. It wasn't like she hadn't thought about it— of course she had. But logic—and, worse, her gut instinct—said it was the wrong answer. Tears prickled, but she willed them back. "I want to," she said, forcing her voice to stay steady. "God, of course I do."

His voice, his eyes, went flat. "But you won't."

"The vortices are unpredictable and we don't know if there's a direct connection between our realms. It could be a one-way trip for me."

"Would that be so terrible?"

The question stung, mostly because, on many levels, the answer was "not really."

If she didn't return to Salem, her father and brothers would spend a couple of months trying desperately to find her, more because it was the right thing to do than because they really missed her, though, and because they would need a logical explanation for her disappearance. And her friends and coworkers would go through the motions, believing deep down inside that she had changed her name and moved to an island somewhere, as she had occasionally threatened to do.

Six months, a year from now, she would be a memory,

maybe a scholarship somewhere. And how much did that thought suck?

"You think I haven't asked myself that?" she said softly. "You think I don't know that I haven't left a single indelible mark on the human realm?"

His fingers tightened on hers. "I'm sorry. I didn't mean to make it worse. But if that's the case, why go back?" His kiss was hard and possessive, and made her burn for him. "Come with me, my sweet Reda."

She wanted to; oh, how she wanted to. But for a change, logic and practicality had it right. "Say I do... then what?" *Please say you know, please say something that would make it make sense.*

But his expression went bleak. "I know it's too much to ask, too damned dangerous. There are, what? A hundred ways for things to go to hell once I get home? A thousand? Which means I'm an asshole for even asking—I should want you to be safe above everything else, right? It should be enough that I see you go into that vortex—" he pointed at where the shimmers were beginning to rotate "—and can have faith that you made it home okay. It should be enough that I've got the memories of the past few days to take with me, to remember when things turn to shit. Which they probably will."

Her throat locked, because he was saying all the things she'd been telling herself, yet she still wanted to shout, *Yes! Yes, I'll come with you.* All she got out, though, was a fractured sigh of, "Dayn."

Eyes firing, he took her other hand and lifted it, so both of her palms were pressed to his chest, folded in his hands. She could feel their heartbeats keeping time, feel the urges of the wolfsbene pounding in her veins as he said, "Maybe I haven't grown up as much as I thought, because every part of me wants to be self-ish right now, and keep you with me. Please say you'll come. I promise that I'll—"

"Don't," she interrupted, pulling a hand free to touch his lips and silence him. "You can't make promises to me. God, you shouldn't even be thinking about me."

"I know. But I can't stop." He kissed her fingers. "Come with me. I need you. I don't want to do this without you."

It was every childish fantasy come to life—the hand-some, powerful prince begging her to run away from her unsatisfying life to live the adventure with him, the dream.

But dreams always ended, didn't they?

"Say everything goes according to plan," she said. "Suppose you and your brothers and sister find one an-other, take out the sorcerer and reclaim Elden. What then? What happens to us?"

"We live happily ever after." His answer should have seemed glib; instead, it made her yearn.

"I'm not a princess, Dayn. I'm just another guards-man's daughter."

She wanted him to look surprised, wanted to think he hadn't seen it. Instead, a spark entered his eyes. "It's no coincidence that the book came to your mother. The stories she told you are straight out of kingdom folk-lore."

"You think she was a guest in the human realm." She did, too. It was only logical.

"Not only that, I think she had the kind of powers that travel in royal lines, or at least the nobility. Why else would my father's spell have sent the book to her? How else would she have known how important it was, or that it was meant for you, not her?" He lowered his voice and leaned in to whisper, "Mindspeak, Reda. I think my father reached out to her the same way he did to me. And he could only do that if there was a blood-line connection, however faint."

Reda's head spun, because she hadn't taken it that far. She might have sagged if he hadn't been there to lean on. Her eyes locked on the love bite at the side of his neck. "You think I'm a vampire." She wasn't sure if her sudden queasiness was nausea or excitement.

"Half or less, and blood drinking doesn't run true. But…yeah, I think the heritage is there."

She shook her head, denying the logic more than the possibility. "You're reaching."

"Maybe. Or maybe I have faith that our feelings mean something, that all of this means something." His gesture encompassed the realm, the vortex and the two of them. "The book didn't come to you randomly. None of this is a coincidence, Reda. And we're not over. I won't let us be."

She saw the kiss coming and nearly moved away, knowing that she couldn't think clearly in his arms—or rather, that the clarity she found there wasn't always based on reason. But the wolfsbene rooted her in place and her traitorous body had her reaching for him, sliding her fingers up into his thick hair and opening her mouth beneath his.

They had made love only a few hours before, but heat leaped through her anew when his lips slanted across hers and their tongues touched and slid. And for the first time, something clicked inside her and a small voice whispered, *Yes. This is it. There's no way you can walk away from this.*

It wasn't the first time she had thought achingly that Dayn could be the love of her life. But it was the first time that she had thought that maybe, possibly, they could make it work. Always before, even if she could believe they would make it through the retaking of Elden, she hadn't been able to picture herself as the consort of a prince. Now, though… Her thoughts soared as he drew his lips from hers, then kissed her cheek, her forehead.

Then he took a step away from her, toward the trail leading up, and held out his hand in invitation. "Come with me, my sweet Reda. Have faith. Be brave."

She flashed on the image of the woodsman asking Red to leave everything and everyone she knew and come away with him, without making any real changes in his own life. Before, she had thought it unfair. Now, she saw that sometimes it was the only answer.

"I— *Look out!*" she screamed, catching sudden sight of a gray-buff blur flying down the lowest section of the trail toward him, then leaping.

He spun instantly to meet the attack, but he had only

just started to pull his sword when the huge wolfyn hit him and took him down with a terrible snarl.

She grabbed for her bow, but it wrenched in her grip, looped across her neck, and she found herself yanked back by the strings, which cut into her. "No!" Panic hammered through her as rough hands grabbed her and dragged her away from where the huge wolfyn—she thought it was Kenar—was ripping at Dayn, tearing at him. She saw blood, heard him shout…and then, worse, go limp and silent. She surged toward him, screaming, "Dayn!"

There wasn't any answer.

He heard her as if from afar, as if in a dream that he didn't want to waken from, because his conscious self was in agony. Dying. Maybe already dead.

*Fight, damn it. You can't leave her to the pack.* The inner voice was his own, the sentiment a noble one, but it seemed too late. He was drifting, his consciousness split from his physical self. He was looking down on himself, watching as Kenar stood atop his deathly still body, lifted his bloodstained muzzle to the sky and howled the victory while the vortex started to pick up speed in the background, going from air to white vapors.

The rest of the pack stood ringing him in a mix of wolf and human forms, with Reda pushed off to the edge and watched by four guards, two of each form. She was white-faced and shaking, tears running down her face as she stared at the carnage. He looked for their sole ally, but Keely wasn't there. Where was she? Had Kenar figured out that she had aided in their escape?

*Gods,* Dayn thought. *Please. Not yet. Give me just a little more time to put things right.* He strained toward his body, trying to put himself back in the ragged flesh that had once been a man.

Sensing a glimmer of pain, he pushed all his energy in that direction, all the magic he could find within his incorporeal self. Agony lashed through him and the scene below dimmed as he was pulled back into the shell of his dying body.

He tried to call more magic, to complete the connection, but he needed something more. He strained and struggled as Kenar barked a command and the pack shifted, eddying as Reda's guards brought her forward. Panic lashed through Dayn, and for a second he thought he felt a flutter of his too-still heart. *Please, gods. Put me back in my body so I can save her and fulfill my oath.*

For a second, nothing happened. Then an inner voice boomed, *Will you sacrifice your future to do it?* The voice wasn't his own, wasn't his father's, wasn't anything he had ever heard before. It was deep, powerful and terrifying, and he thought it came from the realm of the gods, or perhaps the Abyss. It was that all-encompassing.

"Yes," Dayn whispered, somehow forcing the word from between his corpse's cold lips. "Absolutely yes." This was his lesson, his warning—he had started to be the selfish man again in trying to take Reda with him. He wouldn't make the same mistake again. "I swear it."

Power flared suddenly, wrapping around him, yanking him from his distant perch and thrusting him into his dying body. Only it wasn't dying anymore. Magic washed through him, bathing his body and kick-starting his heart, which flopped for a few moments within his chest, but then took on its native, life-giving rhythm.

*Pain!* It hit him like a new vortex, sucking him down and threatening to send him flying once more above the agony of it all. But he dug in and gutted it out, sending all the magic he could muster toward his birthright powers. His gums burned; his secondary canines sharpened and extended, piercing the tender flesh and descending to touch the inside of his lower lip. Warmth flowed through him, knitting bones, healing flesh and organs and beating back the pain. *Faster, faster,* he chanted inwardly. *Hurry!*

Lacking his bird's-eye view, he was forced to crack his eyelids and peer through blurry eyes to see Kenar, now in human form, standing over Reda, who was on her knees, forced there by her human-form guards while the two wolf forms stood back, bristling. Dayn knew all four, knew they would follow their alpha's orders without question. And he dreaded the empty, soulless look in Kenar's eyes as he stared down at her.

"I claim the rights of a guest," she said, lifting her chin to glare at Kenar, face white and drawn. "You have to grant me shelter and safety. It's tradition."

The alpha's eyes didn't even flicker. "That would

have worked on my sire, or even my softhearted whore of a sister, but not on me. I'm pack law now, not a bunch of moldy old traditions that lured a witch and her creatures to come into our realm and attack us. And my law says there are no guests anymore. There are only the wolfyn and their enemies." He turned away, tossing over his shoulder, "Kill her."

Reda screamed as the guards dragged her to her feet.

"Hold!" Dayn bellowed, lunging to his feet and yanking his short sword with one hand, his crossbow with the other. He swept the crowd and snarled, showing his blood drinker's fangs.

Reda's face lit and she gave a low, glad cry. "Dayn!"

The wolfyn flinched back, ears flat and lips pulling back in snarls of their own. All but Kenar, who rounded on him, eyes lighting with cruel joy. *"Bloodsucker,"* he hissed. "Back for more?"

The bastard had left him partly alive on purpose, testing to see if he would heal.

Not letting his hand shake at what he was about to do, Dayn pointed his sword at the alpha's throat. "I claim the Right of Challenge."

Reda's eyes widened and her lips shaped the words *Right of Challenge,* though no sound emerged.

Kenar barked a laugh. "Bullshit. A bloodsucker can't challenge to lead the pack. Only a wolfyn has wolfyn rights."

"I know." Dayn looked at Reda, and said, "Remember this if you remember nothing else good about me—I'm sorry for everything." Because what happened next would destroy the slim chance they'd had at a future. Just like the voice had said.

Exhaling against the sudden stab of pain brought by the knowledge, he did the something he had avoided since his first blood moon, when he had realized what his parents' spell had really done to him when it sent him to the wolfyn realm.

He called on his other magic. And changed.

# Chapter 10

Reda's scream was buried beneath the tumult that arose from the wolfyn as Dayn's form blurred, widened, shifted, shortened…and then crystallized into a huge wolfyn.

Dayn was a wolfyn. *Oh, God. No. This isn't possible. It's not happening.* But shaking her head didn't clear the sight, and she was beyond thinking any of this was a dream. Or, in this case, a nightmare.

Its—*his*—fur was dark, nearly black, which made the reddish shoulder patch and golden dorsal stripe stand out like a visual shout. And when he drew back his lips to snarl at Kenar, his canines were longer than those of any of the others, and wickedly pointed. A vampire trapped, temporarily at least, in a wolf's body.

"Noooo." The word escaped from Reda on a low, anguished moan as the structure of her unreal reality crashed to pieces around her and she saw the past few days for what they had been.

Dayn's brilliant eyes—emerald green, not the amber of the others'—flicked to her at the noise, but she couldn't find any human emotion in them. His words rang inside her: *I'm sorry for everything.*

He wasn't just talking about her being caught up in his family's magic, or even about him having kept yet another huge secret from her. He was apologizing for what he had done to her over the past two days.

The bastard had enthralled her.

*Shame. Rage. Heartbreak.* She didn't know what to feel, what to focus on within the huge wave of emotion that slammed through her as the pack struggled to deal with this new shift in the balance of power.

Kenar recovered quickly from the surprise. He might have paled, but his sneer didn't lose any of its oily, predatory nature. It made her think of the wolfyn in the book, the villain... And that made her see how Dayn wasn't the woodsman, after all.

He was the wolf.

He was the seducer, the tempter. And she had fallen hard for the temptation.

"A challenge?" Kenar waved the others back, and the pack members cleared out. Within seconds, he and Dayn were facing each other in the middle of a cleared circle. "You think the pack will accept you as their leader now? I don't think so. And don't look to Keely for any help this time. She was outcast for helping you. Last I saw, she was hauling ass away from a big silver loner." Kenar's sneer turned even nastier. "He's probably caught up to her by now. Wonder if she's having fun? Those loners don't get a chance at many bitches."

Dayn growled low in his throat and began circling toward Kenar, trying to flank him.

The alpha, still in human form, moved to stay opposite him, openly taunting now. "Were you planning on handing things over to my weak slut of a sister? You think that's going to be any—" He morphed abruptly, dropped to a crouch and leaped with a feral roar as Dayn did the same.

The two huge creatures thudded together midair and went down snarling in a flurry of fur, raking claws and snapping jaws. Blood sprayed and one of the combatants yowled, and then they were surging to their feet, up onto their hind legs to come together again, smashing into each other like fighting rams going for a head butt, only with gaping jaws and wickedly sharp teeth.

Growls and excited yips came from the crowd, and more than one of the human forms went wolf, as if the experience was better in fur.

Reda's stomach roiled; she had to breathe through her mouth to stem the surging nausea that came from the potent mix of fear, disgust and upset rocketing through her.

*Enthralled. God.*

That explained why she had fallen so hard so fast, didn't it? And even now that she knew the truth, she wasn't free of his spell. She couldn't be, because her eyes were fixed on the fight and her heart was lodged in her throat.

She hated the sight of blood wetting his thick, dark coat when he and Kenar next parted. She hated the thought of his lean, beautiful body taking on new scars. And she hated how the other wolfyn were watching him with cold, hard eyes that suggested that even if he won his fight, he wouldn't live to claim his prize. She wanted to put herself between Dayn and the others, warding them off with her body while snarling, *Mine*.

Even more, some part of her drank in the sight of him in his wolf form: how his thick black coat shimmered over his muscles and caught the light as he reared up and lunged for his enemy; and how his eyes flashed like emerald green flame when the combatants came together chest to chest, snapping and snarling. The sight of curving, elongated and wickedly pointed canines stirred her deep inside, and the way he moved so elegantly, like a fighter, like the largest of predators, brought the same whisper of, *Mine*.

And she had to get out of here. Because if she stayed any longer, she might never escape his spell.

But how could she leave? She was surrounded, disarmed, her bow and arrows tossed aside. Mind racing, she scanned the scene. She caught a blur of motion from the trees near the waterfall, another from a stand of middle growth nearby, but then nothing, making her think it had been a bird.

Her captors were all in their wolfish forms now,

glued to the fight as Dayn rose over Kenar and slammed down atop him, driving the alpha to the ground. Teeth flashed, blood sprayed and Kenar screeched in pain. When he next stood, he was panting and dragging a foreleg. Dayn, too, was injured; he was bleeding from a deep gash on his shoulder, and the blood spattering the ground beneath him said that there were other wounds hidden by his dark fur. But he lunged first, drove Kenar back and followed him down with a flash of bloodstained teeth.

The brutal, meaty crunch that followed was the most sickening thing Reda had ever heard, and she gagged as Kenar spasmed and went gruesomely limp.

And then that *slurp-crunch* instantly dropped to the second most sickening thing she had ever heard as Dayn topped it by planting his front paws on Kenar's body, lifting his blood-streaked black muzzle to the sky and loosing a terrifying and self-satisfied howl of victory.

*Awwwooooooo.* The noise reached inside her, making her want to scream and claw at her own skin. Or maybe that was the knowledge that she had lain with a creature, a killer. Her heart tore as she stared at him, his wolf form gorgeous, terrifying…and entirely enthralling.

He howled again and nausea flared suddenly, and she clapped a hand over her mouth and turned away. Two of her huge wolfyn guards flanked her as she ran blindly from the circle with no real destination in mind except *away.* She needed to get away from the sight of his gorgeous emerald eyes, away from the wild, feral glory in his howl, away from the burning desire to turn back.

The guards herded her toward the trailhead, near where her bow and arrows had been tossed. One nudged her toward the weapons. The other turned back to the pack, silver-white fur bristling as if he were protecting her rather than holding her captive.

*Wait. Silver?*

Reda looked down at the wolfyn nearest her, thought she saw something familiar in its eyes. "Keely?"

The creature nodded, then nudged her forcibly toward the weapons, the pathway. She whuffed an almost-word that sounded like, "Go."

And then there was a sudden howl of alarm, a scramble of feet, and Reda looked up to see the pack reorienting on her, Keely and the silver-backed male.

Reda exploded into motion. She grabbed her bow and arrows and bolted for the trail. Behind her, a feral snarl sounded the attack as the Scratch-Eye pack came after her, and Keely and her loner friend tried to fend them off, and only partially succeeded. They stalled some of the wolfyn, but others came on.

Reda ran for her life. Her legs and lungs hurt; the wolfsbene helped, but would it be enough? *Please, God. Gods. Whoever you are,* she thought brokenly as she hit the trail and started up with a half dozen beasts behind her and gaining.

"Hold!" The word cracked commandingly, halting the wolfyn in their tracks.

She couldn't help herself. Recognizing Dayn's voice,

she stopped halfway up and looked back. Her heart shuddered at the sight of him standing over Kenar's body, both of them now morphed back to their human forms, one alive, one dead.

Dayn was wearing the same clothing he had been in when he morphed—how did that work?—and for a nanosecond he looked like the panel in her book that showed the woodsman standing over the slain wolf, triumphant at having saved the girl.

It was the truth, yet not.

Their eyes met, and even across the distance the contact struck sparks inside her. "Oh, Dayn," she whispered, heart hurting.

"For gods' sake go, Reda. Get out of here." He didn't shout the words, but she heard them clearly in her head, in her heart. And she just as clearly saw the pack orienting on him, bristling as the excitement of the fight cleared and they remembered that he was both their sworn enemy and now their leader.

This was about to get ugly, Reda thought. But even as her body—traitor as it was—sent her two steps back down the trail, a full-throated roar of sound and energy geared up above her, drowning out even her own sobbing breaths.

She didn't need to look to know what that meant: the vortex was fully formed. If she was going to leave, she had to do it now.

And, oh, dear God, she needed to leave.

Tears blurring her eyes, she spun and bolted up the remainder of the path.

She heard Dayn shout her name, but she didn't look back. Couldn't. She could only look ahead of herself.

The narrow stone bridge that formed the archway was higher than it had looked from the ground, the drop scarier, the pathway itself narrower—little more than a two-foot-wide span in places and crumbling at its sides. But where only a few days earlier she had balked at the rope bridge, now she strode across the crumbling stone archway without fear.

She wasn't sure if she was too scared to be scared anymore, having been vaccinated by repeated terror, but as she looked down into the dark center of the vortex, her only real thought was, *Well, here goes nothing.* There was no anticipation as she called the spell to mind and visualized her apartment kitchen, which seemed suddenly small and stale rather than safe. But she couldn't stay in the wolfyn realm and she didn't want to go with Dayn anymore. Not now.

She glanced over, saw the pack gathered around Dayn as if awaiting orders and felt her heart break.

And she jumped into the whirlwind that would take her away.

*Reda!* Dayn watched her fall, felt the vortex surge deep in his bones and knew she was gone. He felt it in the emptiness inside him, the hollow spaces he hadn't even recognized until the past few days.

Agony hammered through him—not the pain that had come with the change, but from the way she had looked at him when he transformed, and again when he killed Kenar. The world was better with the bastard dead, but he wished there had been another way. There hadn't been, though, which left him with a pissed-off, leaderless pack and no time to waste.

Tearing his eyes from the archway, he refocused on the pack, not liking the way Kenar's main lieutenants were closing on him, though there seemed to be some sort of commotion going on at the back, over where Reda had broken through. Maybe he had an ally or two, after all. Too bad one or two allies weren't going to do a damn thing when the other forty-something went for his throat.

Pulse thudding sickly in his skull, he spread his hands in a "no harm, no foul" gesture. "Look, I just want to go home. If you'll just let me—"

The wolfyn closest to him shimmered and stretched to his human form to reveal Janus, a thick-necked soldier who followed his alpha's orders unquestioning and knew tradition better than he knew his siblings' names. "You won the challenge," he growled. "But we don't intend to be led by a filthy bloodsucker."

"I don't want to lead you. I just want—"

"I claim the Right of Challenge."

"Damn it, Janus, just listen for a minute. I don't want to fight you."

"Too bad." The other male blurred and retook his wolfyn form, baring his teeth in a feral snarl.

Dayn cursed under his breath, all too aware that he only had so much time before the vortex started to die back down. Hell, the thing could collapse at any moment. Taking a deep breath, he called on his other magic, and—

"Hold, damn you!" a woman's voice called.

Every eye swung to the source, and a murmur of yips and growls rose up at the sight of Keely in human form, pushing through the crowd with a man at her side. Easily twice her mass, he had silver hair despite appearing to be only a few years older than her. He wore the heavy furs and sigil of the Bite-Tail pack, and sent Dayn a steely look as they joined him in the fight circle that had cleared at Janus's challenge.

"Who the hell are you?" Dayn blurted, but even as he said it, the Bite-Tail connection clicked and he put it together. "Roloff?"

"Aye." The big man's low growl carried enough force to quell the pack instantly. He swept the wolfyn with a look. "Keely's father promised her to me, but Kenar broke that bond and outcast me. I claim her by right of the original promise."

And to Dayn's utter shock, Keely blushed.

Not a loner, then, Dayn realized. It had been Roloff, coming around during each moon time, making himself visible and seeing if Keely was ready to go against her brother. And finally, this year, getting what he wanted.

Gods, he would never understand wolfyn politics. But at least someone had gotten what he wanted.

Dayn glanced at the vortex. *Ah, Reda.*

"Do any deny me this mate?" Roloff demanded.

Dayn met his eyes. He didn't embarrass Keely by shaking his head. But he didn't say anything, either.

Keely and Roloff didn't embrace or kiss, but the look they exchanged said that making her an outcast had been the best thing Kenar had ever done for her.

Now, looking entirely in her element, Keely faced the pack. "By right and descent, the leadership of this pack should have come to me, not Kenar. He took control outside of tradition, which means that the challenge was not a true challenge, and this male—" she indicated Dayn "—is not your leader. I am." She swept the pack with a piercing look. "Do any challenge me on this?"

There was dead silence. Janus even looked a little relieved.

After a minute, she nodded. "Good. Then hear me. This man goes with safe passage. None shall touch him." She turned to Dayn, taking his hands and squeezing them in probably the only spontaneously friendly touch between them in two decades. "Go home, Prince Dayn of Elden. Go with my friendship, and the hope that this could be the beginning of a new era of peaceful sharing between our realms."

"You... Wow. Okay." Dayn faltered as he found himself nailed with an ambassadorship before he'd even regained his kingdom. "Yeah. That's ambitious."

"It was what Candida wanted, why she befriended you. So if you don't do it for me, do it for her."

He swallowed hard. "For both of you, then. And for the betterment of our realms, I hope."

"Good. Then go. Get the hell out of here." She kissed him on the cheek, shoved his rucksack, crossbow and sword into his hands and waved for the pack to let him through.

Roloff gave him a cuff on the shoulder that held a good measure of "and don't come back," and the rest of the pack watched him with unblinking amber eyes that said "good riddance." It would take more than Keely's goodwill to convince them—and the other packs—to give the blood drinkers a chance, but the benefits could be huge. Which was just another reason why he needed to get his ass through that vortex and get this brand-new era started.

Still, an empty hollow opened up inside Dayn as he jogged up the trail to the archway. Not because he was sad to leave the wolfyn realm, or because of the changes—and deaths—that had come because of him, or not entirely. No, the ache had curly red hair and blue eyes, and the hollowness came from knowing that the best three days of his life were over.

And the rest of it was about to begin.

His feet weighed him down as he headed out along the narrow causeway, following the line of Reda's footprints in the thin layer of grit. He stopped where she had stopped, stood where she had stood and closed his eyes for a second, trying to mindspeak her and failing yet again. Still, though, he sent his message toward the swirling realm magic, hoping against hope that it might reach her, just as a book of fairy tales once had: *Be well, sweet Reda. Be brave. Live your life.*

Then, without looking down, he stepped off the edge. And plummeted home.

# *Chapter 11*

With Dayn's voice ringing in her ears, Reda blinked awake to find herself hanging weightless, surrounded by strange, shifting fog that was white in some places, while in others it sparkled with rainbows, lit from above with shafts of light that seemed random, yet not. She was wearing her bow over her shoulder and clutching three sad-looking arrows.

"Hello?" she called. "Dayn?" Her pulse thrummed in her.ears. Part of her wanted it to be him, another part not. Maybe someday she would be able to think about him without hearing the sickening crunch of flesh and bone, the shivering howl. Not yet, though. Not by a long shot.

She had thought distance would help, time home alone.

But this definitely wasn't home.

What was going on?

Nerves prickled beneath her skin, not freezing her, but warning her that this wasn't good. She hadn't been conscious for the trip to the wolfyn realm, but based on Dayn's description this wasn't the way the vortex was supposed to work. It was supposed to suck her up and spit her out, no detours. This was most definitely a detour.

*Stay calm. You can handle this.* Making herself breathe evenly, she pictured her apartment kitchen in minute detail, right down to the dishes in the sink and the book on the counter. Then she said her mother's spell. But instead of her kitchen, she got a man's voice.

*Your work is not yet done.*

It sounded in her head, but it came from the fog, from nowhere and everywhere. It chilled her to her marrow, though not because it was a scary; it was deep and well modulated, with an abundance of that formal, faintly stiff tone that crept into Dayn's—

No. She wasn't going there. Not when it made her eyes well and her stomach heave, and filled her mind with the *squish-crack* of a broken neck, the howl of a vicious beast that was part predator, part murderer.

Aware that the voice seemed to be waiting for something, she said softly, "Please let me be done. This isn't my work. It's not my fight."

*Are you so certain?*

Her mind filled suddenly with horrifying images of stone walls destroyed by dozens of club-wielding ettins, armored guards cut to pieces by giant scorpions with razor-tipped tails and claws, a woman carrying a baby, racing across a flagstone floor only to be snatched up from above by a giant spider.

*You are a guardswoman of the blood. You would let this happen?*

"What blood? Who are you?" When there was no answer, her voice sharpened. "For God's sake, what do you want from me? I got him to the arch." She tried to spin in place, but failed. Her heart was hammered with a mix of fear and frustration. "Will you answer a direct question already, damn it! What do you want me to do?"

*Help him reach the castle by tomorrow night. And help him remember his true self or all is lost.*

Her stomach twisted at the dread and dismay that came with the thought of following Dayn to Elden. "And then what?"

*Go home.*

She flashed on the image of a rounded hill very like the one near Dayn's cottage, though without the stones. The spires of a castle were visible in the near distance beyond some trees, and there was a small shrine off to one side. And damned if it wasn't carved with a simplified version of the cover of *Rutakoppchen:* a girl traipsing through the woods while eyes watched from the darkness.

"Do I have a choice?" Her voice cracked miserably and she didn't care. She was crashing off the wolfsbene, beat-up, brokenhearted, and didn't want to have to do this.

*There is always a choice, even when there seems not to be.*

"Great. A frigging fortune cookie," she said.

Then she stopped, hearing her own words echo in the fog, realizing that she was snarking off at a spirit voice she strongly suspected was at least the essence of Dayn's father, the vampire king. More, she was thinking, planning, reacting, having an opinion. She wasn't paralyzed, wasn't leaning back into Dayn's reassuring presence as she had done too many times over the past few days when the going got tough.

She wasn't freezing. She was *dealing*. New strength flowed into her at the realization and, with it, came a fierce sort of joy.

*You are stronger than you know, Alfreda.*

A shiver ran through her. "How did you know my real name?"

*Will you help him?*

A few days ago, it would have seemed ludicrous for her to think she could help a man like Dayn. Even a few hours ago, blinded by her enthrallment, she wouldn't have thought he needed her help with anything save for mutual pleasure. Now, though, she was seeing things more clearly. She supposed shock could do that—either numb her out or wake her up. And now she was awake.

With clearer eyes, she realized that Dayn wasn't as evolved as he wanted to think. He had spent two decades beating himself up for having been distracted by a woman when he should have been focused on his duties the morning of the Blood Sorcerer's attack, only to fall right back into the same pattern with her. Their... relationship? flameout?—she wasn't sure what to call it—had been a distraction, a way to keep himself from focusing on the harder things. She didn't think he had been entirely dishonest with her, either...more that he had lied to himself.

She saw herself differently, too. In the rainbow fog, she suddenly saw a woman who too often waited for other people to take care of things. Granted, her childhood had shaped that, as her father and the therapists had—well meaning or not—blocked off her imagination, her initiative. But that was then and this was now, and she needed to quit being afraid, not just of danger, but of making a mistake, making a *choice*. Back home, she had stopped moving forward, and her soul had begun to wither. In the wolfyn realm, however, she had started doing, thinking, moving, deciding.

Maybe she had made a huge mistake falling for Dayn, had almost made an even bigger one by blindly following him to Elden as his lover. But the first mistake had burned her but not killed her, and the second one wasn't going to happen. If she followed him to Elden, it would be by her own choice, and not as his lover. And if that brought a stab to fresh wounds, heartbreak wasn't fatal, after all.

"Okay," she said to the waiting voice. "I'll do it."

*Good.*

The fog rose up around her, curled toward her and

touched her here and there, tingling where it landed. And then it started moving with more purpose, sluggishly at first and then faster and faster, she found herself hoping to hell that this wasn't going to go into the "mistake" column. She drew breath, but before she could say anything—or even really decide what she wanted to say—the world lurched around her, the fog turned dark and ominous, and *whoomp!* She suddenly found herself standing on a grass-covered hill in the middle of a dense, ominous forest.

Dayn wasn't there. In fact, she was completely and utterly alone. And in realizing that, she became aware that it was the first time she had been alone in days.

She stood for a moment, testing for signs of panic. But while she was tense and most certainly on alert, she wasn't terrified, didn't want to stand still and wait for something to happen.

*Let's get moving,* her instincts said. *Daylight's wasting.*

Overhead, she glimpsed a sky that was a far deeper blue than that in the wolfyn realm, making her blink at the difference. The trees, too, were strange; they were twisted and stunted-looking, though they stretched high overhead to knit their branches into a high canopy of dull brown leaves. The sunlight that filtered through those leaves was a dingy brown color, making her feel oddly dirty.

"Welcome to Elden," she said under her breath. "Doesn't look much like I expected." Both her mother and Dayn had made the kingdoms sound like lush and fertile paradises, like something out of a fantasy movie. But maybe it would get better once she was out of these woods.

Given that realm travel wasn't known in the kingdoms, it stood to reason that the access points would be hidden away, forgotten.

Thinking she'd do best with a good defense, she unslung her bow. And stared.

What before had been a plain but serviceable hand-carved bow was now a slick, high-tech compound bow of the type she had favored in the human realm, but made of a springy, unfamiliar wood and strung with a natural-looking fiber of the proper tensile strength. Her arrows, too, had transformed; she was wearing a sleek quiver that contained a dozen perfectly balanced shafts and offered hooks where she could secure the bow fully strung.

"Upgrades," she said to herself. "Nice." Better yet was the small purse of gold she found in her pocket.

Feeling more optimistic than she had moments before, she struck out in the direction where the light seemed brightest up ahead. She would find herself a village, get her bearings and go from there. If nothing else, she knew where Dayn would be tomorrow night: Castle Island.

Dayn awoke in a darkness so complete that he might have thought he was still unconscious except for the ammoniac smell of guano. It burned his eyes and sinuses and had him holding his breath as he pawed in his rucksack for one of the small wolfyn hand lamps.

It lit, but only partway, emitting a bare and fitful glow even after he dialed it to full power. *Too much science and not enough magic in the gadget,* he thought, not daring to say the words and risk inhaling.

A quick scan showed that the vortex had dumped him in the dead end of a cave. He thought there might have been paintings on the walls, but the smears of guano and the tears blurring his vision made it tough to tell for sure. With only one way out, he didn't have to debate his escape route; shouldering his rucksack, he beat it for thinner air.

The cave curved and curved again before he saw reflected daylight up ahead. He paused short of the last bend and tucked the light away. And then he stood a moment longer, because after twenty years, the next step was a big one.

"Elden," he said softly.

He was finally home. He could finally make things right. And if there was a deep ache within him because he was stepping out of the cave alone, there was nothing he could do about that now. He had made his bargain and his sacrifice. The spirit realm had let him save Reda and send her to safety, and in exchange he had given up any chance for them to have a future. And maybe, probably, that was the way it was supposed to have worked all along.

He took a deep breath and borrowed a particularly fitting human idiom: "Here goes nothing." If he was

lucky and the spell had his back, he would find himself relatively near Castle Island. Better yet would be
to find Nicolai, Breena and Micah camped out waiting
for him. Gods, Micah would be grown now.

Trying not to lock too hard on that hope, tempting
though it might be, Dayn shrugged the rucksack higher
on his shoulder and set out, rounding the corner and
striding out of the cave into the daylight. And stopped
dead.

"Damnation." Another fitting human saying, and
one that was unfortunately all too apt.

The sight that greeted him wasn't anything like
what he'd been expecting, and was nothing he'd been
prepared for. The forest that stretched out before him
wasn't green and lush, wasn't chockful of hiding places
for the forest creatures. It was brown and thin, with no
groundcover and only sparse, yellowed leafy patches
that hardly seemed sufficient to sustain life.

Worse, he couldn't even pretend he was at the edge
of one of the southern kingdoms, near a stretch of bad-
lands or desert. Because as his eyes adjusted to the
painful sight, he recognized the downslope in front of
him, the rise of rocky hill behind him. He even knew
the cave now, though he had never before been all the
way to its end due to the foulness of the air.

He was in Elden, less than a day's march to the
castle. But gods and the Abyss, what had happened to
his land? His forest?

Unfortunately, the answer was an easy one: the Blood
Sorcerer had happened. This was what two decades of

dark sorcery had done to his once-gorgeous kingdom, two decades of neglect. It had killed the land.

"No." Heart sinking so hard his stomach hurt, Dayn took two stumbling steps, then went down on his knees beside a waist-high boulder, where there was a tiny scrap of green struggling to grow in the shade. It was an Elden glory—or it should have been. But instead of producing brilliant blue flowers the exact shade of Reda's eyes, this one had only a single weak bloom in a pale, sad hue.

"I'm sorry." He didn't even realize he was crying until a drop hit the dirt. It dried quickly, sucked into the parched earth so suddenly that he might have thought he imagined it, save that he found moisture on his cheeks and felt the tears in his soul.

He didn't stay there long; he couldn't. But part of him wanted to.

Any faint hope he might've had that this was a localized blight withered as he reached the edge of the forest and saw rolling hills of dusty brown leading to a yellow-hazed horizon, and his last few shreds of optimism died utterly when he hiked himself up into a nearby tree, climbing into the high, swaying branches to get a longer view.

From there, he could see other forests, scattered farms, several villages—though fewer than he remembered—and a dark smudge where he judged Blood Lake to be. And throughout it all, there were patches of brown, green, black, even some furry-looking white and bilious yellow-green, as if the land had died and been taken over by mold and rot.

"Gods help us," he whispered, soul going hollow at the confirmation that it wasn't just the forest that was blighted and dying. It was all of Elden.

And although he had already hated the Blood Sorcerer for the attack on the castle, now that rage dug deeper, grew hotter, became even more personal at the realization that the bastard hadn't just taken power, he had ruined the kingdom, leeching its energy to fuel his dark, twisted magic.

Dayn's forests, his family's people, were suffering, and from the looks of it had been for some time, and he had let it happen. If he had known he would have... The thought process ran aground there, because he couldn't have done anything differently, nothing that would have mattered to Elden. He'd had to wait for the magic to send his guide and bring him home.

Only this wasn't home. Home didn't exist anymore. Elden had become a war zone without a real war, a casualty of the royal family's abandonment, though they hadn't voluntarily abdicated.

On some level, he wished with all his heart that the spell hadn't been corrupted; that he and the others could have come together long before this to take their revenge, sparing the kingdom its torture. On another, though, he knew that it was pointless to wish history changed; he needed to deal with the matter at hand.

Right now, it wasn't about not looking back, wasn't about moving forward. It was about what happened next, about righting the course of an entire kingdom, gods willing. It wasn't about him, wasn't about the things he'd wanted or the people he'd lost.

He shimmied down the tree, feeling its inner rot in the faint slickness of its bark. Then, shouldering his rucksack once more, he hit the road.

And, as his feet carried him down the dusty track, he knew two things for certain. One, he would do whatever he could to set things right in the kingdom, even if that meant giving his life for it. And two, it was for the best that things had happened as they did in the wolfyn realm, because he never would have forgiven himself for dragging Reda into this horror, not just because there was no beauty or magic in his homeland anymore, but because there was no way he could be with her and be what he needed to be.

He couldn't be Dayn the man when Elden needed a prince so badly.

Moragh's new gnome, Destin, tapped on the doorframe of the seedy room she had rented at a grubby inn on the shore of Blood Lake, preferring to not yet be under the sorcerer's roof given that she hadn't yet told him about the possibilities of realm travel, instead keeping that gem to herself as both an exit strategy and a bargaining chip.

"Mistress?" he inquired softly.

"Yes?" she asked without moving, without even opening her eyes. It had taken her nearly an hour of careful preparation to get this far, and she didn't want to have to start over.

"I have spread the word. If the prince returns—"

"He's already here. I can feel him." The spell had reactivated an hour earlier, warning that the wolfyn hadn't managed to take care of business. She hadn't really expected them to, though, not once she learned what Dayn had become, and saw how the archaic wolfyn society worked. They were hidebound, hampered by their own foolish traditions. She had used that to her advantage, though, coercing the pack into slowing down her prey, buying her the time to come back through the stones, recover the Book of Ilth and start making plans for his return.

And the plan she had was a damn good one. It wouldn't just take care of the prince, it would announce her new prowess far and wide. The scholars who had once laughed at her would bow in awe, and the sorcerer…well, the delicious images made her smile and wet her lips with her tongue.

"Shall I send to the castle and have the beast master ready your ettins?"

"No. I'm not going out after him. I'm going to let him come to me." The ugly rumors and hints of a bounty she'd had Destin spread through his network of thieves and cutthroats might take care of the prince for her, but if not, it would slow him down long enough that she would be ready for him.

"Will that be all for now, mistress?"

"Yes. No, wait." She drew satisfaction from his hiss

of indrawn breath and the sudden tension in his stillness. But lately his struggles had diminished all too quickly, his revulsion dulling to a placid acceptance that flattened her pleasure to a mere glow. She had been planning an exciting new game to play with him, but now wasn't the time—she needed raw blood energy and didn't want to have to work for it. "Send to the dungeons for a prisoner, one that nobody will miss."

He exhaled softly. "Yes, mistress."

When he was gone and the door closed, shutting out the stupidity prevalent in the corridors and common areas of any village inn, Moragh cleared her mind and cast about herself, checking the positions of the candles and lines drawn around her with a variety of powders and unguents. Then, satisfied that she was protected, she opened the Book of Ilth, turning past all the realm-travel spells to the final section, to a title page that bore a single word.

*Feiynd.*

Dayn reached the village of Einharr late in an afternoon grown gray from an incoming storm. The warm air was charged with thunder, heavy with moisture and felt strange on his skin after so long in the relatively dry and cold wolfyn realm. Or maybe the strangeness came from the land's sickness; he didn't know.

All he knew was that as he walked through the open gates of the heavy wooden palisade surrounding the village, his skin felt slick and oily, and his gut churned with the deep sorrow that had only grown through the day.

He had walked past roadside ditches filled with bones, most from livestock, but some human, and of the human skulls, a too-high proportion had worn secondary canines. He had been assuming his inability to connect to anyone through mindspeak meant that the wolfyn magic he'd had thrust upon him had fouled some of his purely Elden powers. But the sight of the skull piles had made him consider that he might be the only mindspeaker in range. And that was a damned depressing thought.

He'd passed deserted farms, some burned, others just sitting there, rife with signs of a hasty exit; he wanted to believe that the farming families had fled to other kingdoms, but didn't hold much hope of it. And as he'd gotten in closer to the village proper, he'd passed clusters of small houses and seen signs of habitation, but such poor signs—a few weedy chickens scratching listlessly in the dirt, a thin dog slinking in the shadows, head down, ears flat to its skull—that his heart had hurt anew.

So now, as his boots scuffed the dirt track through the center of the village, raising no dust in the heavy air, he wasn't entirely surprised to see that Einharr, once a thriving community well known for its singing halls and honey beer, was a squalid and run-down version of its former self. Hollow-eyed children peered at him from behind doorways and around corners, flinching away when he made eye contact, and older men and women skulked in windows or on overhung porches, watching him with dull, uninterested eyes.

Twenty years ago, when last he had ridden through here as part of his parents' retinue, the villagers had packed the main street, cheering and jostling to touch the horses and carriages. Now, as he made for the third block in, where the tavern district began—or used to begin, at any rate—his presence seemed to have gone entirely unnoticed. "Seemed" was the operative word, though, because as he continued onward, his nape prickled and his instincts said someone was watching him, that he needed to be careful. Which was a no-brainer, but he needed information, and there was no place better to get it than at the local watering hole.

Picking the one with the most worn-looking steps, as had been his habit when investigating as a Forestal, he stepped up onto the slatted porch, his boots ringing hollowly as he crossed to the heavy, windowless door.

Movement blurred in his peripheral vision; he spun in a crouch, lifting his short sword, but it was just a kid, a skinny, gray-eyed boy wearing ragged homespun and grime behind his ears where he had missed washing. He didn't duck away like the others, but rather stopped dead, eyes widening in shock and fright.

For a second, when the boy did the deer-in-headlights freeze, Dayn flashed on wide blue eyes and similar moments of fear. A searing bolt of grief rocketed through him, warning that he might have submerged his thoughts of Reda, but they weren't gone. Not even close.

Then the kid broke from his paralysis, drew breath and screamed at the top of his lungs, *"Wolfyn!"* He spun and bolted, screeching, "Mama, Papa! The wolfyn's here!"

## Chapter 12

Doors slammed open on both sides of the road and club-wielding men hurtled out from the buildings and flow from around corners, boiling into the street, shouting things like "Get him!" "Cut him off!" "The money's mine!" and "Don't let him get away!"

Cursing, Dayn dodged one club swing, took another on his shoulder and leaped into the road, swinging his sword in a wide arc that was more intended to drive his attackers back rather than hurt them. His mind raced, jammed with thoughts of *Damn that witch,* and *Now what?* He was horrifically outnumbered, but he didn't want to kill the villagers. He was trying to *save* them, damn it!

Looking around frantically while he batted off club

swings with the flat of his sword, he searched for a thin spot, an exit, and found—

"Now!" a voice shouted.

Too late, he looked up to see a heavily weighted net flying down at him, flinging open as it came.

"Son of a—" He spun to bolt, but it caught him hard and knocked him down.

Roaring, he lunged back to his feet, staggering as he fought the tangling lines. He got his sword arm free and slashed out, heard a cry of pain and saw the villagers shrink back for a second. But that didn't last long; they closed in just as he freed himself from the net, leaping away and flailing with his sword. He slapped for his crossbow, but it was gone.

He was surrounded, but the villagers didn't come at him, instead hesitating, keeping their clubs raised as they shouted, egging one another. For a second, their hesitation didn't make any sense. Then he realized: they were afraid he was going to change, didn't know that he'd only succumbed twice in his life and didn't intend to do it again. Not when part of his promise to his father had been to remember his true self, which wasn't wolfyn.

Heart rocketing, he went for his bloodline magic, sending his secondary canines spearing through his gums. Then he bared his teeth and roared at the nearest villager, doing his best impression of Keely on a bad-fur day.

The man shouted and fell back, stumbling into the guy behind him. They both went down and three others shied away as Dayn lunged through the small opening and raced for the open area beyond. For a second he thought he was going to make it, but then the guys at the outer edge of the crowd saw him coming and started closing ranks.

*Zzzt. Thwack!* An arrow whizzed past the men and sank itself in the building opposite. They shouted and fell back as a second missile followed the first, coming even closer to them before nailing a rain barrel.

Dayn didn't stop to wonder who or how; he put his head down and hauled ass for the nearest village gate.

"Close the gate!" The shout went up behind him, and up ahead, two men scrambled from a rickety guard shack and moved to comply, pushing a heavy door that slid sideways on ponderous rollers.

He wasn't going to make it.

Sudden hoofbeats pounded behind him and a familiar voice called, "Dayn!"

And his heart. Stopped. Dead.

His body might have kept running as he looked back over his shoulder, but the rest of him froze at the sight of Reda galloping toward him on a bald-faced bay horse with white-ringed eyes. She was wearing a mix of the clothing he'd last seen her in along with a few Elden-style pieces, including the close-fitting pants and boots typically worn by the members of the cavalry or elite guard. They were old, but the royal colors of his own house still shone clearly.

"Reda," he whispered through a throat gone suddenly dry with mingled joy and dismay. "Sweet gods."

The villagers scattered like blown leaves as she bore down on him. Then she was steering with her knees and weight as she knocked an arrow in a sleek compound bow and let fly, burying the missile in the village gate no more than a handspan from one of the guys who were fighting to get it shut. The two men shouted, took one look at her and dove for cover, leaving the gate half-open and unattended.

"Grab on!" She pulled even with Dayn, offered a hand and, when he locked his wrist to hers, used the bay's momentum to pull him up behind her.

It was a familiar move, one he'd done a hundred times with Nicolai, sometimes even with his father. But the bay squealed and spooked at the move, swerving and then flattening out its haunches as it accelerated to a flat-out panicked bolt that left him sprawled awkwardly on the animal's haunches, being jolted loose with every stride.

"Whoa!" Reda started to haul on the reins, but then glanced back at the villagers, thought better of it and yelled, "Hang on!"

Dayn did his best, getting a good grip on the empty bedroll straps at the back of the age-cracked cavalry saddle as Reda rode the bolt, steering the white-eyed bay through the village gate and out onto the main road, where they thundered for nearly a mile before the animal began to tire, slowing to a bumpy canter, then to a tooth-jarring trot.

Still, though, the horse was restive and upset, refusing to settle, to the point that it was all Reda could do to spin the creature in a circle as Dayn slid down. The brute kicked out and scooted away, but she hauled it back around in a few snorting, prancing whirls, and then it finally started to calm down, blowing elephant-bugle snorts at Dayn.

Who just stood there in the road, staring.

She didn't say anything, either, just met his eyes with a cool expression that didn't tell him a thing. After a moment, she lifted her chin as if to say, *Well?*

"You can ride," he said, which was dead stupid because that was far from the most important thing. But the sight of her astride the wall-eyed bay, carrying a weapon from her own realm and wearing clothes mixed from the other two, shifted his perceptions, jarring him and replacing his image of wide, scared blue eyes.

"I did Pony Club for a bit, played polo now and then in college." She paused. "That and the archery were the closest I could get to living out the fairy tales. Until now."

He had told himself he didn't want her here in this wreck of a kingdom, that he didn't have it in him to protect her and do his duty both. But now that she was here, really *here,* he wanted to fall to his knees and thank the gods and the magic, wanted to kiss her booted toe and work his way up from there, and wanted, somehow, to make things right between them. Because she was here.

The kingdom was a wasteland, Moragh had turned the villagers against him and put a bounty on his head, his siblings were nowhere to be seen and, given how much had been drained from the land, the Blood Sorcerer's powers must be immense.

But sudden, illogical joy wrapped itself around his heart as he stood there staring up at a woman who looked like something from the stories of his own childhood—a goddess of the hunt, perhaps, or a patroness of the king's elite cavalry. Yet at the same time she was the Reda he had known in the wolfyn realm, the one he had made love to, cared for, wanted beyond all reason.

His throat tightened, burning with emotion. "You used the Elden spell."

But she shook her head. "I was sent here."

His blood cooled a degree. "Then how...?"

"Your father. At least, I think that's who it was. He pulled me into limbo, told me I had to help you get all the way to the castle, and that you need to remember your true self. And that if I do that, I can go home for real."

"I know what I am and what I must be—a prince of Elden, with all that it entails." He paused, scrubbing a hand over his face. "Why did he send you with the message? Why not just talk to me while I was in the vortex?"

She looked past him. "I have a theory on that. I got here a few hours ago, bought MacEvoy here—" she indicated the bay, who had leveled off to flat-footed, eye-rolling suspicion "—and clothes that didn't scream 'outsider' quite so loudly. Then I just...I don't know. Started riding. And that gave me time to think."

He was still working to catch up with the sudden

differences in her. The fear was gone—or if not gone, so deeply buried that he couldn't see it anymore. More, she was calm and competent, automatically settling her mount with a touch here, a shift of weight there, and wearing the bow naturally across her back as if it had been made for her. The Queen's Guard would have been proud to have a woman like her. And a kingdom in need of rebuilding could do worse.

*Slow down,* he told himself, all too aware that their entire relationship had taken place at a flat-out gallop, and that a single misstep at such speed could be fatal. "Your theory?" he prompted when she didn't continue.

Meeting his eyes, she said, "I think I'm a test."

"A… Oh." He stared at her. "No. That's impossible."

"Is it?" Looping the reins in one hand, she crossed her arms and just looked at him.

No, it wasn't impossible and they both knew it. More, it made a horrible sort of sense. He was supposed to remember his priorities and his true self. And just as the voice that had come to him as he floated out of his body had demanded a sacrifice from him in exchange for another chance, the magic—and his father—could be trying to teach him the lessons he hadn't yet learned, the ones Elden needed him to master. *Focus. Dedication. Discipline. Humility.*

Gods, no. Not this way. He wanted to make it up to her, to be with her. Their time together had been the brightest spot, not just in the past two decades, but in all the years he had been alive. With her, he had been a man, an individual, a lover, a mate.

*Sacrifice.*

Moving slowly, keeping an eye on the horse, he crossed to her. The bay gave a half rear, but then subsided and held its ground, nostrils flaring as he came up beside them, close enough to touch her leg, though he didn't.

He was viscerally aware of the long curves of her taut muscles beneath the cavalry breeches, though, and the familiar royal crest stamped into the leather at the top of her boot, now wearing a slash that indicated it was part of a rebellion, some sort of organized resistance. And deep down inside him where the wolfyn magic dwelled, arousal and satisfaction mingled at the sight of her wearing his family colors. He wanted to drape her in fine silks in those same colors, wanted to run their slippery softness over her body, then follow the same paths with his hands and lips. He hadn't even begun to deal with her loss, could barely comprehend her return.

But, gods and the Abyss, she could be right that this was a test, a call for him to prove that he had learned his lesson. And a reminder that Elden needed him—or rather, them—to do their duties and hold true to their roles despite their feelings.

Not to mention…what *were* her feelings? He couldn't see beyond her guarded, impassive mask, the one that seemed to say, *This is the situation. What are you going to do about it?* He knew the look from his father's elite security forces, could guess that it went with being on the humans' police force. And it drove home not only her new confidence—or, he suspected, the emergence of a deep-seated confidence that had been within her all along—but also that she had a life outside of him, duties of her own.

When he'd asked her to come with him, he had been so caught up in not wanting their gallop to end, so focused on getting what he most desired, that he'd lost sight of her needs and desires outside of the two of them. More, he had lied to her—by omission, yes, but a grave sin considering the lie. And the fact that he hadn't even considered telling her. Just as he had hidden his blood-drinking self from Keely, he had planned to leave Reda entirely ignorant of the spell-curse that had turned him into his own prey.

Son of a bitch. He hadn't grown up nearly as much as he'd wanted to think.

Aware that the silence was stretching thin, he tried to find the words, but didn't know where to start, or how. Or even whether he should try.

Yes, he needed to try. He owed that to his honor, and to her.

He touched her knee, curving his fingers around the flesh and bone, not meaning the gesture as a come-on, but rather hoping the touch would carry his sincerity to her through the fitful emotional link he had felt once or twice before.

"I got so caught up in the rush that I lost sight of my honor and your right to have the same honesty from me that you had offered me. For that, I am ashamed." He tightened his fingers on her knee. "By the gods, Reda, I'm sorry."

She went white for a second, expression stark, but then flushed hard and hot as her eyes took on a dangerous glint as she leaned down to bat his arm away and hiss, "You're sorry? You *enthralled* me, you unholy bastard."

Shock rattled through him. "I—"

"Don't you *dare* deny it. I may not know magic, but I can take a good guess what being brainwashed feels like." She straightened in the saddle and touched the reins to quiet the bay, which had lit up once more, pawing and tossing its head while its ears flipped back and forth. "When I was with you, nothing else mattered. I didn't care where we were or what we were doing, or even what was going on around us. I would have done anything you asked." She glared through the glint of tears. "Anything, damn you. An 'I'm sorry' doesn't even begin to cut it on that one."

Her words got inside him, making him profoundly wish he had been born a simple man in a simple life, that he had just met her on the street one day, without all the other chaos involved. But that was exactly the sort of thought process that had gotten him in trouble before, wasn't it?

Part of him even wondered if it might not be best to let her think that he had enthralled her. It would probably be better if she hated him—because knowing that she was, or at least had been, feeling the same crazy single-mindedness he was, that the world had threatened to disappear for her, as well, made him want to drag her out of the saddle and hold her, kiss her, talk to her until she agreed to give him—to give *them*—a chance.

But he couldn't do it. He just couldn't. He couldn't leave another lie between them.

"There was no enthrallment," he said, pressing his hand to his chest where she had liked to lay her palm and feel his heartbeat. "I swear it on my soul."

Her eyes narrowed. "There must have been."

"There wasn't." He didn't repeat the oath. She would either believe him or not. *Have faith,* he urged her inwardly. *You know me.* But did she know him enough to believe?

For a moment she didn't say anything; he could almost see the inner battle written on her face. She wanted to believe, but didn't trust him or herself anymore, didn't know what was real and what wasn't—not out in the realms, but inside herself.

He knew her. He understood her. And by the gods he wanted her to trust him. Abyss, he just damn well *wanted* her. This was a mess, *he* was a mess.

Finally, she said, "Could you have enthralled me without knowing, without meaning to?" She looked forlornly hopeful, as though she, too, knew it would be easier if they were at odds.

Or maybe he was just seeing what he wanted to see.

"I chewed the wolfsleep gum to block the wolfyn magic." Using Keely had helped, too, staving off his urges, but he didn't think it hurt anyone to keep that to himself. "What you saw was only my second change. I kept the urges strictly contained, so I would never forget who I was and what I was waiting for."

"And now?" She swept the tree line on either side of the road. "I don't see any wolfsleep trees."

"The magic functions differently in the kingdoms. I'll have to work hard to change here. And I don't intend to. All of the messages I've received from the spirit realm say that I need to be entirely true to myself if I'm going to have a chance against the sorcerer. Which means staying the hell away from the wolfyn magic."

"Yet you changed back at the archway."

He couldn't read her expression, didn't know what she wanted him to say. His better sense said to leave it alone, but he went with the gods' honest truth instead. "You were in danger and I didn't see another option."

"You..." She trailed off, then shook her head. "Never mind. And thank you. For saving my life."

He nodded, but didn't say anything. They both knew he had nearly sacrificed the hopes of an entire kingdom in the process. And what kind of a prince did that make him?

Exhaling, she nodded as if they had reached an agreement. "Right. Okay, then. We should get moving before the villagers get their torches and pitchforks and come after us." She kicked her foot free of the stirrup and shifted forward in the saddle to give him room to climb on behind her. "I'd let you drive, but I don't think MacEvoy likes you."

"He must be able to sense the wolfyn magic." Which

was damned depressing, because one of the things he had looked forward to doing in Elden was once more riding a beast-chaser.

She didn't say anything, but her eyes went sympathetic as she tightened her reins in one hand and held out the other.

He hesitated momentarily, wishing he could say something that would unravel the tangle they had wound up in together, connected yet not, and with so much confusion around them. The perfect words didn't come to him, though. They probably didn't even exist.

Exhaling, he took her hand and swung up behind her, but stayed well back on the saddle skirt and held on to the cantle for balance rather than tucking himself right against her as he longed to do. And, as they rode into the first reddening of dusk, there was only silence between them. They had said what needed to be said, after all. Now they had jobs to do.

*Which seriously sucks,* he thought. But all of a sudden the human words didn't come as easily as they had before, as if the past twenty years were being canceled out now that he was back in his home realm.

The idea was damned disconcerting. Worse, the past three days suddenly seemed a little distant and indistinct, too, as if they had happened to someone else, in another lifetime. It was as if Reda was already gone, like he was already forgetting what they'd had together, when she was sitting only inches away.

"We're coming up in the world," Reda commented

later that night as she poked at the folding bowl she had
suspended on a tripod over the small, sputtering fire.
"This cave is much nicer than the last one. It even came
with utensils."

"Tonight a cave, tomorrow a castle, gods willing,"
Dayn said from the rear of the space, where he was
cobbling together a small horse enclosure from the remains of a large corral.

The huge cavern, which had been the hideout of an
outlaw band that Dayn and a detachment of guardsmen had tracked and arrested just prior to the sorcerer's
attack, offered a small stream, a scattering of useful
items that had somehow escaped the looters, three exits
that let out at various points in the forest and accom-
modations for the bay horse, who she was still calling
MacEvoy after the shop owner, even though the stoner-
quiet personality he'd originally shown her had gone
right out of his furry head the second he saw Dayn.

The horse was too tired and hungry to be in full-on
panic mode anymore, and had gotten somewhat used
to carrying a wolfyn, but even as he hoovered down
the travel cakes his seller had thrown in along with the
tack and clothes, he kept a white-ringed eye on Dayn.

No wonder there weren't any normal horses in the
wolfyn realm. They had probably all died of fright, or
else been eaten. Or both.

Shuddering at the thought and the echoing *slurp-
crunch* noise it put in her head, she glanced over at
Dayn, and caught him looking at her.

They both shied away and went back to their tasks,

but the already tense air between them strung itself a little tighter, as it had been doing, degree by degree, ever since he'd boosted himself up behind her and done his damnedest not to let their bodies touch.

Was it possible to simultaneously exist in both heaven and hell, or whatever this realm called them? She thought so, because she was there right now.

Part of her, idiot that it was, was basking in the glow of having rescued him so grandly, and having him right at hand now. That part of her kept reminding her that they had spent the past two nights alternately making sweet love and screwing each other blind, both equally satisfying, and it relentlessly dredged up increasingly erotic memories as the night wore on. The sensory replays tortured her, turning her insides to molten heat and putting a longing tug between her legs each time she looked at him and thought that it was nearly time for them to hit their bedrolls.

Another part of her, though, said she'd be better off sleeping outside in the cool, foggy night. That part of her was all too aware of MacEvoy's ringed eyes and flattened ears, and knew she should take a cue from the horse—prey animal that it was—and keep her distance.

"Stew's almost ready." She poked at a lump of rehydrated meat floating in a brown slick that looked entirely unappetizing, but smelled great.

"Just let me get these last three rails up."

She snuck a peek, and this time caught him turned away, which gave her a few seconds to stare at his broad shoulders as he fitted the last rails into place and lashed them with the worn rope he had salvaged. The plaid shirt she had taken off of him a dozen times in a dozen different places curved lovingly around his muscles, poignantly reminding her of how it felt to run her hands over him, how his skin tasted and how he seemed to know instinctively how to touch her, as if he really could read her mind, though he claimed he couldn't.

She wanted to believe him, just as she wanted to believe that he was telling the truth about her not being enthralled…but at the same time, without that excuse she would have to admit that she had done it all of her own free will, falling hard and fast for a fairy-tale prince who turned out to be far more complicated than she had thought.

Finished, he gave the enclosure a last check while MacEvoy tracked his every move. Then, satisfied, Dayn ducked through the fence and headed for the fire.

Reda looked quickly away and concentrated on stirring a stew that wasn't going to get better or worse with more stirring. Her hands were trembling, her insides alight with warmth and need. She didn't want to be with a wolfyn, a liar or a manipulator, but she wanted to be with Dayn. And she couldn't have it all.

*Maman, what am I supposed to do?* The question came unbidden; it had been a long time since she stopped asking her mother's spirit for advice. But even as she told herself not to be ridiculous, she still listened inwardly for a few seconds, wondering. Because if she had truly been some part magic, maybe, just maybe…?

There was no answer, though. And as Dayn leaned too close to her and tipped half the stew into a big tin cup he had scavenged and scoured out in the river, her breath went thin and her insides tugged longingly. But at the same time, unexpected tears threatened, making her blink so hard the fire seemed to waver as a new reality solidified within her.

She had lost her maman and Benz. And tomorrow, one way or the other, she was going to lose Dayn. Which would she regret more, being with him tonight... or not?

"Reda," he said, voice choked, "for gods' sake, talk to me." His ragged tone brought her head up and the emerald green of his irises caught her, sucked her in.

She wanted to lose herself in his eyes, in his kiss, in the warm strength of his arms. *But then what?* logic asked, unfortunately making sense. Because if she made love with him tonight, knowing what he was and that he had lied to her, she would always know that she had caved, that she had let herself be seduced without even the excuse of enthrallment.

"I can't," she said on a shuddering breath, turning down not just a conversation but all of it, all of him.

His eyes dulled but he didn't push. He just nodded, rose and took his stew back over to the edge of the corral, where he sat with his back against the wall and his eyes on the main entrance, not on her. But he was aware of her, she knew, just as she was entirely focused on him as the night dragged on.

She was acutely conscious of him eating, then

pulling a few swallows from the waterskin he'd left over there while working. She knew when he set his cup aside and when he stretched his legs, shifted his big body with the soft sigh that meant he was settling in to sleep yet staying on his guard, ready to react in an instant. He closed his eyes but didn't immediately fall asleep. She knew he was awake because she caught his faint responses when she banked the fire and curled herself into a bedroll marked with his family crest, saw a reflected glitter when he cracked an eye to watch.

Her heart told her to go to him, but her head said she needed to stand her ground and resist the temptation, or she would regret it going forward. She didn't want to go forward, though; she wanted to relive the past few nights with one more. In the end, though, she closed her eyes and listened to the *hiss-pop* of the fire because she didn't have the guts to take what she wanted when everything else was so unclear.

She might have ridden to his rescue today, but she was still a coward when it came to this.

## Chapter 13

The Royal Castle of Elden had been beautiful once, Reda saw through the small spyglass Dayn had found in an inner compartment of MacEvoy's saddlebag. From where they stood on the shores of Blood Lake far from the heavily guarded causeway, hidden in a scrubby patch of middle growth near the edge of the Dead Forest, she could see the classic elegance in the castle's turrets and crenellations, in the huge stone sweeps of the battlements and the gracefully engineered causeway that connected the island to the shore. Similar details made the smaller buildings beyond the castle blend in to look like part of the whole.

But although the bones of the royal seat suggested a heritage of loveliness, its current incarnation was dark and dismal, and carried a psychic stink that made her want to recoil.

"Gods and the Abyss," Dayn growled under his breath. "He'll pay for this." She saw stark pain in his eyes as he surveyed the filthy brown, polluted lake.

Here and there, swirls suggested submerged movement, though of what creature she didn't want to know. The island itself looked gray and rotten, and the castle was smog-shrouded and badly run-down, and looked somehow beaten, though she wasn't sure how that was possible. Dark figures moved here and there, some small and human, others huge and hulking, with the silhouettes of creatures she had hoped never to see outside the storybooks—or her own nightmares. Giant, razor-clawed scorpions guarded the causeway, huge crablike creatures scuttled along the battlements and ettins worked on the curtain wall, heaving huge chunks of stone like they were pebbles, though it wasn't clear if they were building it up or tearing it down.

Movement stirred near the base of the castle; squinting, she could just make out human figures walking in chains, linked together and being whipped on by a smaller man in a red-and-black uniform. All six of the prisoners were wearing royal colors and boots, but they were bent and dragging, their body language screaming of pain. Rebel prisoners, no doubt.

"Oh," Reda whispered, and then bit her lip.

"Let me see."

So she handed over the spyglass and pointed. Then she reached over, took his free hand and twined her fingers through his. He tensed and went still for a moment—she wasn't sure if it was from her touch or because he had seen the rebels. But then he exhaled and his shoulders dropped, and he gripped her hand and hung on hard.

And though there was nothing decided between them, when he lowered the spyglass and turned toward her, she went into his arms without hesitation. He clamped around her, just holding her, with his face pressed into her hair as the spyglass clunked to the ground.

MacEvoy snorted and dropped his head to graze, making the bit clink and tugging the reins from her fingers, but those inputs were so much less important than the fine shivers racing through Dayn's body and the fierceness of his grip, which made her feel as if for a change she was the one anchoring him, the one letting him lean.

"We can do this," she said against his throat. "Have faith." They still had nearly half a day to rent or steal a boat, then planned to make the crossing after nightfall.

His laugh was hollow and brittle. "I can't feel Nicolai or the others. I don't think they're here." He pressed his cheek to her temple. "I think that maybe I'm the only one left."

She closed her eyes, heart hurting for him. "You don't know that. And even so, someone has to stop the sorcerer. Things can't stay like this."

He drew away from her, looked down at her so tenderly she almost closed her eyes to capture the moment before it passed. "You're not afraid anymore, my warrior?"

She shook her head, and said, "Honestly, I'm so scared I want to curl up and hide my face in my knees. But I've decided that you were right. Being brave isn't about not being afraid. It's about continuing to function, anyway."

That was the truth she had awakened with that morning, after a long, restless night's sleep. It was a simple concept, really, and utterly logical. And she knew she'd heard it before—not just from him, but also from friends, family, coworkers, the department shrink— but for the first time she really believed it. More, she believed in herself, and knew that she wasn't going to freeze this time. Not tonight, when so much was riding on the outcome.

He framed her face in his hands and leaned in to say against her lips, "Ah, sweet Reda. My precious warrior."

As his mouth covered hers, she knew he was a wolfyn. As his tongue touched her lips, she was fully aware that he had made love to her without telling her the worst of his secrets. And as she parted her lips and let him inside, she did it knowingly. Willingly. Greedily.

There was no enthrallment. There was just the two of them, and the connection that existed despite everything else going on around them.

She wrapped her arms around his waist and held on for a kiss that was less about arousal than about saying,

*Yes, I'm here for you. We're in this together.* Because that was the other certainty she had awakened with—it wasn't about following the orders of a voice in the fog anymore; she was determined to see this through at Dayn's side. Not just because of what might or might not be between them but because it was the right thing to do. This was bigger than the two of them, bigger than anything she'd ever dealt with before. She could do it, though. And she would. She could, in her own way, help save the world. Or at least a kingdom.

Putting that certainty into her kiss, she slid her hands up his back and spread her fingers wide, covering as much of him as she could. *I've got your back,* she thought. *Let's go get this bastard.*

As if he'd heard her, he eased back with a last, lingering press of his lips to her cheek, her temple. Then he turned her so they were both facing away from Blood Lake, and pointed. "See that tall pine there with the three-way split at the top?"

It was maybe a half, three-quarters of a mile away, and looked like a trident. She nodded. "I see it. You want to use it as an emergency meet-up point?"

"No. Your shrine is at the base of that tree."

"My…what?" She turned on him, sure she'd heard wrong.

But his eyes, which had only moments earlier been entirely focused on her, slid past her to the island before flicking back to her face. "I know who I am and what I need to do, Reda. I'm a prince of Elden, first and foremost, and I can't let anything distract me from that."

Her head spun on an inner groan of, *Nooooo*. This wasn't happening, couldn't be happening. "You can't go in there alone. They'll kill you." Her voice cracked on it, her heart bled from it. "If you're trying to protect me, don't. I can take care of myself."

Instead of answering right away, he caught her hand and lifted it to press her palm to his chest, sandwiching it there so she felt the steady beat of his heart. "We each need to live the lives we were born into." He folded their hands together, pressed a kiss to her knuckles and then let her go and stepped back. "Go home, Reda. It's where you belong."

"I…" She just stood there for a second, vapor locked, not from fear but from shock, dismay and a sudden churn of anger. "You son of a bitch. Keely was right, wasn't she? You're a user."

He didn't say anything, just stood there. And she didn't see anything that said he wanted her to stay. In fact, she didn't see anything at all.

Whatever fragile trust they had begun to rebuild— or rather, that *she* had begun to rebuild—shredded in that instant, and disappeared. *Poof.* Gone.

Done. Game over.

When something nudged the small of her back, she jolted hard and spun, which sent MacEvoy skittering back several steps, where he stood, blowing through his nose as if to say, *What's your problem?*

Her startled laugh choked to a sob as she gathered his dragging reins. She didn't look at Dayn, couldn't look at him or she would lose it. "Come on." She sighted on the trident-shaped treetop and gave MacEvoy a tug. "Let's see if there are any decent farms between here and there." If not, she would strip off his tack and set him loose to fend for himself.

She stopped at the edge of the scrub, where it turned to a narrow track that led to the road, and turned back. Dayn stood against a backdrop of the polluted lake and the run-down castle, looking determined, distant and alone. The lone wolfyn. *Oh, God.* Her heart clutched in sudden foreboding, but what more could she say?

So in the end, she lifted a hand. "Good luck, Dayn."

A ghost of a smile touched his lips. "Same to you, sweet Reda." Then, moving with smooth, predatory grace, he slipped from the copse without looking back.

And she was left alone, save for a bald-faced horse and a heavy heart.

Dayn didn't let himself turn back, though he badly wanted to. And he didn't let himself fold inward and curl around the tearing pain that filled the place where his heart had been, though he badly wanted to do that, too. Because for a change he was doing the noble and honorable thing when it came to her: he was sending her away.

The sight of Castle Island had only confirmed the prickle of instinct that had been growing ever since they had set out that morning, the one that had said it was going to take a miracle for him to even reach the island, another for him to get inside the castle. And the odds of him surviving a fight with a sorcerer capable of wreaking so much damage, with twenty years' worth of magic and spells rooted in the castle, were brutally bad with or without his siblings, unless the decades had given them powers that far outstripped his own.

There was a damn good chance that he was going over there to die. And if that was the case he wanted her far away from the island, safely hating him in her own realm. For once, he knew he was doing the right thing when it came to her, the unselfish thing.

So instead of going after her and doing whatever it took to get that shattered look out of her eyes and put her once more back in his arms where the man in him wanted to believe she belonged, he pushed onward toward the section of the Dead Forest known as the Thieves' Woods, in search of a boat.

But as he ghosted along the edge of the Dead Forest, the sense of impending doom he'd awoken with only grew stronger, sending cold chills down his spine and causing him to look over his shoulder time and again.

Then, one of those times he caught a glimpse of movement and his gut fisted. There was something out there. Something big and nasty. And it reeked of dark magic.

Heart pounding, acting on his hunter's instincts, which suddenly screamed loud and clear, he unshipped his crossbow, hesitated and then opened the small, tightly stoppered container at his belt. Carefully—oh, so carefully—he dipped the tips of his last six bolts into the thick black liquid, coating the barbs to an oily shine.

He returned five to their spots on his belt, points hidden. He loaded the sixth onto his crossbow and started walking again, though far more stealthily than before, intensely aware of his surroundings, straining to sense a footstep or breath. Something was out there, but where?

A cloud passed over the sun, shadowing the scene momentarily and then moving on. Wind whispered overhead, sounding strange in the leaves of the dying trees. There was an open spot overhead, letting through sunlight that was dappled with another passing cloud shadow, this one moving unnaturally fast in an unseen current high overhead.

Then it curved back around and went the other way. And grew bigger.

Dayn stopped dead and stared for a split second of disbelief as the shadow grew wings. There weren't any winged creatures that big in Elden. Not unless you counted the legend of the... *No. Impossible.* He heard it in Reda's voice, and suddenly understood the wrenching disconnect of having a childhood bogeyman come to life, even before he ripped himself from his paralysis and yanked his attention to the sky.

"Gods!" The word burst from him at the sight that confronted him.

The huge dark snakelike beast undulated through the sky as if swimming. Then it screeched, swiveled, and folded its wings to plummet toward the earth with its bloodred eyes locked on him. It had small forelimbs with clawed hands, powerfully muscled hindquarters and the head of a scaled stallion. Covered entirely in black scales that gleamed dully in the sunlight, it was gorgeous and terrifying, in the way that only the worst of monsters could be.

Dayn's pulse hammered. It was a dragon. And not just any dragon; it was the Feiynd itself, the assassin of the old magi.

Moragh had summoned it to kill him.

Gods help him.

The Feiynd's mouth split in a silent gape that made it look, for a terrible instant, like it was smiling at him. Wind whistled through its wingsails, sounding like a thousand arrows in flight. And then it folded them fully and hurtled toward him, a living weapon locked on its target.

"Gods and the Abyss," Dayn whispered as his every power and instinct came together inside him at once. There was no point in running when the witch had targeted it on him, no point in hiding. He could only stand his ground and pray as he lifted his crossbow and sighted on one violent red eye.

The eyes could see. They could communicate. They were a route to the head, and from there to the heart.

*Candida, I hope you knew what you were doing. And if this doesn't work, bless you for trying.*

He waited a beat. Had his mark. Saw the Feiynd's mouth open wide.

And fired.

The bolt sped true, but a wing current knocked the projectile off line and it flew into the dragon's mouth, which snapped shut and then opened wide in a thin shriek of pain and anger that lifted beyond the limits of his hearing, hard and high, and so dissonant that it scraped along his nerve endings and made him want to flee like nothing in his life had done before.

Then the noise before the beast crashed through the thin canopy of yellowed leaves and hit the ground, thrown off target by the attack. It landed hard, digging its claws into the earth for purchase and screeching again as branches fell from above and peppered it— and Dayn—with debris.

Then it folded its wings and legs flat against its body and whipped into an aggressive coil, becoming a giant snake that was poised to strike.

Dayn fell back into the trees, hoping to hell they would slow the beast's attack. His heart and mind raced, bringing both fugue and clarity. There was no point in running; he would have to kill the Feiynd here and now. The eyes, he needed to go for the eyes. But they were smaller than he had realized, and set deep within scaly pits. He would have to make the shot of his life. Literally.

Deep within his soul, he whispered, *Father, if you can hear me, if you have any influence on this plane, please help me now.*

As he whipped a second bolt into place, he thanked the gods that Reda wasn't there, because there was no way in hell she could've gone up against the Feiynd. She would have tried, though, because that was who she was.

Aiming the loaded crossbow at one of those tiny, tiny eyes, he sighted. Fired.

The bolt glanced off the armor surrounding the Feiynd's eye pits. It seemed that the creature laughed at him for a split second. Then it screamed at full volume and struck. And Dayn was suddenly fighting for his life, spurred by the knowledge that if he died now, Elden would die with him.

Reda spun back at the sudden eruption of noise coming from the direction of the lake: roars, shrieks and the crashing of brush and trees. Her heart seized. *"Dayn!"*

The second she heard those noises, it stopped mattering whether he'd used her, or if that had been the lie instead, designed to send her running.

At a second terrible clashing noise, MacEvoy spooked and bolted, yanking her clean off her feet. She went to her knees but hung on grimly, and within a few strides, her deadweight had pulled the horse's head around and slowed him to a panting, eye-rolling stop.

"Don't you dare, you pain in my ass." Reda got to her feet, grabbed his bit and dragged his head around so she could glare into one of his white-ringed eyes and growl, "That. Is. Enough. I need you to man up, channel your inner beast-chaser, or whatever it takes, because bolting is not an option for us. Not anymore. Got it?"

She didn't know if her words got through or if it was

more her take-no-crap tone, but he subsided to a shuddering standstill and let her mount.

He propped up on his hind legs in protest, but when she growled he started forward as commanded, went where she pointed. "Good choice," she said, giving his neck a quick pat.

Then, not stopping to think it through or question the logic or emotions, she kicked him toward the terrible noises, praying she wasn't already too late.

Dayn ducked and swerved from one tree to the next, scrambling to load his last crossbow bolt as the Feiynd screeched and snapped behind him.

The Dead Forest was the only thing keeping him alive at this point, slowing the dragon and forcing it to stay in snake form because there was no room for it to spread its limbs and bring its wickedly barbed tail into the attack. But that boon was also a hindrance, as the branches fouled his aim. And there was no way he could fight the creature up close. With a boar pike and a beast-chaser, he might have had a chance. With a short sword and no armor, he would be dead before he got in his first puny blow. His wolfyn form would be no improvement; he might be able to outrun the creature on the ground, but it could fly and the witch had linked it to his life essence.

There was no hope of escape. One of them had to die.

If he could just . . . *there!* Up ahead there was a large

tree with low, sturdy branches, and what looked like a clearing beyond.

Putting on a burst of speed that sucked all but the last dregs of his energy, even with his secondary canines extended and his healing powers maxed, he raced for the tree, leaped and grabbed the low branch and clambered up. From there, he could fire down on the dragon with no interference, maybe even a better angle.

But when he turned back, the beast was gone.

*"Abyss."* That wasn't good.

He was already turning toward the clearing when he heard the thousand-arrow whistle of the Feiynd plummeting from flight. The creature landed in the open meadow just short of the tree in full dragon form, with wings and limbs extended.

Screeching, it reared up on its hindquarters to tower over Dayn's position, taller even than the trees. He couldn't see its eyes, couldn't get a bead on the flexible armpit zone that was often a weakness of armored creatures. All he could see was its scaled underbelly and wide, sweeping wings as it stayed upright for nearly a full second, screaming.

Then, suddenly, it crashed down to all fours atop the tree, tearing through the branches and sending the trunk skewing wildly for a second before it fell, uprooted by the creature's great force.

Dayn tried to fling himself free, but landed just ahead of the outer branches, which came down atop him, pinning him. He ripped free, scrambled to his feet and—

A huge black mass blurred from the side as the Feiynd struck, clamping its jaws on his upper arm and partway across his chest. Its curving, barbed teeth dug in, sending white-hot pain lashing through him.

"No!" His perceptions wrenched and a terrible sense of wrongness washed over him, warning that he was badly hurt. He could smell his own blood over the creature's brimstone breath, could taste it in his mouth and feel it coming from his nose. But at the same time his focus narrowed to two crucial points: he still had his crossbow, and those tiny red eyes were suddenly very close.

He twisted his body and felt more pain, more wrongness, but that didn't stop him from bringing the crossbow up.

Without warning, he was heaved up into the air, still clamped in the dragon's powerful jaws as the beast whipped its neck. Then it let go.

Dayn's inertia tore him from the barbed teeth and he went flying. For a second he was weightless, in a state of almost-pleasure as the old pain of being chomped disappeared and the new pain of being torn up and spit out hadn't yet hit. Then he crashed into the dusty meadow and skidded several feet on the hard ground with the *boom* of impact ringing in his ears.

He tried to get up, but couldn't. Tried to raise the crossbow he still held clutched in one hand, his fingers cramped around the stock, but he couldn't do that, either. All he could do was lie there as the Feiynd reared back on its haunches again, spread its wings and roared its triumph. Then it thudded back to the ground and came toward him, swaggering in dragon form. Its piggish red eyes locked on him and its mouth split wide to show those awful barbed teeth, now stained with his blood.

It took its time, but there was no question what would come next. The stories all said the same thing, after all: the Feiynd never left its target alive.

As it closed to within a dozen of its huge paces, Dayn sought his healing magic, but it was spent. His wolfyn magic, too. He was too far gone, too depleted. His mind raced, but his thoughts were scattered and dull, his plans nonexistent. *I'm sorry, Father.* He had failed, after all. He had come so close, yet was still falling short. And in the end, he was more the man than the prince, anyway, because his last thought as the Feiynd closed to striking range wasn't of his family or Elden, but of his lover. *Goodbye, sweet Reda,* he thought, glad to know that she, at least, was safe.

But as the beast reared up over him, its eyes glittering, mouth gaping wide, he heard the thunder of hoofbeats and her voice screaming, "No!"

An arrow sang, burying itself in the Feiynd's armpit. The dragon screeched and scissored sideways, which sent it crashing aside, away from Dayn. He simultaneously cursed Reda and blessed her, wanted to—

The Feiynd's tail lashed out, whistled through the air and came down hard on Dayn's battered body.

*Darkness.*

\* \* \*

*"No!"* Reda stood in the stirrups and sent another arrow flying at the dragon as it regained its feet. "Get away from him, you bastard!" Beneath her, MacEvoy stayed steady and galloped his heart out, even though his ears were flat to his skull and his body shook with fear.

The arrow bounced, but got the dragon's attention. The thing's head whipped around and it hissed when it locked on her. It was too close to Dayn; there was no way she could get to him with the monster practically standing over his body. Worse, as they closed on the fight, she saw to her horror that Dayn was still and limp, his clothing blood-soaked, his wounds horrific. Far worse than what Kenar had done.

"No," she whispered.

In the moment between one gallop stride and the next, she flashed hard on the sight of Benz behind the counter, the gunman spinning to level his weapon at her and the plan she never executed. Divert and then attack.

A diversion!

Reda didn't stop to think or plan, there was no time, no point. She just kicked free of her stirrups, leaned close to MacEvoy's neck and said, "When I bail, get your ass out of here."

She didn't know if the bay got the message or not, but as they blew past Dayn's body and the huge, glistening black dragon oriented hungrily on what it probably considered horsemeat-on-the-hoof, she screamed, "Go!" And then she flung herself out of the saddle.

The ground was hard, the impact crushing. She tucked and rolled, but by the time she came to a stop, her head was ringing and her right wrist hurt from being jammed, or worse.

She didn't have time to worry about that, though. As she lunged to her feet, she saw that MacEvoy had done his job—intentionally or not—drawing the dragon away. But the monstrous creature only followed the horse for a few strides before it stopped, turned back and reoriented.

Reda fell to her knees beside Dayn, horrified by the ragged, gaping wounds she could see through his torn shirt and the blood that trickled from his mouth. He was breathing shallowly, his eyes rolled back in his head. Sobs backed up in her chest, but she didn't have time for them now. She shook him slightly, hoping for a groan, but got nothing. "Dayn, wake up. We need to go!"

She couldn't carry him and MacEvoy was long gone. Worse, the ground rolled beneath her as the big black dragon headed back toward them, its beady red eyes burning with hunger and hatred.

Moving behind Dayn, she tried to lever him up, but he was deadweight. Worse, she was hurting him, probably doing more damage to his injuries, but what other choice did she have? "Dayn, please, *wake up!*"

All rationality in the world said for her to leave him and run, that the creature wanted him, not her. But logic didn't stand a chance against her feelings for him, so she stayed put, trying desperately to rouse him. His head lolled and his mouth opened slightly, revealing his fully extended secondary canines.

The sight stirred a one-two punch of heat and understanding. She didn't let herself think about it, didn't let herself hesitate. She opened his mouth, set her wrist against those two scalpel-sharp points and pushed.

She cried out at the pain, but then sucked in a breath at the wash of heat that followed, flowing through her body as he moved slightly against her, rousing. Backing her wrist off his fangs, she turned her arm so the bloody spots hit his tongue, which moved, fitfully at first and then with purpose, lapping two strong strokes and then a third.

Doing her best to ignore for now the pleasure-pain of his feeding, she leaned in and said, "Wake up. I need you."

Her heart hammered and despair threatened as the dragon reached them and reared up, shrieking and beating at the air with its wings. Then it slammed back down and snaked its vicious triangle of a head toward them, moving in for the kill, gaping its jaws wide and—

Dayn moved convulsively, jerking upright, yanking the crossbow into position and putting his bolt straight into one fiery red eye.

The dragon bellowed and yanked back, wings flailing so hard that it lifted off the ground and hung for a moment, suspended as it writhed and keened, contorting into impossible-seeming shapes in the sky. Seconds later, it went limp and plummeted to the ground.

It vanished when it hit, sent back to whatever magic had summoned it.

Suddenly, the meadow was entirely silent.

Reda stared at the place where it had been, and blew out a long breath. "Okay. We made it. That was…okay." She wasn't okay, though, because she was far too aware of the deep ache in her wrist and the echo of mingled pleasure-pain within her.

Dayn, too, was far from okay. He groaned as he tried to sit up away from her, then fell back weakly. A muscle pulsed at the corner of his jaw. "We need to get out of here. Moragh will know we killed her creature. She'll send men to find us, or come herself, and I'm in no shape to fight."

That was an understatement. It took all her effort to get him on his feet and keep him there, and he leaned heavily against her. More, as they left the meadow and headed back into the forest, he slid into and out of lucidity, his mumbled thoughts fragmented. "Don't know who I am, he says? I'll show… Wish I could've gone with you, my sweet Reda, wish you hadn't come back… Don't know where they are…"

The "wish you hadn't come back" was a theme. And where before she had told herself he had sent her away to keep her safe, now she wondered whether she was kidding herself. But for a change, instead of immediately assuming the worst, she decided she would wait and see. First and foremost, she needed to get him back on his feet. And although she thought she knew how to do it, the prospect wasn't appealing.

Or rather, it *was* appealing. And that was what worried her.

A short distance into the forest, she found a spot where a big tree had long ago fallen against three big boulders. Time and weather had hollowed out the giant trunk, creating a small sheltered area that would have to do, because Dayn was breathing hard and struggling to keep himself upright.

She eased him into the hiding spot and then walked a quick circuit, but didn't find any sign of the witch, at least nothing that she could detect with her all-too-human senses. Rejoining him, she ducked down and crawled in beside him.

The hollow was dry enough and offered good concealment, but she sorely missed the supplies that had galloped away with MacEvoy, because Dayn didn't look good at all. His eyes were closed, his breathing shallow and pain cut deep grooves beside his mouth.

The thing was, though, he didn't need anything from the saddlebags. He needed blood.

# Chapter 14

Steeling herself, Reda looked down at her wrist. The slices were neat marks, already sealed up through some sort of vampire magic. But what made her the most queasy was the reddish circle painted on her forearm, showing where his mouth had been.

When it had actually been happening, it hadn't really bothered her. Now, though, her stomach roiled, though she couldn't have said why. It hadn't really hurt all that much, and the pleasure had far outweighed the sting. More, she didn't feel any different than she did before, and it had *saved* them, damn it. How was that wrong?

It wasn't until she didn't get an answer that she realized she was waiting for one. She wanted reason and logic to weigh in, wanted to hear from practicality, because they were the ones who could explain why her baseline human self said it was wrong for one person to drink blood from another, yet under the circumstances she couldn't think of a good reason why.

Maybe that was her answer, and the reason why the other parts of her were staying silent—because in the end this wasn't the human realm, wasn't even the wolfyn realm. They were in the kingdoms where magic—and emotion—trumped.

She had heard it all before: *love is messy, it hurts, it's not logical, it defies prediction.* But now she got why those were clichés, got why some people nodded knowingly over them while others looked blank.

Her parents hadn't made any sense together. On the surface, a fey dreamer, possibly even a realm traveler, shouldn't have had anything in common with the stalwart, conservative, linear-thinking major. Yet they had chosen each other, had made four children together. More, when she died, a piece of him had died with her—the piece that had known how to laugh, how to live, how to remember without letting the past take over the present.

Reda had long known that she was a product of her mother's death and the way her father changed. What she hadn't really grasped, though, was that she had also come from a love that had been so strong that it had drawn her parents together despite their differences, and whose absence had made her father a different, lesser man.

Which brought to mind another of those sayings:

throw your heart over first and the rest will follow. He had done that and gotten burned. Had she on some level realized it and held herself at a distance rather than leading with her heart, not wanting the pain he'd lived through, not wanting to cause the pain he had experienced because of it?

When had she ever thrown herself into a relationship? More, when had she put her heart into it first? Maybe she had started to in the wolfyn realm, only to have Dayn's secrets rear up between them. But even there she hadn't given herself fully.

His test might have been proving that he could think of others before himself, but maybe hers had been to do the opposite and learn how to please herself and stop worrying about what other people—including the ones she channeled in her head—thought about her decisions.

"Got it figured out yet?"

Starting, she looked over and found Dayn watching her through heavy-lidded eyes. A flush touched her cheeks, warmed her skin and made her suddenly conscious of her own pulse. "Have I got what figured out? The way onto the island?"

"Whatever was making you look so fierce just now, like you were ready to take on the whole world by yourself. The thought of which, by the way, terrifies me."

Hearing him sounding more like himself, she took a closer look. "You're healed!"

He nodded, shifting and testing a muscle here, a move there. "I can't explain it, but that little bit of your blood helped far more than I would have expected it to. Maybe it's got something to do with whoever your ancestors were, or maybe it's connected to the part of the spell that ties my life force to the island. Who knows? But believe it or not, I'm good to go." He parted his ragged shirt to reveal his chest and flat stomach, made whole once more, save for reddish marks stamping the places where he had been torn to the bone an hour earlier.

If they had been in the outlaws' cave, separated by fences and space, it might not have happened. But she was sitting so near him in the small hollow that it was too easy to stretch her hand across and press her palm to his chest to soak up the feel of the warm, yielding muscle the steady *lub-dub* of his heartbeat.

"I thought you were going to die." She hadn't meant to say it aloud, hadn't meant for her eyes to well up.

He covered her hand with his own, holding her against his heart. "You've seen for yourself that I'm not easy to kill."

"But you could have died back there. You still might."

Reaching up with an arm that had been broken an hour before, he touched the single tear that had broken free, then cupped her cheek in his palm. "Ah, Reda. My sweet, sweet Reda. I wish I could freeze time right now. No more looking back or moving forward, just the two of us together."

She closed her eyes and felt another tear track down her cheek as he leaned in and touched his lips to hers.

And although nothing was different between them, there was something new inside her as she opened her mouth beneath his.

He made a low, urgent noise in the back of his throat, almost a whimper yet so much more masculine than that, as if he, too, so badly needed this yet had been afraid that it wouldn't happen ever again. But it would happen, it *was* happening, and she poured herself into the moment, determined to take what she needed and give everything in return. There was no more second-guessing, no more inner debate; her mind was still and wholly in the moment when she wrapped her arms around his neck and he rose above her, easing her down to the dry, yielding moss. There were no more reservations, no skittering fears of too-sharp teeth or compulsions, because this thing happening between them went both ways.

She felt his wolfyn's enthrallment in the gentle rasp of his weapon-callused hands over her skin as they loosened enough clothing to find each other, and in the shudder of his breath when she softly kissed his cheek, his forehead, the touch saying, *I'm here, with you, and right now nothing else matters.* She felt him control his other, vampire self in the way he coiled tight with pleasure and need when she grazed her teeth along the veins at the side of his neck, nipping lightly over the fading love bites.

And it was because of that enthrallment, because of that control, and because of the time-faded, grief-faded memory of her father twirling her mother across the back lawn and the two of them racing down the wooded path to the forest, looking back over their shoulders like naughty kids—or mismatched lovers who had somehow matched perfectly—that there was no fear as she shifted beneath him and guided his mouth to the side of her neck.

He went very still. Then, with a low groan that resonated deep inside her, he opened his mouth against her skin.

She tried not to tense but did, then relaxed when he kissed her there, laved her with his tongue, scraped his teeth lightly across the sensitized flesh. Then he drew away.

Murmuring disappointment, she opened her eyes to find him looking at her, waiting for her to look at him. The emerald of his eyes had gone lush with passion and his face was flushed, his dark hair tousled, making him look younger and more carefree than she had ever seen him before. But his expression was in deadly earnest when he rasped, "Are you sure?"

His fangs caught the light when he spoke, and the sight kicked new heat into her bloodstream. She wanted them on her, in her, wanted to take the risk body and soul, and know that a piece of her was inside him. "I'm sure. But only if you want to."

"I've never wanted anything—or anyone—more." He pressed his forehead to hers. "Reda, I—"

"Shhh." She pressed her fingers to his lips. "Let's save that for after." Because for all that they were taking their moment together here and now, the immediate future pressed heavily and she didn't want either of them to make promises they might have to break.

He drew back, eyes shadowed, but nodded. "After, then." He eased in and kissed her lips, gently at first, chastely, but then parted his lips as if saying, as she had, *Only if you want to.*

And, oh, yes, she wanted to. Nerves added an edge to the excitement as she opened her mouth and kissed him back, using her tongue to explore the two long fangs that overlapped his other teeth, sliding it along one and then the other as he rumbled a deep groan that released new wetness inside her.

He stroked her body as they kissed, slid her clothes farther out of the way and cupped her, stroked her. She arched into him, parting her legs in wanton demand and then moaning when he skimmed along the outsides of her heated flesh without penetrating. But then he broke their kiss and pressed his lips to her cheek, her jaw, the soft spot below her ear.

She moved restlessly against him, would have cupped him, touched him with some inciting friction of her own, but he had angled his body away to concentrate on her. Which was so unbearably sexy she thought she would shatter. "More," she whispered. "Now. Please, now."

The nerves were gone, leaving only wild heat and need as he grazed one fang down her neck. Pleasure shivers coiled through her until her whole body throbbed with her heartbeat, making her exquisitely aware of the blood racing through her body and running beneath the place at the side of her throat where he opened his mouth to suckle her.

His fingers mimicked the pressure of his lips, rubbing her clit with a voluptuous intensity that pulled the pressure inside her tighter and tighter. She whimpered and moved against him, and where before she might have held herself back, not wanting him to know how thoroughly she was under his control, now she gave in to the sensations, reveled in them, tangling her fingers in his hair and urging him on.

He suckled harder, worked his fingers a little deeper, so she felt his teeth on her throat, his fingers at the entrance to her body. Tingles raced through her, presaging orgasm, and she moaned his name as the pleasure gathered. Tightened. Poised...

Pain lanced through her as he bit down; pleasure rose up as he pierced her with two fingers at the same time, and she was caught amid the two for a breathless instant of shock. But then, between one heartbeat and the next, the pain became heat and the shock became a shuddering groan of "Ohhh, yes," as he sucked from her on a deep and primal level while his hand surged against her with those long, elegant fingers inside her and the heel of his hand gently massaging her clit.

She clung to him, one hand buried in his hair, holding him against her throat, the other curved around his shoulder and digging in as waves of heat and pleasure rolled through her, throbbing with her pulse, and then with his, too, as their heartbeats aligned in rhythm. She felt his heartbeat, his pleasure, knew that had to be the magic of the forming bond. But instead of being terrifying or intrusive, as she had imagined, it was incredible, indescribable. It didn't take anything away from her; it gave to her, shared with her. Just like he did.

The first delicious curls of a monstrous-feeling orgasm tickled at the edges of her senses, and when he groaned deep in his chest, she knew he could feel it, too. He intensified his rhythm, working her, sucking her and gasping against her throat when she whimpered and fisted her hand in his hair, holding him against her, urging him on.

His excitement washed through her, along with a deep, possessive pleasure that whispered in her mind: *You are mine now, as I am yours. We are ourselves, yet we are also one.*

The orgasm caught her, swirled around her, inside her, and sucked her up into a vortex of pleasure so overwhelming that the rest of the world ceased to exist for her—there was only Dayn's mouth and hands, the searing heat that came through their new bond and the glory that whirled through her body.

She arched and gasped, riding the pressure and the spin, and then staying excited when the pulsing echoes faded but the pleasure didn't fade. Instead, it plateaued, as if her body, too, was saying, *Give me more.*

He groaned softly as he withdrew his fangs, bringing a pinch of pain that disappeared quickly when he licked where they had been. Then he kissed the spot, kissed her jaw, whispered her name.

"Don't stop," she whispered in return. She was

replete yet still greedy, and she could feel the need inside him. He was full to bursting, hard enough to hurt, and aching to be inside her. "Come inside me."

His head came up; his eyes fixed on hers, silently asking if she knew what she was commanding. He had fed from her throat, which meant she was primed now to accept his seed.

She nodded slowly, not even bothering to check in with her inner committee. This was her life, her call. And illogical or not, it was what she wanted, what she needed. "Only if you want to," she said to him as she had done earlier.

"Gods, yes." He kissed her, fangs fully extended still, and so sensitive that he shuddered when she licked along the curve of one. As they kissed, he withdrew his fingers and looped her leg over his arm, baring her swollen flesh wide as he moved into position.

Breaking the kiss, she stared down at their poised sexes, unbearably aroused. His engorged cock was hard and heavy, and flushed a gorgeous ruddy red where it nudged her pink folds so intimately. She could feel its throb, feel her heartbeat align with the pulse.

"I want this," he said, bringing her eyes up to his. Then her eyelids fluttered closed as he pushed forward a delicious inch. He leaned in and kissed her closed lids, whispering, "I want you." He seated himself another inch, filling and stretching her. Then, voice deep and reverent, as if he was promising her the world, he grated, "I am yours." And he pushed fully home.

Colors exploded behind her eyelids, sensory rainbows

that said the storm had passed, the air was clear and the past had been washed away. And for now, in this frozen moment that they had stolen for themselves, she allowed herself to believe it, because on some levels it was true.

As she surged against him, counterpointing the powerful thrusts that wrung cries from both of them, she was whole within herself, taking what she wanted and trusting her own instincts over life lessons that didn't work for her, maybe hadn't ever really worked for her. And as he clamped her hips in his hands and anchored her so he could drive deeper, so deeply that she nearly came from the pressure of him hitting her exactly right inside and out, she knew that what they had found together was separate from Elden's problems and his need for redemption. Those things might have put them in each other's orbits, but their deep connection—and now their bond—was their own.

Knowing it, believing in it and him, and this one singular moment they had stolen, she found his mouth and poured herself into a kiss that held nothing back. She was wide open to him, feeling his heartbeat and pleasure and sharing her own in return.

Emotion washed through her, tightening her body around him as a second orgasm gathered, deep and powerful, as they rocked together, not having sex or making love so much as *mating,* sealing the bond that now connected them.

Through it, she knew that he was lost in her, in the moment and the sensations, holding nothing back as he thrust and thrust again, finding a sweet, sweet spot where they fit perfectly, joined intimately. Her body tightened as he stroked harder and faster, then faster still, touching that spot, that wonderful glorious place that wrapped her up, caught her up. And sent her flying.

She threw her head back, rapt in the glory of coming with her body, mind and heart united, and nothing held in reserve. She called his name, praised him, urged him on, drove him wild.

"Yes, Reda. My sweet Reda." He bowed his head as his rhythm hitched and his big body shuddered against her. He surged into her, pressed home, touched the place that was theirs alone, and then he was coming, too, her name reverberating in his chest as he leaned into her, against her.

The sensations washed between them, amping their responses and locking them together in protracted pleasure before leveling off and then, eventually, easing.

"Gods." He pressed his cheek to hers, his breathing still hard and fast. "Dear gods. If I had known..."

It was a first for him, too, she realized. His first time drinking from a woman's throat. His first bonding. And if she had anything to say about it, his first, last and only. She waited for panic, didn't feel any. And smiled, feeling lighter than she had in...well, forever. "I'm glad you didn't find out with anyone else."

"Only you, sweet Reda." He rolled onto his side, bringing her with him so they lay facing each other. They were no longer intimately joined, but she could feel their bond as a small kernel of warmth that moved through her, moving with her blood. It wasn't intrusive or invasive. It simply *was*.

His eyes searched hers. "I'm fine," she said, tightening her fingers on his. "Better than fine."

"No regrets?" His words were soft and slow. Hopeful.

"Not ever, no matter what happens." Her heart wanted to hurt with the prospect of things to come, but she determinedly kept her thoughts there, in the present, with him. Though from the way his lids were drooping, she didn't think she would have him with her, present and accounted for, for much longer. "You, sir, are crashing."

"Too musshh magic." His words were slurring, his eyes going unfocused. He blinked, trying to stay awake, but it was clearly a losing battle. "All that healing. Need an hour. We…we shhhould have enough time."

Whether they did or not, he wasn't going to be any use until he recharged. Fleetingly, she wished for some of Candida's clever potions, but they were long gone. "Sleep," she said. "I'll keep watch." Unlike him, she was wide awake, clearheaded and ready for action.

"Don…don't go anywhere. Not sssafe." His eyes were nearly closed now, his body relaxing toward sleep whether he liked it or not.

"I won't. I promise."

He lifted their joined hands to his lips, kissed her knuckles and then pressed them to his heart. He was smiling as he slipped into sleep, and she smiled, watching him. And in that moment, in that perfect stolen piece of the present, she felt at peace.

*Dayn tightened his grip on Reda's hand as his older brother repeated the words that would make him the king of Elden.*

*Nicolai's voice rolled out across the crowds that thronged the castle courtyard and spilled beyond to the outer reaches and the greensward beyond. The sky was blue and perfect, the castle repaired, scrubbed and hung with banners old and new. Breena stood on Nicolai's other side next to a solid man with their father's features—Micah? Gods—and the sight of them warmed Dayn, made him grateful, as he was every day since the day the sorcerer died, for the spell that had saved them and then brought them back together again, along with several others that Dayn sensed standing near each of his sibs, but couldn't see clearly.*

*With the vow finished, Nicolai bowed his head to receive the symbols of his reign. Dayn's eyes misted at the sight of the vestments their father had worn, but the ache was a good one, free of guilt or recrimination. "He'll be a good king," he murmured to Reda.*

*"He'll have a good second-in-command looking out for him," she returned.*

*"So will I." His lips turned up as he glanced over at her. "Or am I your second? I'm never sure."*

*"We can trade off, at least until our new commanding officer arrives." She brought their joined hands to the faint swell of her belly and he spread his hand,*

*spanning their growing child as fierce love and pos-
sessiveness welled up inside him.*

*Nicolai moved out onto the castle balcony and the
crowd erupted into cheers at their first sighting of the
new king of Elden. As the noise swelled, Dayn grinned,
leaned down and kissed her softly.*

*"There's nothing more important than this," he said,
and kissed her again, silently thanking the gods and
the magic that had brought her into his life.*

The dream fragmented and misted away, leaving
Dayn to swim back up to consciousness. Before he had
even opened his eyes, he knew he had needed the rest,
and the pleasant dream that he badly wanted to believe
was prescience more than wishful thinking. He felt refreshed and recharged, with none of the fuzziness that
had accompanied the crash.

He was a little embarrassed, though not about having
wiped out so thoroughly, but because he hadn't planned
for it. He'd heard of such things, but hadn't ever before
used as much magic as he had over the past four days.
And then to add in a bonding…yeah. Not his best planning ever.

But at the same time, it was the best decision he'd
ever made. He felt the warmth of her in his veins, felt
their distant connection, felt—

*Wait a minute. Distant?* His blood iced at the realization that she felt suddenly very far away.

Something was wrong.

"Reda?" he said as he opened his eyes, even though

he already knew she wasn't there. But he got a second shock when he looked around. It was nearly dark out.

Lunging to his feet, he yanked his clothes to rights and ducked out of the shelter.

The surrounding area was undisturbed, at least as best as he could tell in the gathering darkness. There was no sign of a struggle, no evidence that she had stepped out to relieve herself and been attacked by some beast. And if she'd been taken from right there by human hands, anyone grabbing her would have seen him, and captured him for the bounty. Which meant she had left under her own power.

His pulse thudded in his ears, choppy and upset. She had promised to stay with him, yet she had disappeared and he had slept far, far too long. Gods and the Abyss. This wasn't a dream; it was a nightmare. She had disappeared and he was up against his deadline.

What had happened? Had she regretted forming the bond, maybe even been repulsed once her blood cooled? Had the intensity of their mating sent her into a panicked retreat?

Most importantly, had she fled to the shrine?

"No," he grated, refusing to believe it. Perhaps they hadn't made any promises of forever, but she had fed him, mated with him, taken his seed inside her after the bonding. They belonged to each other now. She had to know that.

Except he hadn't told her, had he? And when he had started to say something along those lines, she had hushed him and changed the subject. At the time, he had thought she was feeling too raw and unsettled from their other confidences to add talk of the future into the mix. Now, though, he wondered whether she hadn't believed there would be one.

He had been so dazzled by the warrior woman astride a fractious bay that he'd lost track that she, too, had spent a long time alone, questioning her worth. How had he forgotten that?

Gods. Had he lost her in truth? He quickly sought their bond; the weak flicker had to mean she was still in the kingdom realm. But for how long? Was she even now working to call a vortex to carry her home?

*Let her go,* said an inner voice. *She'll be safer there, alive no matter what happens on the island. Maybe you could even travel to her when all this is over. Right now, you need to get yourself onto that island. Time is running out.*

He froze. Was this, then, his test? Was he to prove himself by choosing Elden over her? Because despite that logic, his gut said that if she left the realm, he would never see her again. More, it said he had to go after her now, that he didn't dare tackle the island or the sorcerer without her at his side.

*Wishful thinking,* came the scoff. But it wasn't really. It was faith. He had faith in his own gut, faith in the magic he and Reda made together.

*Please, gods, don't let me screw this up.* This time the human slang came naturally.

His heart thudded against his ribs and his stomach knotted, but when he moved, it wasn't toward Blood

Lake, the island or the redemption he'd spent twenty years preparing for. Instead, he headed away, following the thin scuff-shadows that only a trained hunter would see. Seeking the bond magic, he thought with all his might, *Hang on, sweet Reda. I'm coming. Wait for me and we'll figure this out together.*

Because the dream might have been a fantasy, but it had one thing right: she was his priority. He wasn't the heir, hadn't the best of his siblings when it came to anything except his ability to hunt and ride. But with Reda—and *for* her—he had become a prince. A hero, even.

She made him better, and without her, he wouldn't be any use to Elden.

# Chapter 15

Reda swam slowly up from a sleep that felt too deep, with quivers in her stomach that said something was badly wrong. She was lying on a hard surface and her head hurt, but those inputs seemed strange and faraway, her fragmented dreams so much more real.

*Was it all a dream, after all?* she thought, but wasn't sure where the inner voice had come from or what it meant.

Her thoughts scattered like a herd of identical bald-faced bay horses, snorting and blowing as they swerved and collided. Past and present mixed together: *she was a little girl of six or seven, sitting cross-legged in the woods opposite her maman, leaning in, wide-eyed. "Tell me more about the magic. Please?" She was a rookie cop going in low while her ride-along partner went high, and then laughing her ass off when they plugged a pair of homicide cops with red paintball splashes. She was ten years old, stumbling into the woods in her nightgown. "Maman? Maman, where are you?" Twenty-six, standing over Benz's grave, knowing that he wasn't in there, that dead was dead.*

The graveyard had smelled of cut grass and apple trees. Now, though, she wrinkled her nose against an ammoniac taint and the smell of animals. More, the noises were wrong. The graveyard's silence was broken by restless noises that made her think she was in a barn: sniffs, snuffles and low chuffs, the movement of big bodies in straw.

Where was she? What was wrong with her? What was going on?

She struggled to open her eyes. Then the fog started to clear…and she realized they were already open, covered by a fetid rag that was tightly tied around her head. There was another jammed in her mouth, which was dry and foul. Light and air seeped in around the edges, but just barely.

Crying out, the noise muffled and nasty, she yanked up her hands to tear at the blindfold. But chains rattled, cuffs dug into her wrists and her hands stopped short of her face.

She realized now that she had never known true terror before.

"No!" She thrashed upright, slammed against a stone wall, rolled off what proved to be a narrow cot, hit the cold stone floor awkwardly on one hip and shoulder, then got hung up on the chains. Her feet weren't bound, but her wrist shackles were fastened to the wall, giving her only a few feet of play.

Twisting so hard she felt muscles pull, she got her hands to her face and plucked at the knotted rags with weak, trembling fingers. *Breathe,* she told herself when the numbness spread and her moves slowed, threatened to stop entirely. *Damn it, breathe!*

The most recent of memories broke free: *lying curled up against Dayn while he slept; hearing a twig crack in the distance, then the voices of men talking in low undertones as they searched the forest; learning from them that Moragh had used up her magic summoning the Feiynd and couldn't track Dayn by his father's spell anymore, but knew he had to be near where the dragon died, injured.*

Her nose was closing up from the smell, cutting off her air, sending panic higher even as she tried to slow her brain down. *One thing at a time. Do the gag first. The knot is in the back.* But. She. Couldn't. Move.

More flashes: *the men moving on; her trying to wake Dayn but failing; the debate—she had promised to stay with him, but they would be circling back soon. Her slipping from concealment, heart pounding with no real plan other than to lead them away. Not into the Dead Forest, but where? The shrine, she had thought, she could lead them to the shrine. Would a vortex scare them and buy her some time to double back?*

The stone was cold and hard beneath her, the knot

tight and greasy. She concentrated on those inputs, made herself relax and suck on the thin trickle of oxygen leaking through her gag, then try the knot again.

The memories were coming faster now, clearer: *her following the men, her mouth sour and her heart drumming against her ribs; finding them and circling around to where she could lead them to the trident-topped tree, and then...*

*A blow from behind. A man kneeling on her, pushing her face into the dirt. A coarse, terrifying discussion about what to do with her, then the decision to bring her unspoiled to the witch for questioning. Another blow, then darkness.*

*Darkness.*

She sobbed against the gag, curled around herself, fingers useless on her bonds. The low, ragged noises stirred the creatures around her; from a little distance, echoing as if down a corridor, she heard metal dragging on stone followed by a low, rumbling feline growl that didn't sound like anything she'd ever heard before. Then, farther down, a bugle that was part elephant, part trombone.

This was no barn. The noises belonged to creatures that would be kept in a zoo.

Or, in this realm, in a bestiary.

"No," she whispered into her knees. "Please, no." She didn't remember if the questioning had happened yet, but the too-deep sleep and numbing fog made her think of the vortex magic. Had the witch bespelled her? Had she blabbed? "Dayn?" she called, torn between equal fear and hope. "Are you there?"

There was no answer from her fellow prisoners; not even a growl. But faint warmth stuttered to life within her, moving slowly through her body, surging with the beat of her blood.

He was alive. She let the thought fill her, chasing away some of the chill and unlocking her muscles. Did he know she was on the island, captured? Or did he think she had taken off on him? She didn't know how much he could sense through the bond. Her thoughts churned with new unease: Would he turn his back on duty and come after her, or would the kingdom's needs outweigh the bond? She didn't know which she would prefer; she only knew that she hated being part of the inner war she imagined him fighting. He was an honorable male, her bound mate. Yet he was also a prince of Elden.

She should have left when she had the chance, she knew. But although that would have been the better, more honorable thing to do, all she could think was, *Hell with that.* She wanted Dayn, wanted a future with him even if she had to fight for it. Because she loved him.

"Love," she whispered softly as the small kernel of warmth unfurled from a point to a glow, and then to new strength flowing through her with the beat of her heart. *Yes,* she thought. *This.*

She loved him. Not because he was a woodsman, a prince or a hero, but because he was a vampire and a wolfyn. It didn't make any logical sense, went against everything rationality told her she should feel. But her heart didn't care about any of that. She loved him, pure and simple. She didn't need to have faith in the feeling, didn't have to believe in it for it to exist; it simply was.

That revelation spurred her, got her moving again. Her hands stopped shaking; her stomach unknotted and she uncurled herself from fetal uselessness. The chains clanked and dragged as she repositioned herself against the cot, using it to support her weighed-down wrists as she craned and went to work again on the knots, starting with the top one this time.

It gave almost immediately, and the blindfold fell away. *Success!*

She blinked against the sudden blaze of light, squinting until it resolved to rather anemic amber firelight coming from torches set in brackets outside her cell.

Because that was most definitely what it was. The space was the size of a large box stall; indeed, there was an iron hayrack in the corner, and places to hang buckets. But the door wasn't made for a horse or donkey—or none that she had ever seen before. It was made of iron bars that ran floor to ceiling, with no lock, no hinge, no nothing. Magic.

She sank back, heart thudding as bile rose.

"Oh, Dayn. Help me." Her lips shaped the words, but no sound came out. She hoped—prayed—he could sense her need through their bond, though. Because there was no way she was getting out of this one on her own.

\* \* \*

*Dayn. Help me!*

At the sound of her voice, his head whipped up from the faint trail he'd been following. "Reda?"

His feet kept moving, but he turned inward as their bond suddenly grew stronger than before, amped by the fear he felt in her, along with an echo of hopelessness that terrified him. She was in trouble!

Adrenaline fired through his veins and his secondaries broke the skin, bringing the added aggression of his blood-drinking ancestors. "Hang on. I'm coming," he said, both aloud and in his heart. "Hang on. Don't leave. Don't—" He broke off, stopping dead at the edge of a churned-up patch of forest, where booted footprints were layered deeply and skid marks showed the impression of a human body just about her size. *"Reda!"*

The impressions were hours old, the body that had made them long gone. "No!" Gods, no. Who had taken her? Thieves, outlaws, soldiers? All equally dangerous, equally horrifying.

Pulse thundering in his ears, he sent magic into the bond, acting on instinct because he didn't know much about the connection or how it worked, especially with someone from the human realm. *Reda, where are you?*

There was no answer. Only the fear.

He took two running steps after her. But then he stopped, heart hammering. This wasn't going to work. He needed to move faster, couldn't risk losing the trail. Reda needed him, and she needed him now.

Deep within him, magic spun up. Not his blood-drinking

powers, but the other. *Be true to yourself. Know your priorities.* It was his father's voice, but he wasn't sure if it was a memory or a message.

He stood for a moment in the center of the churned-up clearing, hands fisted at his sides, body shaking with the pull of the forces that were trying to tear him apart. His birthright demanded that he not give in to the lure of the wolfyn form. And his sibs, his honor and the people still living in this blighted land needed him to get his ass to Castle Island before the zero hour, which was approaching fast. Every shred of logic and rational thinking he possessed said that had to outweigh Reda's need. More, if he changed now, if he gave in to that magic, he put himself that much farther from his true self.

It felt like that was already happening, though, every time he thought about not going after Reda. She was his mate, his love, his other half. Without her, he wouldn't be living; he would be simply existing, as he had done for the past twenty years in the wolfyn realm. Without her, he wasn't himself.

He looked up into the night sky. "I'm sorry, Father. I wish I could be the kind of son you wanted, the kind of prince Elden needs. But I can't. This is who I am."

And he changed.

Pain flared through him, familiar even though it was only his third time making the transition. He gritted his teeth as flesh stretched and tore, tendons realigned and the ground grew suddenly closer to his eyes as his body reshaped itself into that of a huge wolf. A hunter.

And today, if needs be, a killer. Because he would kill his own countrymen if that was what it took to keep his mate safe.

Rage and feral aggression flowed through him, calling to the beast within, and he threw back his head and howled.

Birds fled from nearby trees and several large creatures crashed in the brush, fleeing the predator that was suddenly among them. He didn't pay any attention to them, though; he was wholly focused on the scents that suddenly flooded his system as he put his nose down and bolted along the trail.

In his father's time, the smells of oiled leather, honed steel and grain-fed horses of a cavalry detachment would have been a relief. Now, though, the details coiled new fear inside him, chilling his blood and warning that she hadn't been taken by thieves or outlaws, but by soldiers.

The sorcerer had her.

He hit the road and turned toward the lake, running with his head up now, both because the scent was so strong and because he knew where he was going—which was where he'd been going all along. Not home, but to a reckoning.

He flashed on his father's memories of the castle's fall—blood splattering the stones of the courtyard, ettins fighting their way up to the second level, where the families lived, the king and queen despairing. Only it wasn't his parents he saw now; it was Reda standing alone, trying to fight her way free of the creatures that grasped and clawed at her.

In the waking dream, she looked straight at him. He didn't hear her voice, though, and the bond had gone frighteningly dim. Hurry. He had to hurry! Ignoring the panicked scatters of the villagers, he blew through a town and then blasted along the edge of the lake, body flat to the ground, claws biting into the ground, legs eating up the distance to the heavily guarded causeway. He heard shouts up ahead, saw a ragged band of men assembling, hastily armed with broken pikes and ancient-looking swords.

He didn't have time for this, didn't want to hurt them, so he just put his head down and charged, bulling through their line and sending them flying. An arrow whizzed in from the side, but he snapped it out of the air and broke it in his jaws, the moves automatic, instinctual, as if he'd always lived in this body.

Shouts followed him onto the narrow causeway and a rasping horn blared an alarm. On either side of him blurred the polluted waters of Blood Lake; up ahead, the huge, scorpionlike creatures formed ranks, clashing their claws and whipping their tails as if to say, *Bring it on!*

Hatred hazed his vision red. He had seen them through his father's eyes kill the soldiers who had been his friends, his comrades. The feral fighting instinct of an alpha male said to kill; the priorities of a mated man said to get the hell to the castle.

As he neared them, he gathered himself to leap over

the huge creatures, saw their tails whip back and forth in expectation. Four strides. Three. Two. He coiled, faked a spring and ducked under the closest two, slashing at their legs on the way by.

The things screeched high, anguished screams, and the causeway behind him exploded to slashing, clacking chaos. He heard a couple of splashes, but didn't look back. He was done with looking back.

He shouldered two bristling soldiers into the lake, and this time the splashes were followed by bloodcurdling screams. Then he was off the causeway, onto the island and charging toward the castle.

More shouts and another horn blast came, but they didn't seem to be aimed at him. The castle was stirring with movement, as if he wasn't the only unexpected arrival.

Dayn missed a step as he realized what that could mean.

It was happening, after all. He had returned in time, and unless he missed his guess, he wasn't the only one. His heart surged and he accelerated toward the castle.

A crossbow bolt thrummed toward him and buried itself in the dirt; a second carved a furrow in his haunch and he missed a few steps. But healing magic surged within him, hot and hard, as if he were suddenly drawing strength from the soil of Castle Island. Within seconds the injury had closed up and he was running once more at full tilt toward the outer bailey and—

He skidded hard, nearly falling when the trail he had been following suddenly swerved and headed away from the castle, toward the cluster of buildings at the other end of the island.

The sounds of footfalls and armor clanks rang out within the castle, calling to him. But his bond with Reda called harder. He could sense her now; he could feel her fear and despair. *I'm coming,* he sent along the bond. *Hang on!*

And he bolted away from the castle, toward the woman he loved, because he finally knew who he really was: he was hers.

# Chapter 16

The trail led to the bestiary, which unlike the castle seemed deserted, at least of humans. Still in wolf form, Dayn slunk through the open doors at one end of the L-shaped building and padded up the long, barnlike aisle, which was flanked on either side by barred doors instead of the sliders he remembered.

The fur of his ruff bristled and his senses were maxed out. He could feel Reda's energy, but he couldn't track her using the bond. He could only look in every stall-size cell, his bile rising higher with each one as he caught sight of the beasts he had studied, the ones he had once tracked and hunted in all their wild glory, chained and contained, with much of their beauty stripped away.

A jungle liger lay chained to the wall; bare patches on its haunches showed where it had chewed its own fur away. A pair of demidragons slept huddled together in a corner, their normally dark scales bleached pale from cold and the lack of sun. A huge spider hung from the ceiling with its legs folded around its body and its multifaceted eyes glazed. The creatures seemed dispirited and uninterested…or, Dayn realized with a chill shiver, like they had been leeched of their life forces.

The sorcerer fed off everything, it seemed.

Then there was a fierce growl from up ahead, one that had Dayn's hackles rising instinctively as he drew even with the doorway, where a smallish wolfyn male was pressed against the iron bars. The unfamiliar wolfyn's ears were flat to his head, his amber eyes crazed with hatred.

"I'm a friend," Dayn said in the simplified wolf-form language Candida had taught him on the sly. "I can help."

The wolfyn didn't show any recognition. Instead, he snarled at him and then danced back to snap at the bars, dig at them, and then pressed forward again, trying to get at Dayn. There didn't seem to be any humanity left in the small male. Which, perhaps, was a blessing.

His snarls, though, had stirred up the other creatures, which stomped and shifted restlessly, starting to growl and snort.

"Hush," Dayn snarled. "They'll hear." He moved on, caught a faint whiff of flowers and spices and charged to the end of the aisle, heart rocketing. "Reda?" The word was a two-syllable chuff that sounded very like the wolfyn word for *heart*. Which was only fitting, as she had taken his.

He skidded to a stop in front of the cell that carried her scent. And stopped dead.

It was empty, the bars fully retracted into the floor and ceiling through some magical means. She was gone.

And the air beyond that point stank of fear and pain. The smell slammed into him, shutting down his senses. He couldn't scent her from there, couldn't track her.

*"No."* His stomach dropped. Frantically, he searched for the bond, felt her, but didn't like what he felt. There was anger, which was good because it said she was fighting whatever was happening to her. But there was also terror and despair. And that wasn't good at all.

"They've taken her." The deep, resonant voice came from the opposite cell, and spoke a tongue he knew, though had never spoken successfully.

Heart galloping like a coal-black herd flowing over a green meadow, Dayn whirled and charged to the cell, which was so deeply shadowed that all he could see was a huge, indistinct shape in the corner. He pressed against the bars and said in the same language, "Where?"

And his wolf-form tongue said the word in a way his human tongue had never managed.

The huge shape moved, turned and came toward him, hooves ringing on the ground and striking sparks of metal on stone. The torchlight from the aisleway glinted off a long, metallic spiral and lit the blink of fiery orange eyes nearly lost beneath a long, flowing forelock.

It was the biggest damn unicorn Dayn had ever seen.

"Let me out and I'll show you." The stallion's eyes took on a hard, vicious gleam that reminded him that while the creatures might tolerate the wolfyn, they sure as hell didn't like them.

Then again, they didn't like anyone. And captivity really pissed them off. "I've got a better idea," Dayn said. And hoped to hell he wasn't about to make a fatal mistake.

"Go see what all that commotion is up at the castle," Moragh snapped in her servant's direction. "It's upsetting the beasts."

"Yes, mistress." The gnome bowed his way out.

The training hall—at least that was what Reda thought it was, based on all the open space and racked weapons—echoed with the hollow thud of the double doors shutting behind him, cutting out the distant blare of horns, the nearer snorts and stomps of the caged beasts.

The witch turned back, eyes glittering dangerously. "Now. Where were we?"

Reda just glared. Her head hurt and the large stone chamber around her kept going in and out of focus, but she held doggedly on to consciousness, clinging to the stone-cold fury that had come over her when the guards had opened her cell door and she had made a break for it, only to be struck down and dragged to her destination.

Pushed beyond fear and terror to a new place deep inside herself, where a hard and determined soldier of a woman existed, she wanted nothing more than to grab Moragh by her hair and dunk her head in the vat she was so carefully tending over a fire in the center of the big stone room. Or Reda could go for any number of the weapons displayed around the room; she wasn't picky. What she was, however, was trapped in the center of a strange symbol drawn on the stone floor in glittering powder. It generated a magical field of some sort, an invisible wall enclosing her. She flattened her palms against it now. "I don't know where you were," she said in answer to the witch's question, "but I was thinking about the scene where the wicked witch gets it, and wondering if I could get a vortex to drop a house on you."

She didn't let the bitch see the terror beneath her bravado, didn't let herself think about anything beyond stalling for time. Dayn was on the island—she could feel his nearness through their bond—and he would come for her as soon as he could. She knew that just as surely as she knew she loved him.

And that she had to stay alive and whole until he arrived.

Moragh sneered. "You've got a smart mouth on you. Must come with that royal blood of yours." She narrowed her eyes. "What are you, a quarter-bred Medinian? Can see it in the eyes." She bared her fangs and dragged her fingertips across the leather-bound book she clutched open to her chest. "All the more power for me. When I'm done with you, I'll be damn near invincible. Realm travel, magic, science—it'll all be mine."

"You…" Reda faltered. Her grandfather Medina had been a huge bear of a man, equally prone to laughter and moodiness, and everyone had said she had his eyes.

Something screeched outside, a high, keening call that raised the fine hairs on Reda's arms.

Moragh darted a glance in the direction of the bestiary. "Don't know what's gotten into them."

"The lost children are here," Reda said matter-of-factly. "They're going to kill the sorcerer." Her heart drummed against her ribs. *Hurry, Dayn!*

"Let them. Soon I won't need the Blood Sorcerer anymore." She lowered the book, scanned a page and then set the book aside to pick up a jewel-handled knife with a viciously sharp-looking cutting edge. Then, as she advanced on Reda, she recited a string of syllables in a low, sibilant tone.

"Don't—" Reda's voice cut out, her breath cut out, *everything* cut out as the magic that had held her trapped abruptly closed in on her, coating her skin. Panic lashed—she wanted to fight, attack, retreat, do *something*, damn it—but the magic held her, controlled her.

At a gesture from the witch, the grip of the magic forced Reda to drop her to her knees, spread her arms out to the sides and tip her head back, baring her throat in a terrifying position of obeisance.

*No,* Reda screamed inwardly. *Nooo!*

Her mouth dried to dust as Moragh advanced on her, continuing to recite strange syllables that didn't make any sense to Reda, but coiled inside with hard, hurting intensity.

And suddenly, she wasn't cold and controlled anymore, wasn't confident, because for the first time since she had broken from her craven shell, it was painfully, elementally clear that being brave wasn't always enough.

Benz had been brave, and that hadn't saved him. He'd needed his partner to have his back.

*Dayn, hurry!* But she didn't know if the words got through, if anything got through. Panic bubbled in her, leaking weak tears from her eyes.

Moragh's chant rose in its intensity as the witch stopped directly opposite Reda. Her eyes were burning with power, her face frighteningly beatific as she set the knifepoint at the hollow between Reda's breasts.

Pain pricked and a drop of blood welled up. The sight made the love bites on her wrist and neck throb with memory, made the rest of her ache with sorrow. *I'm sorry, love. I tried to hold on long enough.*

The witch ended her chant with a flourish, drew back the knife and—

*Bang!* Moragh gasped and spun as the double doors flew open with a gunshot crash that reminded Reda of the ettin bursting into Dayn's cabin. Only this time the creature that filled the night-dark doorway wasn't a three-headed giant; it was a huge black unicorn with a flowing mane and tail, hugely spiraled horn and murder in its fiery orange eyes.

And astride it rode a fairy-tale prince.

He wore a rebel's tunic over his shirt and brandished his short sword as the huge unicorn lunged into the hall and flew toward Moragh. The witch screeched and backpedaled, bringing up her own smaller knife.

*Dayn!* Reda didn't know if she managed to say it aloud or if the word sounded just in their heads, carried on the love bond that suddenly flared fierce and proud. He heard her either way; his eyes locked on hers for a brief second, with a look that said everything that she was feeling.

The unicorn swerved to miss Moragh, did a sliding stop and bumped Reda, knocking her aside as Dayn performed a flying dismount that sent him right into the witch.

The second Reda's feet left the powder-drawn symbol, the magic snapped out of existence. And she was free! She scrambled to her feet, backpedaling as the unicorn's huge head swung toward her and the light glinted off its spiral horn.

Dayn landed swinging, but Moragh ducked and spun away, coming for Reda with the knife outstretched. The unicorn oriented, lowering its massive weapon, but Dayn got there first. He flung himself on Moragh and they went down together, rolling and struggling.

And then not struggling anymore.

Reda surged forward, heart stopping for a second and then pounding back to life when he moved, shifting to extricate himself from the witch, who lay on her back, both hands gripping the handle of her own knife, which had been driven into her heart.

"She's gone," he said, voice rough with whatever it had taken him to get to her.

Reda waited until he looked at her. Then she smiled. "I'm not."

His expression shifted, then cleared. "Ah, Reda."

And then it was easy to cross to him, reach up and touch his dear face. "You left the others to come find me." She wouldn't have asked it of him, but it mattered.

But he shook his head. "I came for you first, dear heart. I don't want to do this without you. Past, present, future—none of it matters if you're not at my side."

Her heart lodged in her throat as everything she had ever desired—even things she hadn't realized she wanted—suddenly opened up in front of her. And, even better, she didn't want to look at them yet. She only wanted to look at the man standing in front of her right then and there.

"I love you." The words weren't scary and they didn't hurt, she found. But they mattered.

His face smoothed and his eyes lit. "My sweet Reda." He drew her into his arms and kissed her, so his lips were against hers when he said, "By the gods, I love you, too. You're it for me. You're my life, my love, my one and only. I wasn't born to be the king and I don't want to play politics. I just want to be a man who's in love with his mate."

She kissed his jaw, nipped his throat and felt him

quiver against her. "You're talking of kings and politics like the battle is already over. Sounds to me like it's just getting started."

"Duty calls." He broke away from her as the unicorn moved up near him, then gathered a handful of the long black mane and swung himself aboard. Leaning down, he reached a hand for her. "And it's calling for both of us. From now on, we're a team, no matter what."

As if that had answered a last lingering question she hadn't even been aware of having, the last of the tension eased her heart, leaving only the warmth of their bond—and her love for him—behind. She took his hand and settled herself gingerly into position on the unicorn's broad, powerful back. "Is he yours?"

The creature snorted disgustedly as it started out, moving easily despite the double burden and the slippery stone floor.

"I think it's closer to say that we're cautious allies."

She laughed and moved up to snuggle behind Dayn and slide her arms around his waist. As the big black creature carried them down the training hall, she asked casually. "What's a Medinian?"

"The royal family of High Reaches." He shot a curious look back over his shoulder. "Why?"

"I'll tell you later."

He smiled. "I like the sound of that. 'Later.' Yeah. That's good."

She pressed a hand to her stomach, where the warmth of their loving bond had concentrated itself in a happy glow. "My gut tells me there's going to be a later, that it's all going to work out okay."

"Mine, too. And it also says that your gut is going to be saying to you something else in the next few weeks."

"What?"

"Tell you later."

Laughing, she pressed tight to his back and wrapped her arms around his waist. "Sounds good. Now, let's help the others take care of 'now' so we can get to the later."

"Deal."

He covered her hands with his and the two of them moved in unison as the huge black unicorn cantered off, metallic hooves ringing on the stones as they headed for the castle, the coming battle…and the rest of their lives together in the magical kingdom of Elden.

\* \* \* \* \*

*Next month, don't miss the fourth installment
of Royal House of Shadows.
It's Micah's romance in
LORD OF THE ABYSS by Nalini Singh!*

# PARANORMAL

Dark and sensual paranormal romance stories
that stretch the boundaries of conflict and desire, life and death.

## n●cturne™

### COMING NEXT MONTH
### AVAILABLE NOVEMBER 22, 2011

**#125 LORD OF THE ABYSS**
*Royal House of Shadows*
**Nalini Singh**

**#126 SOUL WHISPERER**
*The Trackers*
**Jenna Kernan**

# REQUEST YOUR FREE BOOKS!

## 2 FREE NOVELS FROM THE PARANORMAL ROMANCE COLLECTION PLUS 2 FREE GIFTS!

**YES!** Please send me 2 FREE novels from the Paranormal Romance Collection and my 2 FREE gifts (gifts are worth about $10). After receiving them, if I don't wish to receive any more books, I can return the shipping statement marked "cancel." If I don't cancel, I will receive 4 brand-new novels every month and be billed just $21.42 in the U.S. or $23.46 in Canada. That's a saving of at least 21% off the cover price of all 4 books. It's quite a bargain! Shipping and handling is just 50¢ per book in the U.S. and 75¢ per book in Canada.* I understand that accepting the 2 free books and gifts places me under no obligation to buy anything. I can always return a shipment and cancel at any time. Even if I never buy another book, the two free books and gifts are mine to keep forever.

237/337 HDN FEL2

| | |
|---|---|
| Name | (PLEASE PRINT) |

| | | |
|---|---|---|
| Address | | Apt. # |

| | | |
|---|---|---|
| City | State/Prov. | Zip/Postal Code |

Signature (if under 18, a parent or guardian must sign)

### Mail to the **Reader Service:**
**IN U.S.A.:** P.O. Box 1867, Buffalo, NY 14240-1867
**IN CANADA:** P.O. Box 609, Fort Erie, Ontario L2A 5X3

Not valid for current subscribers to the Paranormal Romance Collection
or Harlequin® Nocturne™ books.

**Want to try two free books from another line?**
**Call 1-800-873-8635 or visit www.ReaderService.com.**

* Terms and prices subject to change without notice. Prices do not include applicable taxes. Sales tax applicable in N.Y. Canadian residents will be charged applicable taxes. Offer not valid in Quebec. This offer is limited to one order per household. All orders subject to credit approval. Credit or debit balances in a customer's account(s) may be offset by any other outstanding balance owed by or to the customer. Please allow 4 to 6 weeks for delivery. Offer available while quantities last.

**Your Privacy**—The Reader Service is committed to protecting your privacy. Our Privacy Policy is available online at www.ReaderService.com or upon request from the Reader Service.

We make a portion of our mailing list available to reputable third parties that offer products we believe may interest you. If you prefer that we not exchange your name with third parties, or if you wish to clarify or modify your communication preferences, please visit us at www.ReaderService.com/consumerschoice or write to us at Reader Service Preference Service, P.O. Box 9062, Buffalo, NY 14269. Include your complete name and address.

*Lucy Flemming and Ross Mitchell shared a magical,*
*sexy Christmas weekend together six years ago.*
*This Christmas, history may repeat itself when they find*
*themselves stranded in a major snowstorm…*
*and alone at last.*

*Read on for a sneak peek from*
*IT HAPPENED ONE CHRISTMAS*
*by Leslie Kelly.*

*Available December 2011, only from Harlequin® Blaze™.*

EYEING THE GRAY, THICK SKY through the expansive wall of windows, Lucy began to pack up her photography gear. The Christmas party was winding down, only a dozen or so people remaining on this floor, which had been transformed from cubicles and meeting rooms to a holiday funland. She smiled at those nearest to her, then, seeing the glances at her silly elf hat, she reached up to tug it off her head.

Before she could do it, however, she heard a voice. A deep, male voice—smooth and sexy, and so not Santa's.

"I appreciate you filling in on such short notice. I've heard you do a terrific job."

Lucy didn't turn around, letting her brain process what she was hearing. Her whole body had stiffened, the hairs on the back of her neck standing up, her skin tightening into tiny goose bumps. Because that voice sounded so familiar. *Impossibly* familiar.

*It can't be.*

"It sounds like the kids had a great time."

Unable to stop herself, Lucy began to turn around, wondering if her ears—and all her other senses—were deceiving her. After all, six years was a long time, the mind could play tricks. What were the odds that she'd bump into *him*, here? And today of all days. December 23.

*Six years exactly.* Was that really possible?

One look—and the accompanying frantic thudding of her heart—and she knew her ears and brain were working just fine. Because it was *him*.

"Oh, my God," he whispered, shocked, frozen, staring as thoroughly as she was. "Lucy?"

She nodded slowly, not taking her eyes off him, wondering why the years had made him even more attractive than ever. It didn't seem fair. Not when she'd spent the past six years thinking he must have started losing that thick, golden-brown hair, or added a spare tire to that trim, muscular form.

No.

The man was gorgeous. Truly, without-a-doubt, mouth-wateringly handsome, every bit as hot as he'd been the first time she'd laid eyes on him. She'd been twenty-two, he one year older.

They'd shared an amazing holiday season.

And had never seen one another again.

Until now.

*Find out what happens in*
*IT HAPPENED ONE CHRISTMAS*
*by Leslie Kelly.*
*Available December 2011, only from Harlequin® Blaze™*

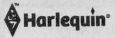

FROM *NEW YORK TIMES* BESTSELLING AUTHOR

# GENA SHOWALTER

*Dating the Undead* by Gena Showalter and Jill Monroe includes tips, tricks, recipes and quizzes that will answer all your relationship questions about your Immortal Man.

Coming January 2012!

Aden Stone should be dead—but when his vampire girlfriend, Victoria, saves his life, she puts everything they care about at risk.

TWISTED is the third installment in the *New York Times* bestselling Intertwined series.

Available wherever books are sold!

HINGS2TITLEMM